Fire is the Test of Gold

A NOVEL

Elizabeth Randall

BROTHER MOCKINGBIRD

Library of Congress Control Number: 2022939488

For information please contact:
Brother Mockingbird, LLC
www.brothermockingbird.org
ISBN: 978-1-7378411-9-7 Paperback
ISBN: 979-8-9863305-4-9 eBook

For Bob,
my friend, my flame, my forever.

"Fire is the test of gold; adversity, of strong men."

\- Seneca

Prologue
THE NIGHT BEFORE- TRULY

The first death threat showed up on his Facebook page. It couldn't have been there long because a few minutes later when he looked again it was gone, blacked out, with some message about content. Then the second one popped up. Then the third.

He sat there for a long time staring at the screen of his laptop, stomach churning, trying to configure the new parameters of his life. In appearance, Truly was nothing special. He had a slightly doughy face, a short haircut, and a genial expression. He was also a lanky man with the stooped shoulders of a swimmer. In church, when he knelt and offered up prayers of penance, he looked guilty. Yet, his composure was evident as he reached for his cell phone and pressed the screen a couple of times. He held it to his ear for a few seconds. It rang, and then it was picked up.

"It's me," he said. "Tomorrow morning. Meet me at 11." He listened for a minute. "Just a reminder. Jetson Park. The Magellan boat ramp."

Truly knew he could ask his wife's cousin, Jay, to do anything for him. But not necessarily on time. He put the phone down and sat there with his elbows on the desk, his hands shading his eyes. Not that there was much light beyond a naked overhead bulb in the small enclosure in his garage that passed for an office. He built the bench out of materials from Warehouse

Depot, put up some shelves, and a shower curtain to cordon off space. He had a portable air conditioner in the summer and a space heater in the winter. When the garage door was open, he could hear the sounds in his house, Darlyn singing, the rattle of pots and pans near dinnertime, the TV, the doorbell. He was the man of the house, and he didn't even have a room of his own, just a lousy corner of the garage.

Truly glanced at the screen again, at his Facebook page with his profile, cheek to cheek with Ruby, Darlyn pressed in close, holding the brim of her hat in a jaunty salute. A beach day with a cloudless blue sky, sand dunes, and sea oats; the image of familial bliss.

"Tru-lee."

Darlyn stood in the doorway of the garage, outlined by the bright familiar glow of home behind her. He didn't even have to look at her to see it.

He said, "What is it," without lifting his head. He heard her exhale and smelled the familiar odor of her cigarette.

"Suppa." She waited. Sometimes when Truly looked at Darlyn, just glanced at her without looking too deep, he found it hard to believe she was his wife. She was pretty with curly black hair down to her waist, close-set blue eyes, tanned skin. Her figure, in spite of a not-too-distant pregnancy at the age of 43, had snapped back with only the faintest silvery traces of stretch marks on her abdomen. If all he had to do was look at her, there was no problem. But then she would open her mouth. Her religious zeal grew more acute with each passing year. Religious music blared, day and night from her smart speaker.

Truly minimized the page on his screen. "Hang on," he said. "I'll be just a minute."

"Tru-lee?" It was a question this time, and one he knew he would have to eventually answer. But not now.

"I said I'm coming." He heard the hiss of her breath, the exhalation. Then she turned, headed back toward the kitchen. He heard a crash, and Ruby started to cry. Darlyn said, "Alexa, turn on "My Revival." A shrill female soprano began to sing.

"Hey, could you shut the door?" Truly called. No one answered. Still, he sat there. Remembering.

Two weeks ago, his old man was hit by lightning out of a clear blue sky while fishing on a dock down the street from the house. Truly saw the lightning strike from his picture window. The old man landed face-first in the water. Truly charged out of the house, waded out into the retention pond, lifted his father whose head was lolling, white foam at his mouth. Truly carried him like a wet sodden child and dropped him on the sand. Then he performed CPR long enough to get the old man's heart going.

They both knew it was temporary. After that, there wasn't much left to do other than preside over the old man's death bed. There was too much internal damage to hope for recovery. Truly held the old man's hand and sat with him. Dying, as it turned out, was a long and tedious procedure, not at all like the IED victims, the sniper casualties in war. There was nothing peaceful or pretty about dying in a hospital bed either, Truly discovered. There were burns, tattoo-like marks of branching electric discharges on skin. In terrible pain, the old man's heart gave out after eight hours.

All his life, it was Truly and the old man, just the two of them, yet, in all that time, the old man accumulated nothing to leave behind except debt, and a single engine twenty four foot center console boat docked at Fort Canaveral.

Truly checked the boat out. It was a tight little vessel, although nothing fancy. No VHF, no GPS, single engine. Just an anchor, life vests, and an emergency kit. He had never been on it in his life. Truly knew nothing about boats.

In fact, it surprised him that the boat was now his. His father was a man who owned the same pair of shoes, resoled for thirty years, a man who didn't trust credit cards and barely trusted cash. He didn't play the greyhounds, bolita or cockfighting. Yet at the end of the day, it appeared all that was left was the impractical twenty-four-foot center console runaround.

Darlyn wanted the boat, but Truly said, "First off, I have to make sure it runs. I want to give it a final big hurrah for the old man. I'm taking it out for a sea trial to scatter his ashes. We can sell it from there."

His cousin-in-law, Jay, agreed to take it out with him. Truly lived in the house where Jay grew up, where Jay still lived, although he was almost thirty years old. Jay knew how to drive a boat. The kid was fifteen years his junior, young for a wingman. Young for his age, too. And reckless. But that was another matter.

Truly maximized his Facebook page, which carried his father's obituary. In the comments were three explicit threats on his life:

mess with us and we'll do something worse than kill you
you better run because we're going to destroy you
you will not live through this

Death. Well, what of it? He was the one who lifted the old man in his arms and carried him to the sand, worked over him until he breathed, carried him to the car and drove him to the hospital. Heard his last words. All of them.

But before that. When the old man first regained consciousness. If Truly thought really hard, it seemed he heard something, a whisper, almost a breath, an edge of a word. He concentrated. The word floated into his mind as though he had dislodged it through sheer mental acumen.

Early.

He grimaced and logged out of his Facebook page.

1

SARA - EARLY THAT MORNING

Wiping the hair out of her eyes, Sara said, "That was a pleasant surprise."

Later she would wonder if she had, in fact, been too happy. Maybe she had tempted fate. Maybe she had always tempted fate. She was what was known as the all-American girl even though she was, technically, at twenty-five, no longer a girl. Still her red hair, green eyes, reedy body, and features arranged in moderate size and proportion on her perfectly oval face made her the kind of trophy girlfriend any man could proudly display on his arm. Even her head-to-toe freckles made her look down to Earth, the kind of woman who knew how to run a 5K, work for a living, and change the oil in her car. But it was 2019 not 1960, and Sara was no one's trophy, even if her new boyfriend did make her a little weak in the knees.

Jay surprised her this morning by slipping into bed with her. Three weeks, and he already had a key to her house. Their coupling was quick, frantic, and primal. They nestled under the covers now; their naked bodies curved against each other. Sara was having one of those moments she was sure to remember when she was old and the memory of passion still had the ability to warm her.

"I'm happy," she thought, snuggling, her back against Jay's chest. Usually Sara dated older men, preferring their maturity to the antics of feckless generational cohorts. When she was in college, she and her guy friends would stay up all night talking. They were colleagues, equals. But four years out of college, guys her age were suddenly more interested in an escort and a sex partner than in deep conversation. These days, she didn't even need to be a good conversationalist because there wasn't much conversation. There was texting and tweeting and liking and clicking the heart icon on Instagram. Sara hadn't known what she was missing until she met Jay.

Some men transform from adolescence into veritable male Adonis's in their 20s and 30s. Sara thought of Johnny Depp, Brad Pitt, John Legend. Except for the Adonis angle, Jay was just another underemployed millennial, not that different from other guys except in looks. His looks were spectacular. His looks occupied her thoughts day and night. His smile. That shirt he wore to the beach. And then took off. Yes, gorgeous Jay distracted her from all other thoughts. And when they were together, there was little conversation. They didn't need conversation.

Jay was one of the technicians at InterTech where she worked as a software trainer. She had seen him in the break room, but she never talked to him until he showed up at her cubicle one day. She was staring at a company newsletter on her desktop until her eyes glazed. Between training classes, she always took a day or two to catch up on correspondence, which basically entailed looking busy and doing nothing before preparing for the next update to the proprietary software InterTech marketed. It was one of the perks of the job, which was more than augmented by the sixteen hour days and seven day work weeks she put in during a new training cycle.

"Sara Shyrock?"

She swiveled her chair, and there he was. Encircled in his arms, remembering, Sara had to bite her lip.

"Hi," Jay had said and smiled. She wondered if he knew how easy life was for him with a smile like that. Her cubicle was so small, she had to get up and let him sit in her chair in front of the laptop. She stood behind him. His dark hair curled just over his shirt collar, and she had an impulse to stand on her tiptoes and brush it back. The infamous and gorgeous Jay.

She heard about him, of course. He crashed through the office with the force of a sexual H-Bomb, if you believed gossip. Half the women trainers already slept with him even if they were married. The other half wanted to. But that day, he was all business, trying to repair a system error before she had to document it. Without even turning around, he said, "Let me just run defrag on this, and it'll be good as new."

"I should have done that," Sara said,

"It's okay."

"No, I feel stupid. Dragging you over here for routine maintenance." In truth, Sara filled out the work order with the express intent of meeting Jay. She had just broken up with her boyfriend.

"You can make it up to me," Jay said,

"Really?"

"Let's grab some lunch."

They ate soggy sandwiches from the canteen on the first floor with mayonnaise dripping through the air holes of the bread. Sitting on hard plastic chairs on the strip of sidewalk dominated by a huge silver ashtray, set apart for smokers, Sara endured the stares of coworkers who spotted them from the hall beyond the big plate glass window. She and Jay were like exhibits in a zoo, apparently. She bit into her sandwich and chewed. Swallowed. Looked at her watch. She was cooling on the whole Jay phenomenon. Except when she looked at him.

"Don't you have to be at work?" Sara took a sip of her Diet Coke lifting the aluminum can to hide her face. Perhaps if she could get away from the magnetic force of his appeal, she could think straight. As it was, she was tempted to brush some lint from his broad shoulder. Run a finger along his perfect jawline.

"Trying to get rid of me?" Jay asked. Sara could tell from his tone he didn't believe it.

"No," she said. She felt short of breath. "But you make me uncomfortable."

"Why's that?"

"I don't know you."

"Would you like to?"

"I.. what?"

"How about dinner tonight?"

Sara seemed a bit at sea. "Sure. I guess. Why, though?"

"You probably faked the work order. It happens a lot. But that's okay."

"Is this where I'm supposed to curl up and die?"

Jay chuckled. "Now, now. Play nice. Besides, I think you're cute."

"You do, do you?" She paused, trying to think of a reason not to go, of a way not to fall into this treacherous detonation with the office sex bomb. "Just so you know, I split the check. Always." Sara learned this from her grandmother who used to say, 'There's no reason on God's green earth for a man to pay for a working woman's dinner on a date. Pay for your own. If he tells you to make it up to him by cooking him dinner, he's trying to put you in your place." Sara's grandma went to college in the seventies and marched for the Equal Rights Amendment. She did not put up with crap from anyone.

Sara found her advice to be true. If it was her companionship men were after, what did they care if she paid for her own lasagna? She was used to some men arguing this point, which often led to her turning down the date, period. If her most basic dating rule was an issue of contention, there was no point going forward. But Jay seemed amused. "Damn," he shrugged. "That lets out asking for sexual favors."

Sara said, "For you, maybe."

They burst out laughing. Sara saw a couple of women from training, women with manicures, pedicures, and heels, looking their way through the glass. Their asses jammed into their tight Ann Taylor business suits, they glanced at her, then away, as they returned to the tricky business of walking in stiletto heels. Sara stopped laughing and straightened up abruptly.

"So where do you want to go?" she said.

They went to some steak place where Sara found that just being near Jay raised her adrenalin so much she completely lost her appetite. That was three weeks and three pounds ago.

Sara waited the requisite three dates before she slept with her swanky new boyfriend. Since then, she got together with him every chance she got. Like now. Jay kissed her shoulder and let his lips stray to her neck.

"Stop," Sara said. "We both have things to do." She expected him to protest. She waited for him to protest. When he didn't, she turned over to face him.

"I'm not going to work," he said. "Truly and I are taking the boat out today."

Sara stroked his tan shoulder, let her caress linger over his biceps. He caught her hand in his.

"We're going out," he repeated, somewhat weakly. Sara stretched out full length and touched her toes to his. "We fit together perfectly." She brushed her lips against his lips.

Jay grabbed her around the waist and crushed her to him in an excruciatingly deep kiss. When he released her, she was limp. He flung the sheets off and got out of bed. Sara reached for him, her hand trailing along the perimeter of the bed.

"Don't go," she said.

"I have to," he called from the bathroom. He was standing in front of the closet door, which was a full-length mirror. He flexed an arm and glanced over his shoulder at Sara. Her gaze drifted lower to the scars on his legs. He'd told her they were from a skirmish in the war, which meant he was brave as well as handsome.

She rolled out of bed and stood behind him, her arms clenched his torso. "I can't believe you're leaving," she murmured.

He stood apart from her almost politely. "Only for now," he said. He folded up his pants, and Sara thought she heard a clang as something hit the ceramic floor. She opened her mouth to mention it, but he turned toward the drumming of the shower.

She ran a hand through her hair. She wanted to ask, "You'll be back?" They were at that three-week juncture in a relationship when it was just as easy to drift apart as it was to stay together. Sara opened her mouth to ask the question. Then closed it. This was not the time. He was in a hurry. And she was definitely a chicken. Jay thrust aside the shower curtain and tested the water by turning it on and off several times. Finally, he straightened up and pulled back the curtain, the old-fashioned shower stanchions rattling.

She shouted over the drumming water, "Do you want breakfast?" She never ate breakfast. Nor could she cook.

"Oh, no," he said, "no thanks. Coffee, though. If you got it."

"Okay," she said.

The bathroom was starting to steam up. "Do you want the door open or closed?"

"Open," he said. He drew back the shower curtain and grinned at her. Even dripping wet, he was gorgeous, his dark hair curling around his head, his eyes sapphire blue. That cleft chin. Sara got a grip on herself. "Uh," she said. "Yeah, absolutely." She walked across the room and picked up his Hard Rock Orlando t-shirt and slid it over her head. "Coffee coming right up."

"Atta girl."

She ambled out of her bedroom, down the stairs, and into her kitchen, a rather large L-shaped affair, marooned from the family room by poor design and no architectural planning. Sara was famous for impulsive buying, and her house was no exception. It was impossible to watch TV or join a conversation in the family room from the kitchen. She planted a large round wooden IKEA table in the middle of the kitchen, where friends or family sat while she heated things up in the microwave.

Dreamily, she reached up to her Formica cabinets and opened them to reveal bone china and crystal glasses. She stood on tiptoes to reach the shelf above where the mugs were stored. Her hand hovered for a moment. Should she select the round plastic mug with the corporate logo, the one with her name on it, or the celestial mug with constellations that emerged when warmed by hot coffee?

Her hand closed around the sturdy blue ceramic cup, the one she used when she was writing lesson plans. A hand closed around her hand and helped her grasp the handle. She stood perfectly still. She hadn't heard the water shut off, yet here he was pressed close behind her. His other hand slid up her T-shirt and around her waist.

"I thought you had to go," she said.

"Not right this second." He bent, his breath warming her ear, "There is something about a pretty girl wearing my T-shirt. And nothing else. "

He had his jeans on, but his chest was bare, and he smelled like soap. Lifting her t-shirt to her chin, his hands strayed down her belly, pressing her close, his wiry chest hairs tickling her back. She turned and stood on her toes kissing him, opening her mouth, touching her tongue to his. Holding her waist with both hands, he leaned into her kiss and backed her up to the kitchen table. They toppled the napkin holder. A small ceramic salt shaker in the shape of a boat fell on the tile and shattered.

Sara hoisted her T-shirt up to her neck and over her head. Jay grabbed it, threw it on the floor, and lifted her arms around his neck. He ran his hands up and down her back as they kissed, then bent to take the nipple of her breast between his lips. She heard him fumble with the zipper on his pants and then the rustle of denim as Jay dropped his jeans to the floor, although he didn't step out of them. He slid his middle finger inside her.

Sara moaned, backed up, and lay flat on her back on the kitchen table, her legs dangling above the floor, her hands sliding down and gripping two of the table legs. She heard Jay's breath hiss, and as agile as a panther, he moved in, one knee then another straddling her legs. She reached for him with one hand and arched her back. The table wobbled.

"Um," he said.

"What?"

"Forgot the rubber."

"Oh, shit."

They were both panting. Each waited for the other to move, but all that happened was they inched even closer. Then closest of all. Sara lay flat, reached down, clutched the legs of the table again. "Just this once," Sara thought. Jay loomed over her for a second, as she made up her mind. Sara slid forward on the table, which creaked furiously for a few minutes. Then there was silence. Jay's full weight was upon her. Sara said, "My back."

"Sorry." Jay managed to extricate himself and zip up his jeans. Sara used her arms to lift off the table. She stepped around the broken saltshaker and bent to pick up the biggest pieces.

Jay was already busy at the sink, washing his hands. He picked the celestial cup off the top shelf and poured himself coffee. Orion's belt lit up its perimeter. He grinned at Sara and winked. "I will never look at this table again without thinking of you. Or any table most likely."

"I'll say." She straightened up and threw the shards of glass in the trash. She liked that he planned on seeing the table, and her, again. A fan of Jane Austen, she tended to view all her relationships romantically and with an eye towards permanence. "Will it always be like that?" she asked. It was one of those loaded questions. It just slipped out.

Jay, turned, grinning, both hands holding the mug.

"That depends," he said.

Her face must have fallen a little, because he walked over and pulled her close, facing him. He reached and brushed her bangs up with the palm of his hand. "That depends," he said, "as long as we never do it again in bed."

She hugged him tightly. "That can be arranged. As long as my furniture holds up."

Jay kissed her so thoroughly she had to stand on her toes. "My God," she thought, "I love him."

After he left, she leaned against the front door fiddling with her hair. On her way to the shower, she bumped into furniture. She was late to work. She arrived in time to fudge her entry time in the book by the elevator, which recorded everyone's comings and goings. Roosevelt, the doorman, gave her a friendly wave with his white-gloved hand as the elevator doors came together. He would never rat her out.

Then a hand inserted itself in the gap between the elevator doors, and they opened. Galvin Steele entered, immaculately dressed, hoisting an umbrella. Sara punched the number three button savagely and the circle lit up. Galvin worked on her floor. Galvin was in management at InterTech.

The elevator began moving up. Sara took out her phone and stared at it. Galvin said, "Hi Sara."

"Hello, Galvin." She did not look up.

"You look very pretty today."

Sara did look up. "What am I supposed to say to that?"

Galvin's eyebrows came together in a perfect arch. "Say?

15

I don't know. 'Thank you Galvin?'"

Sara flung her phone into her shoulder bag and stared straight ahead.

"You can't stay mad at me forever, Sara," Galvin said.

"I most certainly can. And I will."

The elevator doors pinged, then opened, and Sara was the first one into the hall. Looking around, she saw she was only on the second floor, but, rather than backtrack, she headed for the stairs and pounded up the additional flight. The hallway opened onto the purple expanse of carpet, a company color. She emerged from the stairwell, just in time to face the elevator doors opening to reveal an amused Galvin Steele.

Jackie Moates was manning the reception desk at the other end of the hall, which suddenly seemed far away. There was no ladies room to duck into either. Her knees stiff, she hurried past the elevator. She hadn't gone far when she felt his hand on her arm.

"Stop," she said, loosening his grasp and turning to face him.

"We need to talk," Galvin said. "Can we do that?"

"You had your chance." She resumed her bolt to the reception desk and made it this time, although Galvin stayed on her heels.

Jackie lifted her eyebrows at Sara and glanced up at the brass clock ominously ticking in the background. 10:00 a.m.

Sara decided a direct offense was best. A corporate receptionist was no different, after all, from a hair stylist or a bartender in terms of knowing their clients' business. She walked up to the desk and said, "Is Mr. Montana in?" Nick Montana was the owner and general manager, someone who, occasionally, seemed aware of his employee's comings and goings.

Jackie said. "He hasn't made his rounds yet." Unsaid, but hanging in the air was the caveat, 'He never makes his rounds.'

She turned to Galvin. "How are you this morning, sir?

"I'm somewhat mediocre, sorry to say."

Jackie was a middle-aged woman who wore her short brown bob of hair like a helmet. There was nothing whatsoever about her to suggest she had a vestibule of empathy circulating anywhere in the hard nut of her soul. Sara gave her credit for trying, though. Jackie's mouth widened into a cross between a smile and a grimace. Then she just stood there like some slack jawed dinosaur trying to decide whether the berries were poisonous.

"Sara, here," Galvin inclined his head, "won't give me the time of day." Sara snorted and started for her cubicle.

Jackie's mouth shut with a snap. Through stiff lips, she said, "You ought to be careful how you speak about the trainers, sir. They are all in that MeToo."

Sara turned abruptly on her heel. She walked up to Galvin, walked up close, and held a finger up to his face. "You want to know what time it is Mr. Steele? I'll tell you what time it is. It's time to, it's time to…"

But Galvin was already unlocking the conference room. He opened the door and held out his hand. Sara breezed by him. "Turn on the lights. Otherwise, everyone will think we're up to something."

"Aren't we?" Galvin asked. But he turned on the lights. Then he stood there on the other side of the table. Just looking at her.

"You're making me nervous," Sara said.

"I don't mean to. But you won't take my calls or return

my texts. It's been weeks."

"You took your ex-wife to your best friend's wedding."

As if the confession took a lot out of her, Sara sat down heavily in one of the conference chairs, a swivel, which immediately sank below table level. She sprang to her feet.

"That's it?" Galvin asked.

"Yes? Yes."

"Well, I don't buy that at all."

"What? Why not?"

"You didn't even know Kyle. Meryl and I grew up with him. And the bride had a strict guest list. I didn't want to get Kyle in trouble."

"Sounds like a lot of excuses."

Galvin put his umbrella down and moved around to Sara's side of the table. "I think your excuse is a lot lamer. In fact, maybe that isn't why you broke up with me at all.

Sara deliberately walked past him and stood by the door. "What are you talking about?"

"You're dating Jay Hicks. Were you seeing him when we were together?"

"No." She opened the door.

"Okay, then." Galvin picked up his umbrella, smiled and walked past her into the hallway. "Good to know." Slinging the umbrella over shoulder, he started to walk away.

"Can the door stay unlocked?" Sara asked, shutting it.

"Sure," Galvin said, turning. "Seeing a lot of him, I suppose."

"Who? Oh." Sara couldn't resist a bit of boasting. "Jay stopped by this morning."

"On a Tuesday morning?"

"Well…yes."

"I hope he's taking you somewhere nice this weekend." He sauntered off in the direction of his office which was at the end of the hall. When his door was open, he had a direct line of vision to her workspace. "Like Claudio's," he said over his shoulder.

Claudio's, an upscale bistro on the swanky side of Lake Ann, was where Galvin and Sara used to spend their Friday nights. Without saying goodbye, Sara turned and headed down the purple path to her cubicle. Once there, she sank into her own swivel chair, which supported her weight and was at eye level to her computer. She reached under her desk and pressed the power button on her hard drive. The screen lit up with a picture of Sara kayaking on the Wekiva River. She was alone except for the leathery hide of a gator. She tried not to formulate the thought that Galvin's words were invoking. Jay never took her out on the weekend.

It was always week mornings and weeknights. On weekends he had a download at work, or there was a guy's night out, or there was some other…excuse. He discouraged texting, saying he preferred the personal touch. Most of their 'dates' were arranged at work or were 'surprises' like the tryst this morning. They rarely went out. She chalked it up to the newness, the excitement of a new partner.

How could she have been so blind? Sara cursed herself, pounded her thighs with her fists. She was such an idiot. Jay had all the classic signs of a cheating man.

She had accused Galvin of having an affair with his ex-wife. But with Jay the tables had turned. Now she was the girl on the side.

2

DARYLN - MORNING

Darlyn charged through an arched doorway hung with a swinging door like the ones in saloons. Her kitchen had a huge stone fireplace with a swept hearth. The rest of the immense kitchen was granite and tile except for the sink and the refrigerator, which were stainless steel. The kitchen was custom built and took up most of the downstairs floor.

A little girl sat on a receiving blanket spread out on the grate and played with an empty cracker box. She was singing to herself and coughing a little, probably because she was in a fireplace, however clean it looked. Her pinafore was smudged with ashes.

Darlyn sat down at the long kitchen table, set for three. She lit a cigarette and left it burning in the ashtray when she saw steam rising from a pot. She walked to the stove, stirred something and said, without turning around, "Ruby! Stop coughing."

The little girl held her breath, sputtering. The red barrettes on her braids trembled.

Darlyn turned around. "I tole you and I tole you. You don't have a cough. Who died on the cross for you?"

Ruby shook her head mutely, turning a little purple.

"He earned his stripes for you, so you could be forgiven for sins. If you are coughing it's because you are bad. SO, YOU ARE NOT COUGHING."

Darlyn employed exactly three tones at home: icy silence, banshee, and shattered glass. Truly entered, picked up Ruby and returned to his seat with the child. "Have some water," he said, picking up a plastic glass and holding it to her lips. She sipped.

"She's coughing because she's sitting on that cold, damp floor," he said to Darlyn.

She glowered at him. "She is coughing 'cause she is filled with sin."

Ruby's gray eyes met his, and her baby mouth turned up in a toothy smile. "That's my girl," he said.

"Give her a bath?" Darlyn asked. "I'm cooking here."

"Sure," Truly said, rising and shouldering the child. "Who's coming?"

"Jay. A course."

Truly stopped at the doorway, frowning. "He's going out on the boat with me today. And he better not be late."

Darlyn looked over her shoulder. "Don't tell me."

Truly shrugged. Darlyn watched as he left the room. Then she reached for her phone and touched the screen a few times.

He picked up. "Yeah?"

"Whatcha doing now?" She heard running water.

"Shower."

"At home?"

"No."

"Are you at that harlot's house again?"

"Calm down." He paused. "Where's Truly?"

Darlyn said, "That is what I'm calling about. He is giving Ruby a bath, running a little late. Don't you be. "

Jay said, "Yeah. I gotta go." He clicked off. Darlyn,

frowned, put her phone in her apron pocket and moved back to the large cast iron cookstove, stirring oatmeal in a Dutch oven pot on the range. She kept a black plastic ashtray by the stove and took puffs of her cigarette as she stirred, the smoke and the steam forming a toxic cloud. Darlyn imported the stove from England and a pretty penny it cost, too. But she hadn't cared because the Lord told her she would be rich soon. Then Truly's daddy died, and it turned out he was broke. Living on credit, who knew how long.

She should have known because getting mowed down by a lightning bolt on a perfectly clear day was too obvious a sign of divine retribution to miss. But she would not speak evil of the old man, because he was with the Lord. Whether he was above Him or below Him was another matter entirely. He was FBI, but he'd taken early retirement when he was in his fifties. The old man never lost that apologetic look, that way of asking questions as though he knew in advance the answers didn't matter.

And Truly. She didn't believe in dishing dirt on her lawfully wedded husband, but he hadn't worked, not really, since his last contract ran out. He used to get good freelance jobs all the time. Now it seemed all these projects were finished.

Darlyn did not think herself a worldly woman. She only wanted what she felt she deserved. And as a beautiful woman who served the Lord, she felt she deserved a whole lot. Darlyn ascribed to the Jim Baker/Joel Osteen brand of Christianity, called prosperity gospel. There was no doubt in her mind her financial and her physical well-being were the will of her Lord God and Savior. After all, she lived in a 2900 square foot home, and she was sure the Lord would deal with the bills piling up.

She wasn't even a little bit worried. She hummed with the religious music blasting out of her Alexa device, which is where she picked up her pronounced southern accent.

There was the dull background noise of a bulldozer and half a dozen workmen on the plat next to hers, digging nonstop to put another McMansion up right next to hers. The construction noise, and the work men's comments were now a staple of her daytime regime. There was one workman who was the biggest, brawniest workman of them all, and Darlyn had been watching him for days.

He was six foot six, black as the devil, and built like a mountain with all its ridges, crevices, and summits. Darlyn eyed him through her wide-open blinds as she stirred the oatmeal. Would he be amenable to the words of the Lord? She could tell him how God used his past life and heartaches for good. She could read stories of God's grace and redemption. She felt her heart quicken, and her skin break out in goosebumps as she stared at the young man wielding a pickaxe, and she thought of the grace of the Lord in that temple of a body.

Her mind made up, Darlyn let the stirring spoon fall into the oatmeal. She turned on the cold-water faucet and grabbed a plastic pitcher she kept on the counter. She filled it with a quart and turned the old-fashioned white ceramic faucet to the right, shutting it off. She could hear Truly upstairs talking to Ruby in her bath. Darlyn's religious twangy guitar music accompanied by shrill sopranos filled the house, but outside the construction noise had ceased. "Mid-mornin' break," she thought.

She reached up, pulled open a cabinet door, and grabbed a container of Crystal Lite lemonade. Peeling up the plastic lid with her fingers, she withdrew the scoop and dug into the powdery synthetic dregs. She poured two scoops into the pitcher, stirred it with a finger, and then tossed in a couple of ice cubes from the dispenser in the fridge.

In a few short steps, she was at the door, flinging it open and stepping out onto the porch. Sure enough, the men were sitting around, kicking their legs from a perch on a flatbed truck, crouching by the curb, lounging against the 'dozer. Her African god was standing, he and all the other men, about a half dozen of them. They turned and faced her. The crouching men stood, holding cans of beer behind their backs. Darlyn smiled a smile of Christian charity, beamed her sunny benevolence on one and all. She opened her mouth to offer these burly men some refreshment, but her mouth was too dry.

The tall guy Darlyn had trouble keeping her eyes off, said, "Ma'am?"

Darlyn licked her lips. "You all must be thirsty," she said, stepping down from the porch. She stumbled a little and the tall man stepped forward and put his hand on her elbow to steady her.

"That's fine, that's fine," Darlyn said, straightening, still smiling. "But thank you...?"

"Link," the man said. He stood right where he was, and Darlyn had to move away and step around him to find a place to put the tray with the pitcher and the plastic glasses down. She looked around and finally settled the tray on a tree stump. As she straightened, she thought she detected appreciation among the men for her efforts to hydrate them in their thirsty work; they were all smiling at her and at each other. She poured the lemonade into a plastic cup and passed it to Link.

He took it with a 'do I have to' expression. The men

holding beer brought their cans out from behind their backs and cautiously sipped. Link tossed the lemonade back, and Darlyn watched his throat muscles as he swallowed. He straightened up, grimaced, and wiped his mouth with the back of his hand.

Darlyn said, "What's that you're building there?"

Link said, "Rich man's house." His voice was higher than she expected.

Darlyn almost dug the toe of her Ked sneaker in the sand, but she rallied, looked him in the eye and asked, "Don'cha like building houses?"

"If it were a hospital, I would be fully into it," Link said.

Darlyn said, "That's right noble of you. Do any other type work? Besides construction?"

The other guys were grinning at Link who seemed aware Darlyn was addressing her comments solely at him. "I have a pool cleaning business," Link said.

Truly came down the steps carrying the stroller with Ruby in it. He put the stroller down and threaded between the men to get to the sidewalk. "Bye momma," he said, waving at Darlyn. Ruby gave a little cough. Darlyn grimaced and waved back. She turned to Link.

"Dang," Darlyn said. "If that don't beat all. Truly dropped a wrench on the pool pump, and now it does not work at all."

Link stared at the other men intently as they began to snicker. "Yeah?"

Darlyn said. "I would so appreciate a knock on the door 'fore you leave today. Maybe you can take a look at it."

The other men all turned away, faces contorted with laughter.

"Yeah," Link said, "I don't think..."

"See ya then." Darlyn waggled her fingers at him. "And please bring the tray." She turned and climbed the steps to her big home, pleased with her efforts to help this man by finding work around her house for him to do. Crossing to the stove, she shook a cigarette out of the pack she kept in a ceramic pumpkin on her counter. With the cigarette between her lips, she brought the lighter to the tip, contemplated her afternoon, and inhaled deeply. Live and let live, that was her motto, and she was sure her consideration would convey just that blessed message.

3
GALVIN STEELE-MORNING

Back in his office Galvin was tempted to throw his raincoat on the floor and his umbrella across the room. Instead, he shrugged his way out of his coat, slung it on the coat rack he kept in the corner of his office, and hung the umbrella on the next rung. Then he sat down at his desk, folded his hands, and narrowed his eyes in the direction of Sara's cubicle.

What Sara didn't understand was that ex-wife or not, Meryl was a friend, and that wasn't going to change. He had known her for half his life, which included ten years of marriage. They met at FSU, freshman year, and by the time they were sophomores, they were living together in a leaky sixty-year-old shag carpeted apartment. Married the day after graduation, they embarked on a placid matrimonial sea where they were compatible in every way except, as it turned out, in one crucial area.

Galvin discovered this crevice months into their new marriage. Meryl emerged from the bathroom one morning as he was knotting his tie and preparing to begin his corporate career as a member of the helpline crew at InterTech.

"I'm late," she said flatly.

Galvin didn't even turn around. "No, you have time. It's only just seven."

"No, I'm late, Galvin. Was there a leak in the rubber you didn't tell me about?"

He whirled around, the smile on his face fading as he met her eyes. "No," he said. "No leaks."

"Then what the fuck," she said and slumped down on the bed.

Galvin tried for reassuring. "It's early. Maybe you will start today."

Meryl sighed. "It was supposed to come yesterday. I'm never late."

Galvin sat down next to her and put his arm around her. "I'm sure it's nothing."

They were silent for a few seconds. "But," Galvin said. "If it is…something. I have a good job. "

Meryl leaped to her feet, cutting him off. "I'm student teaching. Then I'm job hunting. I can't start my first professional job pregnant."

Galvin stared at her, and his mother's words echoed eerily. "You're too young," she'd said when he told her of his plan to marry.

How had Meryl and he never discussed this? Had each of them assumed, since they got along so well, that having children was an issue on which they would just agree?

Galvin chose his words carefully. "So, you would end the pregnancy."

Meryl was opening her drawers, taking articles of clothing out and slamming the drawers shut. She turned around to face him wide eyed. "Of course."

Galvin decided to get all the bad news at once. "What about down the road, once you, I mean you and I, are more established in our careers?"

Meryl shoved one leg into her pantyhose. "Shoot. I just

don't see myself with kids. I practically brought up my brother and sister."

Meryl was the oldest of three children and the daughter of alcoholics. Meryl's upbringing was textbook poverty, and his childhood was textbook middle class. His mother was an elementary school principal, and his dad was an engineer who designed military equipment for government contracts. Galvin had his own room filled with books and video games, a state-of-the-art desktop computer, and a bed in the shape of a race car. He would have traded it all for a brother or a sister.

Galvin was an only child. At the playground, he watched siblings race around, intent on games he couldn't comprehend. Galvin's parents were a little older, an indulgent couple who doted on their only child. Their home was orderly, stable, silent. Galvin assumed he would start a family young. He wanted lots of kids.

But Meryl was not pregnant on that long-ago morning when she fretted about missing a period. And now look at him. Nearly forty, childless and single. He couldn't blame Meryl. He hung on for ten years, hoping she would change her mind, or that he would.

She hadn't. He hadn't. So, they divorced and somehow never broke off friendly contact. Still, since then, he had not met one woman who understood his relationship with his ex-wife. Meryl, on the other hand, played the field regularly and with no apparent handicaps.

Galvin tried. If ever there was a man meant to be married it was him. He was neat, precise, even tempered. He liked a routine. His desk and his desk drawers were uncluttered. Unless he had a business date, he ate the same lunch every day at exactly noon. Maybe someday he would alternate the daily peanut butter and jelly on whole wheat. Ten years ago, he had switched from grape jelly to strawberry.

His one passion was antique sports cars. He owned a 1975 convertible MGB and even though it mostly stayed in his garage, he spent whole weekends trying to keep it running. Oh, he dated women his friends fixed up for him. They were nice enough, but nothing seemed to click. One date ordered the most expensive item on the menu, drank a whole bottle of wine, and fell asleep, snoring, on the ride home. Another woman gobbled popcorn during a movie, cramming it into her mouth, letting it spill into the crevice between her breasts, and popping even those stray pieces into her mouth. Another was rabidly political, another wanted to save the wolves. His last fix-up tried to borrow money from him.

Like the other women he dated, Sara was all wrong for him. They met during her interview when he sat in with another manager to screen new InterTech employees. Galvin gave her high scores during the interview. Two weeks later management attended training classes when InterTech bought out a small independent business and appropriated their software. Under the fluorescent light in the chilly white walled training room, he was the student, and Sara was the trainer; Galvin finally understood the power of a good teacher. Also, he couldn't take his eyes off her.

He lingered after the session to ask a few questions about the software she demonstrated. She answered seriously, earnestly, her face upturned to his. In spite of her appeal, he couldn't quite bring himself to ask her out. Clearing his throat, he asked, "Is it okay to come to you with questions?"

"Of course, "she said, and turned away to answer her phone. He wondered who it was. Anyone as attractive as Sara had a busy social calendar.

Galvin started emailing her the next day and the days that followed, asking perfectly legitimate questions about the software. Eventually, the tenor of their conversations became more...personal. She sent him her recipe for crepes (practically the only thing I can cook, she messaged) and he recommended a mechanic for her twelve-year-old Saturn. He began coming to work late so they met in the lobby and went up in the elevator together. Jackie raised her eyebrows at him when he passed her desk with Sara in the morning.

Finally, one afternoon after he requested her presence to explain the software licensing to him, Sara said, "So, at this point, I think you know as much as I do."

She rose to go, and Galvin sat there, trying to think of some way to make her stay. She paused in the doorway as if reading his mind. "What?"

Galvin had a window office, which, when the blinds were open, as they were that day, looked out on a sunny pasture devoid of livestock. The glare caused her to squint and shield her eyes with the flat of her hand. Seeing her distraction, Galvin said, "So what's your schedule look like this week?"

Sara shrugged. "I have training…"

Galvin interrupted, "No, I meant evenings."

Sara stopped squinting and looked at him. He had a feeling she was looking at him differently than she had a few minutes ago when he was just a thick-headed manager who couldn't get with the program. God, he hated dating! Forcing himself to speak slowly and distinctly, he said "How about we meet up on Wednesday at Claudio's?" Claudio's was the most expensive steak house in town. He had planned to invite her for weeks.

Sara touched her hair and then let her hand fall to the side. "I eat with my Gran on Wednesdays. And aren't you married?"

"No," Galvin said, shaking his head. He said, "no," again for good measure. He held up his left hand and wiggled his ringless fingers at her.

Sara said, "Because my last boyfriend, the last person I dated, told me he was single. And he wasn't.

"I'm divorced," Galvin said.

"That's good," Sara said, "because this last guy? He had a girlfriend for years. I ran into her at a party, just by chance? We were talking about this guy we were both seeing. He started to sound very familiar, the more we talked, if you get my drift. He turned out to be the same guy. What are the chances? He made excuses to one of us when he was seeing the other."

"Despicable," Galvin said.

"I know, right? That's the one thing I can't stand," Sara said. "Well, actually there is more than one thing. But that's the worst. A cheater."

"How about Tuesday? Is 8:00 okay?"

They didn't sleep together on the first date, but they spent a long time saying good night parked at Claudio's under a huge oak tree. Dating Sara made Galvin feel ten years younger. Almost her age, in fact.

Galvin was a realist. He saw right away, she was all wrong for him—too young, too pretty, too messy— her desk in the office and her desk at home was littered with crumpled

Kleenex, jolly rancher wrappers, post-it notes with cryptic reminders, loose pens and pencils, coins, and paper clips. In her home, there were always dishes in her sink, coffee grounds half on the floor, half in the garbage, crumbs on the cutting board, lint in the dryer. But he was drawn to her energy, her beauty, her intelligence, her...Galvin recalled the few passionate nights and lazy mornings they'd had together before Sara called it off.

"Sir?"

It was Jackie. He didn't have a private secretary, but Jackie fielded his calls, without his permission.

"Phone," she said. Galvin glanced at his desk phone and saw the red-light start blinking.

"You didn't need to walk all the way down here to tell me that, Jackie. Just transfer it."

"You're welcome, Mr. Steele. "

"Thanks." Galvin watched her walk heavily towards the reception desk, her endemic ankles flowing over the tops of her orthopedic shoes. He knew little about Jackie's life, but she did seem to have an eerie prescience about showing up when he took personal calls. He shook his head and picked up the phone.

"Steele here."

"Galvin." It was Meryl. Just hearing her voice steadied him. Yet she rarely called him at work.

"Is anything wrong?" There was a breathless quality to her words, something pent up about her pace.

"No, everything is right. I have the most unbelievable news." This was definitely unlike Meryl who was almost as predictable as Galvin.

"Well, don't keep me hanging."

"Oh, Galvin. I'm getting married."

Galvin realized he was holding his breath and slowly exhaled. "That's great. Who's the lucky man?"

"Oh, you know him. It's Jim, good old Jim. And I'm pregnant. Can you believe it?"

No, Galvin could not believe it. He put a hand up to his forehead and then slowly lowered it. "Great," he said. "Just great."

"I wanted to give you the first heads up, so you wouldn't hear it from Kyle or any of our old friends. You'll come to the wedding?"

"Of course." Although he wasn't sure he could. In fact, he wasn't sure he could even continue the conversation much longer.

"It's going to be in October," Meryl went on. "You and I eloped. A proper wedding is so much harder to plan. And of course, there's that little love bundle coming."

"Well, life is short," Galvin said.

"Don't I know it. I'm already eight weeks. What do you think of the name Emma?"

"You'd better ask Jim. Meryl?"

"Yeah?"

"I thought you didn't want kids. Or a kid. Even one kid."

"Oh, Galvin. That's ancient history."

He let it go. There was a pause.

"You can bring a guest to the wedding. Are you seeing anyone?"

Galvin felt a sharp pain in his chest. "Not at the moment."

"Well," Meryl said, her voice brisk, "weddings are good places to meet women."

"My last girlfriend broke up with me because I took you to Kyle's wedding," Galvin said. "Sara. I told you about her."

"God," Meryl said. "I'm sorry."

"Well..." Galvin took a deep breath. "Congratulations. You, me, and Jim will have to catch up soon."

"Of course," Meryl said. There was silence. He could not think of a thing to say.

"Are you all right, Galvin?"

"Never better," he said. "Give Jim my best."

"I will. Bye now."

Galvin clicked off and placed the phone in its holder. Then he got up and stood in the doorway of his office staring down the expanse of purple carpeting. At the end of the hall, he could see Sara talking on her phone, her head flung back, her legs crossed. Slowly, he closed his office door and leaned his head on it for a minute.

He had just learned a piece of information he never anticipated. Meryl did want kids. She just didn't want kids with him. He walked over to the window and looked out. There were two ponies in the pasture, a brown one and a white one. He had never seen them before. Perhaps, he just hadn't looked. They gamboled on the grass.

There was so much he hadn't seen.

4
JAY-MORNING

Jay made it out of Sara's in record time and hopped into his Spectra red '82 Buick Regal. She lived in Lake Ann, and he had to touch base with Truly, then drive an hour to dock at Jetson Park, the second time that day. He had already been there once, taken something from the boat, and it was in the trunk of his car now. He shouldn't have stopped at Sara's. Jay was late.

He shifted to fifth gear and roared up the interstate. There were some dark clouds unfurling over the Lake Ann horizon, and he checked the weather on his phone, steering with one hand. "Siri," he said. "Weather for Fort Canaveral. "

A voice with a British accent reported: Wind Advisory issued...Strong winds and rough waves will create hazardous conditions for small craft.

"Shit," Jay muttered and threw the phone on the passenger seat. It landed screen up, and briefly flashed a text message from Sara. He was a fast reader. It said, "Please call me as soon as you see this."

The Buick Regal was a stick, so it was hard to drive and text at the same time. Jay liked mechanical things and the activity of driving. He liked action, period. He grinned thinking of the morning. It was only a couple of hours since he'd had Sara on her kitchen table. She just couldn't get enough of Jay the Juice.

Sara would have to wait for an answer to his text until he got to the dock. He needed to keep his mind clear with bad weather looming. Truly didn't know how to steer a boat. Jay scratched his chest absentmindedly, and his hand wandered to his pocket. He froze. He scrabbled madly at his trousers and chanced a peek down the crack between the car seats.

It was gone. His lucky amulet. He clenched and unclenched his fingers around the steering wheel. Where the fuck had he left it? He went over the past few hours in his mind. Sara's bathroom. The shower. Folding his pants. It must have fallen on the tile floor. He hoped the steam didn't hurt the oval blue ceramic amulet, the engraving on the other side. Usually, he protected it from the elements.

Sure as shit, he'd left it in Sara's bathroom. Probably on the floor behind the toilet. Great. He'd never left it anywhere before. But when Darlyn called, nagging him as usual, he'd managed to break in and ask about Truly. "He is giving Ruby a bay-ath," Darlyn said, inflection rising on the last word as though Jay objected. Far from it. Jay hung up and bounded down the stairs after Sara.

Now what. He thought about turning around and going back for it, but that was a negatory with bad weather looming, and Truly waiting and all. Jay banged his hand against the steering wheel, and the small car swerved, almost touching the Ram truck looming over him in the other lane. The guy at the wheel honked, and Jay gave him the finger. Then he zoomed right to the nearest exit, drove down the ramp, and pulled into a Hess station. He picked up his phone and speed dialed Sara. She picked it up on the first ring.

"Hello, handsome."

Jay smiled. Even though he was secure about his looks,

it didn't hurt to hear it from a pretty woman. Jay hadn't always had that all-American boy next door appearance women found hard to resist. No one, as Darlyn reminded him, thought Jay handsome as a baby. Strangers' 'new-baby-smile' faltered for a fraction of a second as they took in his too large features—big nose, big ears, bulging eyes, and thick lips. As a young teenager, he didn't attract girls. He was bony and his high cheekbones gave him an undernourished look. But by age fifteen, he filled out; he had muscles from wrestling training and a tan from water skiing all summer. By twenty it wasn't just the girls after him. Grown women and grown men made passes. He had aged into those prominent features; his bone structure was perfectly symmetrical. It was manly. Every year, he became all the more striking.

Jay was used to juggling women, and it startled him that morning to realize Sara was the only woman he was presently hooked up with. Her veiled hints about the future were his cue to back off. It had been a bad idea to date almost all the trainers. But, there was a new one he had his eye on— blonde, curvy, snappy dresser, big baby blue eyes. Gabrielle, he thought her name was.

Sara was quite a woman. But he had years of freedom ahead of him.

"Hello, beautiful," he said into his phone and smiled because Sara certainly was. Thinking about their hot morning together, his voice deepened. "What's up?"

"Nothing much. Just working. I wanted to hear your voice.

Jay said, "Listen, I left something—"

"Jay?"

Uh-oh. Her tone had serious conversation embedded in it. He decided to get off as soon as possible and just text her about the amulet.

"Yeah, listen, you're not coming in too clear..."

"What are you doing this weekend?"

His hand on the phone tightened. "Why?"

"I thought maybe you could come with me to visit my Gran? She likes it when I come by with a friend."

Jay was acutely aware that the execution of the invitation was breathless and too long. She had rehearsed it. "Oh," he said. "Well, can I let you know?"

"Are you busy?" Sara asked. The girl was digging in, Jay could tell. He wasn't going to get off the phone without a fricking good excuse. "God," Jay thought. "I should have broke it off a week ago."

Jay was good at breaking up with girls he dated from the office. He was a master psychologist when it came to ending relationships amicably. Every woman was different, but most fell into particular categories.

For the self-centered woman, he described a fatal illness like heart disease, even cancer. In one case he told a dim yet possessive young lady there was schizophrenia in his family, and he was starting to show symptoms. Then he'd tell them he couldn't subject them to his slow decline; reluctantly, they'd agree.

For the materialistic woman, he made it clear that technician grade three was the highest he cared to go career wise in the corporate hierarchy, and that he came from a poor family. For the prim and proper woman, he invented prison time and a long line of family felons. Sometimes the schizophrenia angle worked well here too. For the maternal woman, he'd tell them he was sterile.

Of course, since their work environment was one stewing petri dish of gossip, rumors reigned when Jay's name was mentioned and these 'facts' were aired in strictest confidence. So far, all of his exes assumed Jay hadn't wanted to tell her predecessors the awful truth, and he fully confided only to her and her alone.

But Jay hadn't figured out an excuse for Sara yet. For one thing, he was enjoying her company too much. For another, he didn't think any of his dodges would work on her.

Because of her attachment to the grandma who raised her, he could tell she was loyal and wouldn't be deterred by poor health. Her materialism extended to her own career, and she had a better job than he did, which she seemed to enjoy. And Sara was not the least bit prim and proper as evidenced by their escapade atop the kitchen table that morning. There was no indication she desired to rear children in the near or distant future, despite the fact they'd both forgotten a condom that morning. If anything, it proved they were too irresponsible to have children.

Sara was smart and attractive. For the first time, he felt a real challenge in escaping the clutches of an impending relationship. He was up to it. But not this morning. Too much going on. "Truly and I are watching Ruby this weekend," he said.

There was a small tic of time. "Where's Darlyn?" she asked.

Jay noted she didn't ask to join them. Not the maternal type then.

"Yoga. Visiting her mother."

"I don't understand," Sara said. "Wouldn't the grandmother like to see Ruby?"

Jay mouthed the word 'shit.' "She's the yoga teacher," he improvised. "Very flexible old lady."

"Jay,"Sara began.

"Sara?" he said loudly? "Sara?"

"I'm right here, Jay."

"Bad connection, Sara," Jay said. He pressed the red button on the phone screen, put the little red car into gear and scanned the traffic. He was going to have to ghost her, plain and simple. Jay pulled back on the gear stick and depressed the clutch. Once he got his amulet back. Then he stepped on the gas and the car roared into action.

"Jay the Juice," he said and maneuvered the red car into the left lane behind a gray SUV. He saw the driver check him out in her rearview, two babies strapped into the back seat. Suburban mom. His favorite kind. Jay gave her his best smile.

5
TRULY-MORNING

By the time Truly finished Ruby's bath and got her dressed in her pink toddler overalls with bunny faces on the pockets, he had some time. He thought he might take the child for a walk around the block in her stroller before brunch or breakfast or whatever Darlyn was calling that gruel she was cooking up on the stovetop.

Lifting the child into his arms, he clomped down the short staircase to the hall and opened the front door. Darlyn was chatting with the workmen next door, offering them a drink or some such. Truly opened the hall closet and removed a rickety umbrella stroller and with one hand, unfolded it and kicked the back hinge into place. He plopped the child into the sling back seat and arranged the little awning over her head. He grabbed two ball caps from the rack on the wall, picked up the stroller with the child in it and walked it down the steps. He settled the pink sparkly sequined cap on Ruby's head and donned his own ball cap, brim forward.

Darlyn, a cigarette dangling from her lips, barely turned around.

"Goin' somewhere, hon?"

"Just around the block," Truly said. He nodded to the workmen and rolled the stroller down the driveway around their parked trucks. Squirrels sprinted down the driveway and through the grass like pets. Truly stopped, waved to Darlyn and said, "Bye Momma." Ruby had taken her hat off and was inspecting it closely. She coughed. Truly took off, heading towards the east side of the neighborhood.

Harrison Parke was an old-fashioned Florida suburb built in the late eighties. Originally platted as a neighborhood of townhouses, the city still owned swaths of people's backyards on the outside chance that County Road would ever widen. Giant live oaks, tilting pine trees, and towering palm tree roots upended local driveways and cracked the sidewalks.

Truly quickened his pace. Ruby's little head bobbed up and down as Truly maneuvered the spindly wheels of the stroller around uneven layers of concrete. Beads of moisture dotted his head by the time he rolled to a stop in front of a sky-blue two-story house on the other side of the mile-wide circle that comprised eighty-two high-end homes with zero lot lines. He took out his phone, texted for a minute, and the door to the blue house opened.

"Bev," he said, and she turned his way.

She was a slender woman in her forties with shoulder-length wavy chestnut colored hair and skin the color of dark honey. She wore shades, white shorts, a white t-shirt, ankle socks and white sneakers. Walking briskly down the driveway, she extended her hand a few feet away. "Truly?"

"Over here," he said. "I can't come in today. I have the baby with me."

"Oh, Ruby," she said. Moving towards his voice, she grasped his hands holding the handles of the stroller and then crouched down at eye level with the little girl. She smiled.

"Bef," Ruby said, jamming her fingers in her mouth. She looked up at Truly and then back at Bev. She reached out a tentative hand and touched Bev's face. In turn, Bev traced her fingers over Ruby's chubby cheeks and through her wispy silky hair. "Hi Baby."

"Buh," Ruby said. She smiled, displaying white kernels of new teeth. Bev gave the child a soft kiss and straightened up. Truly moved the stroller into the driveway and drew Bev along by the hand, behind the ficus plant. He looked around quickly. Seeing no one, he turned her towards him, cupped her face in his hands and kissed her. He drew back a little and let her trace his face with her hands. "I'm going out," he said. "Today's the day." He glanced over at Ruby who had fallen asleep, her head tilted to the side, her thumb in her mouth. He put his arms around Bev's slim frame.

She pushed his hair up off his forehead. Her words were rushed, her voice soft. "I know this isn't the time and place. But for the first time in my life, I feel as though I can see. I feel as though I can see every day of my future. Our future. And I want it. I want to be a part of it more than anything."

"I want it too," Truly said, gripping her shoulders. "My God. "

Bev smiled and, as always, Truly thought it odd that she was so beautiful, and she'd never even seen an image of herself as an adult.

They met at one of those neighborhood poolside ordeals Darlyn insisted they go to. Darlyn, wearing a seventies era halter top, mingled, as he sat by the pool staring at the multi-colored lights that illuminated the water. Toby, the host, explained in excruciating detail how much it cost, the mechanics of the job, and so on. It was the kind of thing, the only kind of thing, neighbors in Harrison Parke discussed. Grills, lawn maintenance, air conditioners, roofs, gutters, pipes were the minutia of suburbia that constituted a life. The women exchanged recipes, rearranged furniture, compared window dressings, and bragged about their kids.

Truly collapsed into the lawn chair when Toby moved on, as if the man had sucked the life out of him. People reveal certain parts of themselves to other people, and Truly thought Toby revealed nothing that could be interpreted as friendship; he was more of an infomercial.

Truly knew he was not the sort of husband anyone would throw a birthday party for. It was always those beefy red-faced men, like Toby, whose blonde wives organized suburban gatherings. Everyone offered insincere birthday wishes, drank too much, and drilled down on small talk for a couple of hours. It was meant to be a tribal thing, communing with folks who lived nearby, but instead it was as boring as a year-old *Reader's Digest* in a dentist's office.

"Do you have a light?" the woman on his left asked. In the flickering light of the pool, her skin was ebony. Long wavy hair came down over her shoulders. A slim woman, she was dressed in a clinging white sheath made of silk. She wore shades.

Truly carried a lighter to these parties to fuel the inevitable bowls of weed the men smoked in the garage while the women put out the food. He lit her cigarette. He asked, "Why the glasses? Where's the glare?"

She smiled. "I wear the glasses because I'm blind. My eyes, I've been told, are not especially pretty." She waited a few seconds. "I'm Bev, by the way."

Truly heard of her, of course. Bev, described to him by his neighbors, was some sort of strange species—unmarried and disabled. He would not have guessed the poised woman to

45

his left was the same person.

So Truly didn't say anything—he didn't know what to say. He was peculiarly conscious of the woman sitting next to him, her arm near his. She smoked heavily, in silence, as if abstracted, a thin line creased above her level, dark brows. Her hair was dark, but a softish brown, not black, and her skin was smooth. Her breasts would be black; why Truly had this thought, he could not for the life of him say.

Truly said, "I like the live oak in front of your house. This neighborhood is mad for taking down trees. My neighbor took down a healthy Crimson Bottlebrush. When I asked him why, he said, 'It was spoiling the view of the house.'"

Bev shook her head. "I'm incredulous."

Truly, leaned forward, lowered his voice. She wore a citrus scent. He gazed at her face and wondered about her eyes behind the dark glasses. Were they milky, opaque? He decided to flirt with her. Why not? He did it all the time with the neighborhood matrons. It was harmless fun. He rubbed his palms along the legs of jeans, and his breath caught a little in his throat. His lips were inches from hers. He knew that she knew that. She was motionless as though she were under a spell. Truly spoke into her ear, his breath soft. "Hey, incredulous. Do you believe in love at first sight?"

"Now you're giving me a line," Bev said. "And now I've heard it all." She pushed him away, sat up abruptly, and made her way into the house, weaving, relying on memory as to where everything was.

People were drunk, tottering against each other, smiling, laughing. Pandora, practically indistinct, played: *We are the Septarians, we are the wizards of time, we can speed things up, we can slow it down.*

No one noticed her. She bumped into a drunk man wearing a paper Burger King crown. They both staggered.

Truly shouted, "Bev," but the party noise was an uproarious hum, and she didn't hear. Truly leaped to his feet, strode into the living room, and pushed the crowned neighbor hard onto a sectional couch where the man rolled to his side. Then he lost sight of Bev. Over the heads of his neighbors, he glimpsed the white dress, and he stepped on some feet to lunge forward and just catch the door as she walked into the bathroom.

"Bev," he said so she would know who it was. Then he shut and locked the door and held her shoulders to the wall and kissed her as though his life depended on it.

Bev was stiff at first, but then less so. Truly dropped his hands and tugged on the short hem of her silken sheath. He lifted it up to her waist. Then above her breasts. He watched her face, not her body as he did this. Someone banged on the bathroom door. 'S'matter? Ya fall in?'

Bev started to move away, but Truly said, "Whoa, whoa." He ran the back of his hand across her chest. No bra.

Their neighbor banged on the door again. "C'mon!"

Bev whispered, "Are you drunk?"

"You didn't answer my question."

Bev didn't ask him what he meant. She said, "I have no sight."

Truly let the hem of her dress drop, covering her breasts, hips, thighs. He took her hands and held them to his face. "See."

She traced his jaw, ran a finger over his nose. With one hand, he reached and gently removed her sunglasses. Bev dropped her hands. Her sable-colored eyes looked opaque. Almond shaped. Fathomless.

The pounding on the door stopped. He put the sunglasses back on, looping them gently over her ears.

"You go out first," he said. "I'll follow in a minute. But don't go."

Bev stopped, her hand on the door.

"I want to walk you home." Bev smiled then, over her shoulder, as she turned the knob and slipped out. Truly turned and looked at himself in the mirror as though he were a stranger. Later, he wondered if that was when he fell hard for her, or if he felt that way the minute he saw her.

Now, a year later, he stood in her driveway, his hands cupping her elbows. "I'm going to make it happen," he said, his voice deeper than usual. "This is not some middle-aged affair. I am not stringing you along."

Bev stepped back and gestured towards Ruby's carriage. Truly knew Bev situated objects in her mind in order to maneuver without sight.

"We're not leaving her with Darlyn," Truly said. His voice sounded rough. "That's the plan."

"Just checking," Bev said.

Something caught his eye a few yards down the street. It was a black cat, perhaps a stray, sauntering down the sidewalk. As he watched, it slid under a car and crouched there, its eyes shining.

"We can talk later," Bev was saying, and Truly suddenly became aware of the time.

"I have to go," he said. A plane flew overhead, and he heard a lawnmower sputter a few doors down. He bent and kissed Bev on the cheek and turned to go, grasping the handles of the umbrella stroller. She clutched his sleeve.

"I love you," she said.

Even though Truly knew it was impossible, it seemed to him Bev stared directly at him from behind her dark glasses. It was as though she was the only person who had ever really seen him in his whole life.

6
SARA-MORNING

After Jay hung up on her, Sara sat at her cubicle, staring at the phone in her hand. She wasn't aware she had stared at it for several seconds until she heard some trainers rounding the corner in the angular maze in which they all worked. Their heels sank so far into the plush purple carpet, they tottered. Their talk sounded like headlines nobody bothered to read.

"Her makeup is every shade of wrong."

"I know! She looks so 2010s."

There was the sound of the Women's lav door opening, and the voices went on for a bit, echoing, "No puking today, okay Karen?" And, "God, I hate this fat around my waist."

Shut up! Sara thought. She swiveled to her desk, propped her cell up on her Skyhorse phone stand, pulled her chair in. She sat there with her fingers poised over the keyboard.

Usually, her work drew her in, built on itself, assumed form and structure. Until she took this job with InterTech, Sara had no idea she excelled at research, organization, writing, and teaching. She scored high on her SATs and ACTs in high school, but her grades were mediocre. She ended up with a Liberal Arts degree from a Florida University. She moved around for a year or two out of college and ended up telemarketing while commuting to downtown Jacksonville. But she was always cruising the internet for work. It was hard for millennials to get ahead, but Sara wasn't someone who let crushing odds intimidate her.

A college professor Sara liked emailed her the Glass Door job advertising the InterTech training position. So, Sara mailed off her resume, heard back, did a phone interview, and was finally invited to appear for a live interview.

That was how she met Galvin. He was professional and somewhat intimidating. "Why do you want this job?" he'd asked. She could tell he thought she was just another young woman, who would move in a year or two to somewhere more exciting than suburban Lake Ann. A woman in her late twenties could do whatever she wanted—decide she wanted to go back to school, or start an internet business, or even can salmon in Alaska.

"I want to stay local," Sara had said. "I have a grand-mother who lives in the area."

She thought that softened him a little, because he leaned forward and said, "You're close to her?"

Not one to mistake body language, Sara leaned in too. Behind him, in the field below his window, she could see a white and a brown pony running around, circling the inner fence.

"She's like a mother to me," she said looking into his eyes, which happened to be the color of acorns.

A presentation was required to clinch the position, and Sara blew it out of the park presenting like a pro in front of Galvin, his boss, Nick Montana, Jackie Moats, and the director of training, a woman who looked just like Delta Burke and whose name was, in fact, Danielle. Sara's performance came from somewhere inside herself. She was prepared, but it seemed she was born to do this. She put the presentation together about improving memory, using several techniques she researched and used with Gran.

Galvin told her there were over 200 applicants for the position, but Sara was everyone's first choice. It was good to know she had talent, but it took her a little while to warm up to him. The trouble was, he didn't know he was good looking, or he didn't care. He was like an Abercrombie model, in a buttoned up, white collar shirt. Well defined features, a sharp jaw, and angular cheekbones. The tanned complexion of his skin went well with his amber eyes. His hair was prematurely gray, but his face was unlined, and to be honest, he kind of took her breath away until he opened his mouth and revealed that he was an arrogant nerdy guy who always had to be right.

He corrected her almost every time she said anything. His mansplaining was infuriating. Still, they were compatible physically. At odd moments, she still vividly recalled one afternoon when they literally made love for hours. It was so intense she could barely breathe, and she told him that she loved him. And then what had he done?

She asked him to a Gordon Lightfoot concert—he loved those Canadian crooners. He said, no, he had to attend a wedding. One of his best friends. In all innocence, Sara asked him if he could bring a guest.

"Oh, yes," he said.

She just stood there looking at him in the doorway of his office. She even smiled.

"Well?" she said.

Galvin's smile faded. "I'm going with Meryl."

Sara just stared. She thought the blood may have drained from her face, but maybe she was being dramatic. "You have a date with your ex-wife?"

He had actually laughed. "It's not like that."

Sara stepped past the threshold and faced Galvin directly. "Are you really divorced?"

"Of course, I am!"

"I am starting to doubt that." Sara turned and walked back to her cubicle, which wasn't any kind of grand exit since it was only a few yards away.

Galvin was right on her heels; Sara didn't turn around. She sat, facing her computer screen. She reached down and pressed the Power button on the hard drive with her middle finger.

"Look here," Galvin said. "Kyle is a good friend of ours. We've known him since college."

Sara spun her swivel chair around and faced him. "You honestly don't see anything weird about this?"

"What? You want me to take you to an event that would bore you?" One of the trainers loitered past Sara's cubicle.

"Will you lower your voice?" Sara whispered furiously.

Galvin tried to assume a more casual stance, leaning his hand against the crest of the beige cubicle. It shifted slightly, and he moved his hand, shoved it into his pocket. "Am I supposed to hate my ex-wife?" he whispered.

"No," Sara whispered. "But she is not supposed to be your date to an important social event."

"You have tickets to a concert. You're busy. Besides, it's not important," Galvin said.

"If it's not important, take me," Sara said. It was, she realized, the first time she stood up to him, insisted on her way.

Galvin's face turned a little red. "That's ridiculous." He paused. "You're ridiculous."

"Oh, I am, am I?" Sara jumped to her feet and looked Galvin square in the eye. "Take me to the wedding," she said.

"Or we are through."

Galvin raised his voice a little. "Is that an ultimatum?"

"You can call it whatever you want," Sara hissed. "Because I am through arguing with you."

She stalked off to the Women's room, and they had not spoken, texted, or called each other the rest of the week. That weekend, Galvin escorted Meryl to their friend's wedding. Sara ghosted him ever since.

Now she was involved with the office stud, who was probably dating three other girls, which is why his weekends booked way in advance. Sara felt empty. She didn't like feeling this way. Maybe she misinterpreted Jay's call. Maybe his phone dropped the connection.

"Sara?"

She looked up and saw Jackie standing solidly in the opening to her cubicle. It irritated her that Jackie called the men 'sir' or by their surnames, and addressed all the women by their first names.

"You have a call."

Jackie only showed up to announce personal calls, like some kind of rebuke. Sure enough when Sara looked at her desk phone the red light was flashing. Her heart leaped. Here was proof Jay really suffered a dropped call. He was calling her back on her office line, a more secure line.

"Thanks Jackie," she said, flashing a brilliant smile to the grim woman, turning now to resume reconnaissance at the reception desk.

"Don't thank me," Jackie said.

Sara snatched up the receiver. "I'm so glad you called back."

There was silence. Then a female voice said, "Sara?"

Sara flew down to earth with a painful thud. Her caller was clearly not Jay. "Who is this?"

"Why," the voice said, "this is Meryl."

Sara was nonplussed. "Who?"

"It's Meryl," the woman on the other end of the line said. "Meryl Steele. Galvin's ex-wife."

7
DARLYN-MORNING

Darlyn was alone in the kitchen when Jay showed up. He came in as he always did, as though he were doing her a favor. He yelled at her smart speaker, "Alexa, stop." The sound of Christian rock abruptly ceased.

Darlyn frowned, put down her spoon and flexed her fingers. "Don't yell, idiot."

Jay settled on the bench next to the table. Darlyn regarded him stonily. She rose from the picnic table and returned to the stove, lighting a cigarette. Something was bubbling in a big pot. "Dang, Jay. Lucky for you, that Truly is runnin' late."

Jay shrugged. "Whatever." He threw a set of keys on the table. "Those are yours."

"Is it done?" Darlyn asked.

"Yep. Keep Truly outta the bedroom. Make sure it's gone, time we get back. What's cookin'?"

"Oatmeal. Not enough for you."

Jay rose. "I'll just get some coffee." He went to the cabinet over the stove and selected a coffee mug. He held it under the large silver urn on the counter and pushed the lever forward. The coffee gushed into his cup, steam and the aroma of brewed coffee rose into the air.

There was a clatter at the threshold, and Truly emerged, pushing a sleeping Ruby in her stroller.

"Dang, Truly, her neck is all bent."

Truly glanced over to Jay, who stood. They both nodded. Then Truly turned, stooped and gently lifted Ruby from her umbrella seat into his arms. She snored softly.

"I'll be right back," he said.

Darlyn slopped a ladle of oatmeal into a bowl and placed it on the picnic bench. She rummaged through the drawer for a spoon, just as Truly sat down heavily on the bench across from Jay. "She's asleep," Truly said to no one in particular.

"I could see that when you got home," Darlyn said, joining the men holding a cup of coffee. "So what time ya'll pushing off?"

Truly gulped a spoonful of oatmeal, made a face, and glanced at his watch. "Eleven."

Jay drank his coffee, and Truly finished his oatmeal in two big spoonfuls. The men rose simultaneously, leaving their dishes on the table.

Truly opened the coat closet, lifted a cardboard container from the overhead rack, and fit it into his tackle bag. He came back and faced Darlyn. "If you get a chance, later," he said, "can you throw some chlorine in the pool?" He bent to kiss her cheek. Darlyn could tell she surprised him when she lifted up her arms and embraced him around the neck. Then she stepped back. "When d'ya think you'll be back?"

"I don't know," Truly said. He looked over at Jay. "What would you say?"

Jay shrugged. "We have to go out three miles to scatter the old man's ashes. Sea is a little rough today."

"I'll text you when we get back," Truly said. He yawned.

Jay shook his head. "Buck up, bro. Here we go."

He gave Darlyn a brief wave, three fingers, a gesture at once friendly and indifferent. He jammed a black ball cap on his head and headed towards the door.

"I'll get some more coffee on the way," Truly said.

The men left. Darlyn cleared the dishes off the table and piled them in the sink. She had help coming in a couple hours, around the time Ruby would wake up. She walked down the beige Berber carpeted hallway to her room, scented with lavender and lilac wall flowers. The color of the walls were a creamy white, barely yellowed in spite of Darlyn's constant exhalation of nicotine. There was a shiny silver bedspread on the king-sized bed, covered with small lacy pillows and two oversized shams. A canopy with teal-colored curtains added height, making the bed the showpiece of the room.

Humming a little, Darlyn closed the curtains, allowing a little filtered light into the room, and removed her clothes, carrying them with her into her bathroom and throwing them into the white wicker hamper. The bathroom was as big as a small apartment with a stall that stretched across the length of the room with a nozzle on each end.

Darlyn took a hot shower, toweled her long hair dry, combed it, piled it on her head, sprayed it, and shoved her arms into Truly's ratty terry cloth robe. She lit a cigarette the second she was out of the shower, balancing the lit end away from the counter on the edge of the sink. Smoke and steam circled hazily near the light fixture in the ceiling. She was just cinching the sash when she heard the doorbell ring. Darlyn shoved her feet into some old Keds and ran down the hallway to the front door. She opened it.

The work site was deserted now, but on her doorstep stood Link, the construction worker with a pool business on the side. He carried the tray with the plastic cups. He seemed to occupy the entire door frame.

"I can come back later," he said in his squeaky voice, taking in Darlyn's wet hair. "Or you can just let me in the gate, and I'll take a look at the pump for you."

"Oh, don't pay me any mind," Darlyn said. "You jus step on up here and walk through the house."

Link hesitated, looked around as if for support and wiped his big feet on the welcome mat by the door. Then he stepped into the house.

8
GALVIN- MORNING

It was turning into a long day for Galvin. The minutes felt like hours, and the hours were interminable. He spent the morning with the door closed, on the phone with customers. He wrestled with paperwork. Normally he took grumpy satisfaction in getting the work done, but today it was just one long slog. The routine of his life was suddenly unbearable.

Around ten o'clock, he talked to a customer in Alaska. The customer's name was Gus, a man so amiable Galvin had trouble getting off the phone. After their business was concluded, Gus said, "If you ever wanna leave the lower forty eight, man, come on up here."

Galvin considered. "Why would I want to do that?"

"I don't know. I thought you were single."

"I am."

"Well, this is the place to come to if you're free. It's the great frontier, man. It's fishing, mountain climbing, bush planes, adventure."

"What are you talking about? Isn't it cold as hell?

The man laughed. "Not in the summer. And I admit, it's not too pleasant in the winter. It's the kind of cold that can stop you in your tracks and kill you if you don't walk fast. Your face and other body parts actually freeze."

"Oh, that just sounds great."

"Well, it makes you appreciate twenty four hour a day

summers. The solstice here is really something. Dancing in the street. Nubile maidens." Gus laughed. He was a graying stooped man in his early 50s with two divorced wives and alimony.

"I'll think about it."

"Do that. We can use good men around here. The women all wear thigh high boots and not much else in the summer."

Galvin laughed, but after he got off the phone, he stood facing his window, with his hands clasped behind his back. It wasn't time for his peanut butter sandwich quite yet. The ponies weren't out that morning, racing in circles around the perimeter of the fence. He missed them. Lately, he felt as though he were facing a dark tunnel instead of a clear path.

He turned to his computer and googled Alaska. Pictures of yellow and purple wildflowers displayed on his screen. The entire region was an enormous, rough and rocky wilderness with glaciers. Its rugged range separated the southeast passage from the rest of the country. Its waters were a deep glossy aquamarine studded with bluish pieces of glacier. The pictures stirred something deep and visceral within Galvin.

Abruptly, he got up from his desk, pushed back his chair, opened his office door and strode into the hall. He turned left on the purple corridor and walked about 100 yards to the door marked Danielle Biggs. He tapped on her door.

She looked up and smiled. "Galvin," she said as though she were announcing a celebration. Danielle had an unusual beauty that made walkway models look irrelevant; she was robust and real. By ordinary social standards she was overweight, but no one ever looked at Danielle without feeling that there would be something lost by less of her. Her eyes were as hazel as pea soup and her black hair was a long curly mane that swept her shoulders. She wore bright red lipstick and a bronze shade of shadow on her eyelids. Unlike the trainers, she wore flowery Eileen Fischer dresses with smart boxy jackets. And flat shoes. There was always a glint of gold at her throat, a locket with a diamond chip in the center.

Galvin gave her a half smile and said, "Hey, do you have a minute?" She was his equal, a manager, and she was close to her team of trainers who conferred with her often on matters professional and personal. Galvin's job was more bean counting and less people orientated. He sometimes felt as though his job was less important than hers.

"Sure." Danielle saved something on her computer screen and shut the lid on her laptop. She slid forward a glass mason jar filled with peppermint discs wrapped in plastic "Candy?"

Galvin waved the jar away. "This'll just take a minute." He sat down in the chair facing her desk, lounging, taking care not to put his hands on the arms. Danielle told him years ago that she kept loosening the screws on one chair arm or another so it would fall off if the sitter leaned on it. "Then, whoever it is has to apologize," she said. "It gives me the upper hand."

Danielle put her fingertips together and made eye contact. "So, what do you want to talk about?"

Suddenly, Galvin was not sure. "This will sound crazy." He sat up, as if to leave. Danielle raised her eyebrows and waited.

Galvin took a deep breath, exhaled and sat back down. "Don't we…do we…have an office in Alaska? I was talking to a customer there. Gus."

Danielle touched the locket at her throat. "Our Seattle office takes care of our Alaska customers.

"Oh," Galvin said. "In that case. I just thought. Maybe."

But Danielle was already on her feet, pacing a well-worn path next to her desk. "Goodness. It's so funny you would mention this. Because I'm supporting the opening of an office in Anchorage."

Galvin gripped the arms of his chair, which promptly loosened and fell to the floor. "Oh," he said. "Sorry." He stooped and tried awkwardly to reattach it.

Danielle laughed a deep and throaty sound. "Just leave it on the floor. Galvin, this is amazing. It's like you read my mind. But why do you want to relocate?"

"Well," he thought, "ex-wife is getting married. Starting a family." He looked down. He couldn't just blurt that out.

Danielle perched on the side of her desk. It wobbled slightly. She waited. When Galvin didn't respond, she said, "Weren't you seeing someone in the office?"

"Sara." Galvin sighed. "That's pretty much over."

Danielle leveled her gaze to his. "I think we should discuss this Alaska thing. Maybe this evening." She crossed her feet at the ankles and swung them back and forth like a schoolgirl.

"Really?" Galvin asked. He felt a little mesmerized.

"Yes," Danielle said. "I really think so."

"Well, great." Galvin tore his gaze away from hers and stood. "I'll just come by your office at the end of the day. Or should we just meet somewhere?"

"We can go in my car," Danielle said. "There's this great little place in Lake Ann I've been dying to try."

"I live in Lake Ann," Galvin said. "What's the name?"

"It's…wait." Danielle walked around to her desk and looked at her desk calendar. "Claudio's. Have you ever been there?"

"I'll see you at six," Galvin said.

9
JAY-LATE MORNING

Jay felt no apprehension even though his weather radio said thunderstorms were moving offshore that afternoon. Wind can increase rapidly in thunderstorms. Big deal. He had gone to war for God's sake. And he knew exactly how he got out of it alive.

Truly. This trip was partial payback.

He always knew he was going into the military. What else was a poor boy from an indifferent family to do? He enlisted at eighteen, his senior year in high school. Darlyn barely looked up from the television to say goodbye. Both his grandparents were dead by then.

In 2010, he landed by helicopter at night in a village, near a band of settlements with poppy fields. The Americans were going to blow it up. But soon they were getting shot at from every direction. Jay felt as though he were fighting the entire country alone. Some men were blown up by a roadside bomb. He heard an explosion, and then Truly was screaming on the radio.

By the time the medics got to him, he was spread eagle on the side of a canal with shrapnel shredding his legs. There was blood everywhere. The pain was unbearable. Truly gave Jay morphine and tried to joke. "What a great job we're doing. Bringing peace." After the drug kicked in, they both laughed.

Eventually, a pilot landed. By then Jay was quiet. He lived. He was not disabled, just scarred. Well, a lot of people had scars. He was honorably discharged. There was a picture of him in the Lake Ann Sentinel.

Truly received a purple heart. There was no question Jay would have died without Truly. There was no question Jay would do anything for him. It's why he still lived at home. It's why he quit drinking. Darlyn and Ruby were kin, but when a man saves your life, you owe him your own. As if he were, you know, a father.

So that's why he was on a pier on a workday preparing to set out in bad weather on a small boat with one engine and no radio. Well, at least they had their cell phones. He glanced at his screen and saw another text from Sara, which was kind of uncool. *Call me when you get in*, she texted. He never pegged her for desperation.

There were things on his mind. Jetson Park smelled of tar, a toxic reek, in the midmorning heat. Next door, the cruise ship terminals set up shop with super yachts, which could hold a small city aboard its freshly painted and swabbed decks. Coming in and out of Jetson Park was challenging to maneuver because the deep harbors were dominated by foreign entities just like everything of value in Florida. Still, Jay loved boating, the beach. Too bad the old man hadn't left the boat for him. Truly didn't even know how to steer. Truly didn't know a lot of things. Jay protected him. Today was no different.

In Fort Canaveral, he passed the Survey Tower and pulled into the lane with the visitor's booth for Jetson Park. A man in a uniform noted his year-round pass and waved him on to the forty five acres east of Fort Canaveral, a large L-shaped complex where the hulks of cruise ships stayed in harbor. Jay parked between two white lines in a deserted parking lot. He got out, threw his keys up in the air and deftly caught them.

People on bikes passed him as he walked to The Water's Edge, a yellow a-frame store with a tin roof painted green and pavilions with picnic tables planted under scraggy palm trees. Two prominent green dumpsters stood near the entrance next to a Porta Potty. They passed a homeless lady with purple hair shuffling through the dust with a backpack.

For a minute, Jay forgot he was here with Truly to scatter the old man's remains. He wanted a beer. One of Jay's secrets was he was in AA, Alcoholics Anonymous. It was the main reason he didn't stick with relationships. It was one of the reasons he didn't go out on weekends, amateur nights, when everyone drank too much. Women his age, in their twenties and thirties, wanted to party.

Truly was already at the register, buying some beer. "Hey man. Should we get bait?"

Jay shook his head. "In and out, bro. I didn't bring my reel neither."

He opened the glass door of the standing cooler, stood indecisively for a moment and grabbed a bottled cola. The men paid for their purchases and walked outside. The landscape was barren, dominated by cranes, boxy buildings, wire fences, big cylindrical drains with grates over them. An empty tennis court was one long heat wave on a clay turf.

A scorched summer hellscape. Truly and Jay strolled down the pier, where people fished the Intercoastal over one side of the rail. Others squatted, barefoot, cleaning snook. There was a tang of fish blood in the air. On the other side, bordered by striped granite boulders, snowy egrets pecked, and sea turtles swam after minnows. Jay saw one baby turtle with barnacles on its shell. Some dark clouds rushed the horizon, hemmed it in. Pelicans bobbed in the water or perched on concrete pilings. A gull flew by with a French fry in its beak. "I'll barbeque you, you fuck, " a woman screamed after it.

"It's a rough world out there," he said to Truly.

Truly nodded, lost in thought. Then he yawned. He had a day-old beard, and he wore a stained pair of yellow bathing trunks, a fruit of the loom undershirt, and a blue ball cap. He carried a small blue tackle bag by the straps.

"Speaking of which, you looking kinda rough, Tiger." It threw Jay off a little. He was usually the sloppy one, the impulsive one, the risk taker.

Truly clapped his shoulder. "Feeling kinda rough, Billy Ray," he said, imitating Ackroyd as Winthorpe in *Trading Places*.

Jetson Park was a place of action, never a quiet respite. Sometimes, Jay thought, it was like the prelude to an action movie. A guy wearing a red ball cap, fishing on the jetty, turned up a boombox blaring Kenny Rogers. A tugboat roared past, a helicopter chuffed overhead. The men walked down the dry cement towards the dock, bobbing with the incoming waves. Truly maneuvered the trailer down the launch, and the boat bobbed with the same rhythm. Jay checked his watch. It was exactly 11:00 a.m..

A Ford F-150 pulled up. There was a park logo on the side, and the gal in the driver's seat looked efficient and wore a ball cap. She didn't get out, just rolled down her window.

"Ya'll have year-round passes?" she shouted. She had lank hair and dark skin. Her eyes were hidden behind tinted aviator glasses. Likely they were rimmed by cratering crow's feet from years of sun damage. Jay knew this kind of civil servant already, just from the tone of her voice.

"I do. Wanna see my receipt?"

The woman in the Park truck just went on as though Jay hadn't said anything. "Because no one, I repeat, no one, is to use this dock unless he is a bona fide year-round pass holder. "

Truly waved in a friendly way. "Got it."

"I'd get a move on too, if I was you. It's gonna come down hard." The woman in the park truck nodded to herself, adjusted her shades in the rear-view mirror, backed up without looking and roared off looking for other pass holders to harass.

"Asshat," Jay said.

"Give a woman a little bit of power." Truly broke off to yawn hard.

"Are you okay?" Jay punched Truly lightly in the arm, which caused him to sway.

"Sure I am."

Jay held up his hand and felt the light sprinkle of rain on his palm. Drops dimpled the roiling water. The twenty four-foot center console skiff bobbed near the pier. They always called it 'the boat,' but it actually had a name, written in broad black paint strokes on the helm.

Early Byrd

The Early Byrd had a 60 horsepower Mercury four stroke engine and a flat bottom. There was no anchor, but there was a trolling motor, which would enable the boat to circle a small area without moving. There was no GPS, no radio, no flare guns. But they'd probably still have phone service three miles out to sea, to throw the old man's ashes, legally, overboard.

Truly said, "Let's roll. I'm gonna park the truck and trailer. See if you can start that cocksucker."

Jay noticed Truly was slurring his words, but he didn't want to ask him again if he was all right. He would just keep an eye on him. He climbed aboard, checked to see if the boat gear shift was in neutral by moving the black handle left and right. Then he crouched, turned the key in the ignition with his left hand and heard the water running through the engine as it roared. The rain started coming down in earnest.

10
TRULY-LATE MORNING

Truly found himself thinking about the old man as he and Jay walked toward the boat. Arthur Ravija wasn't one of those dads who spun kids around by their arms until they were dizzy. He was the kind of dad who tucked him in at night, and read him stories. Mostly illustrated parables from the Bible. Truly had memories like that about the old man.

There were other memories. Since the old man couldn't say no to him, he let Truly stay up on school nights to watch horror movies. Like *Psycho, Night of the Living Dead*, and *Nightmare on Elm Street*. Truly almost flunked third grade because he couldn't stay awake in class, and he kept having nightmares as he lay with his cheek flat on the desk, waking up screaming.

Truly's hair was sandy colored and frizzy, but the old man's straight dark hair rested flat atop his bony head. His own skin was white and smooth while the old man's was a hide, a disorderly mess of leathery wrinkles. Truly had large hands, capable of putting things together and taking things apart. The old man's hands were withered, and his fingers were skeletal. He was always the quietest person in a room.

What he remembered was the old man being bossed around by repairmen, cops, and bosses. He was perpetually calm, and he backed down immediately with a tense face and a voice that went barely above a whisper. It was truly a paradox. The old man, as a federal agent, literally had a license to kill.

What did it take to spur him into lethal action?

Truly missed having someone else in the house to temper the nonstop fussiness, the protectiveness in which he was raised. Truly was, by nature, mild mannered. But he forced himself to fish, hunt, and play football, intuitive activities for which he was not suited, and he did not enjoy. But he felt damaged by witnessing the suppression of the old man's temper, and the consequent abuse he sustained. Yet all that respectful distance and subservient behavior took its toll. The old man had issues.

Once, Truly had to answer sustained ringing at the doorbell. When he opened the door, the old man fell to the floor. The floor was tiled, and the old man fell heavily stretching out his right arm to break his fall. There was a crackling sound, and shock so fierce the old man went catatonic. He was twelve at the time, but Truly never forgot the sight of the old man's bone protruding from his forearm.

He called an ambulance, and the old man went to the hospital. Truly told the doctors and nurses the old man slipped and fell in the bathroom. He did not want to get his father in trouble. The old man said, in a wave of delusion, his broken arm was the result of a witch's spell.

In time, Truly came to terms with the old man's shrinking disposition, the effeminate posturing. Then he dragged him from the water, he sat by his deathbed, and he held his hand. His duty was fulfilled. He thought it odd, though, and strangely unsettling, that the old man, a good man, was struck by lightning.

11
SARA-LATE MORNING

Sara held her phone away for the second time that day and stared at it. She heard a tinny voice squawk out of the microphone, "Hello? Hello?"

Sara quickly put her cell phone up to her ear and said, "Sorry." Then she silently cursed herself for starting the conversation by apologizing. She knew who Meryl Steele was. Had Galvin put her up to the phone call?

Sara took a deep breath and tried to recover ground. "I'm just surprised to find you on the other end of the line."

Meryl laughed, not an unpleasant sound. "I'm as surprised as you are."

Sara decided not to parry. "To what do I owe the pleasure?"

Meryl must have made a similar decision. "I called Galvin a few minutes ago to invite him to my wedding. I told him he could bring a guest, assuming he would bring you. He said you all had broken up."

"Correct," Sara said in her best corporate tone. She was embarrassed by what was coming.

"Galvin said you broke up with him because he took me to Kyle's wedding."

Galvin, that rat. Now, Meryl would tell her that she was silly to make a fuss. Keeping her professional tone, she said, "Also correct.

"Well." Meryl paused. "I don't blame you one bit. What an ass."

"Well…yeah," Sara said. She slowly exhaled.

Meryl went on. "Jim was out of town, and I just assumed Galvin had no other plans."

"I asked him to take me," Sara blurted out. "He said I'd be bored."

"Well, that's beside the point, isn't it?" Meryl said. "But Galvin is like that."

"Like what?" Sara felt as though Meryl was about to turn over a stone, giving her some insight she could keep.

"Oh, we're so much alike. Stubborn, fussy, and opinionated. We got along, but Galvin kept pushing for kids, and I didn't see us as great parents. The two of us would put too much pressure on a kid."

"Is that why you broke up?" Sara asked.

"I'd say it's a big reason," Meryl said. "Because, Sara? He's a very nice man. I just wanted to reach out, I wasn't going to say this much, but you sound like an intelligent person. Galvin is smart. And loyal. And, uh, funny, and way cute for a buttoned-down type. If he tends to be sort of anal, you know, at times a pain in the butt? A person with a more relaxed personality could temper that."

"Did he ask you to call me?" Sara asked.

"Absolutely not," Meryl said. "But he did sound a little shaken when I told him about the baby."

"Oh. Congratulations," Sara said.

"It is pretty awesome," Meryl said. "I'm going crazy, but Jim is just as laid back as he can be. 'Merl,' he says, 'couples been having babies forever.'"

Sara laughed, feeling a flicker of warmth towards Meryl. After her disappointment with Jay earlier, she was more inclined to forgive Galvin. "So, am I invited to this wedding?"

"Gosh, yes," Meryl said. "That would be great. Love to meet you."

"Ditto," Sara said.

12

LINK- LATE MORNING

Link bent his knees and deposited Darlyn's tray on the foyer floor. Then he looked around, at the Berber carpet, at the ceiling, everywhere except at Darlyn. "Pool straight ahead?"

"Jus ya hold your hosses, big fella," Darlyn said. "There's somethin' I wanna show you."

"What." It wasn't even a question. He finally looked at Darlyn, the abundant hair extensions, coupled with the bathrobe and sneakers.

Darlyn gestured towards the back of the living room. "Why don't you set here for a minute? Cool off? I can be right back in a jiffy."

"Look, I'll just…" But Darlyn was gone, and with a grunt of resignation, Link entered the white carpeted room. There was a lush sectional sofa, also white, with lacy ecru throw pillows. A modern glass coffee table all chrome and angles, positioned strategically six inches from the sofa, was close enough to pick up and put down a drink on the square glass coasters etched with roses. A few cruise magazines and an old Bible flanked a vase of white silk roses. A fake fireplace dominated the center of the room, and Link stared at it a minute, scowling at the mantel, at the family pictures in silver frames. He was afraid to sit on the spotless couch after working all day, so he moved over to the blonde wooden bookcase.

Link was a big reader, particularly of poetry, but the

75

bookshelves were filled with red leather-bound books that looked as though they had never been opened. Link slid one off the shelf and tested the heft of the tome in his hand, The Complete Works of William Thackeray. He turned the pages until he got to Vanity Fair, one of his favorite books.

Link wanted to be an English teacher. This ambition was drummed into him by his own English teacher who mothered him in tenth grade when he moved to Lake Ann, a scared skinny kid, in a new school. He'd taken Ms. Perez's "Writing for College" class. Most of the kids in the class were Advanced Placement students. They wrote about family trips to Hawaii and missionary work in the Dominican Republic. He was a bit flashier being from South Florida—big pants, gold around his neck, a grill. But Ms. Perez smiled at him, so he got up and read his essay about walking in on a robbery at a convenience store in West Palm Beach. Link wrote that he put his hands in the air, but the guy holding the gun said, "Link?" And gave him a ride home.

It was all bullshit, of course. The closest he ever came to a robbery was not returning a library book on time. But Ms. Perez's room became his refuge, the place he went after school at least once a week to tell her about his victories and his failures. She smiled and made time for him. "You are an awesome kid, Link," she'd say. Soon, he was calling her Mom.

Link's parents uprooted him in high school from a suburb in Royal Palm Beach to move to Lake Ann because his mother got a judgeship and his father a position as law professor at Collins College, which didn't seem like a college at all to Link, more like a refined version of Disney. Or Disney's interpretation of a southern college— all pastels and live oaks, lush grass, and

Spanish revival architecture. The point was, his parents were in the prime of lucrative, engrossing careers. Link was expected to be self-reliant, responsible. Like his parents, in fact.

But he was a kid, eighteen years old, and he couldn't think beyond the moment. He turned out to be popular at Lake Ann High School. He had that 'new kid' persona, and he ended up having a good time. He graduated from high school with a low grade point average and no extracurriculars beyond football, where he was okay, but not pro material, not like those athletes doing the mud bowl in Belle Glade. Link's SAT and ACT scores did not break 1000.

He couldn't get into Collins University even with his dad working there. His parents had ethics, so they refused to pull any academic strings on Link's behalf. When all was said and done, he couldn't get into any school except a state two-year college. He lost touch with Ms. Perez.

Link dreamed of applying to a college somewhere far away like Hawaii. There had to be a university on one of those volcanic islands. But it would take money, out of state tuition, which was why Link was finishing up his two-year degree, working construction and running a pool cleaning business on the side. His strict parents thought the hard work was good for him, but he was tired of manual labor. He daydreamed about reading Keats to rapt students seated in the shade of a palm tree. "Bright star, would I were steadfast as thou art." Oh, he was motivated.

Darlyn was gone a long time, and by the time she returned, Link was so absorbed in reading he didn't hear when she reentered the room.

"Hey."

"What is it," he said without looking up.

"Hey, honey." He looked up then. What he saw would have set off strident alarm bells, if such a thing were scientifically possible, through psychic force.

Darlyn wore a filmy white robe with fur on the cuffs and high heeled satin bedroom slippers. And that was pretty much it, Link thought, except for a tiny ring pierced through her navel. She looked, for all the world, like a lewd Barbie doll. Darlyn lifted one foot and planted it on the sofa, George Washington-on-the-Potomac style. Only she wasn't wearing breeches. She stared at Link.

Very deliberately, Link shut the book and placed it on the book shelf. Then he turned, lifted two hands, palms out.

"Lady," he said, "you are really barking up the wrong tree."

Darlyn almost stumbled from her perch on the couch.

"Beg pardon?"

"Look," he said. "I don't even dig women."

Darlyn frowned. "Don't knock it if you ain't never tried it."

"It doesn't work that way," Link said

"Well, I got something to show you anyway," Darlyn said. She removed her foot from the white couch and moved over to stand in front of Link. Close. Link stepped back, but Darlyn advanced. Finally, his back was literally against the wall.

"What about the pool pump?" Link asked.

Darlyn shook her head. A few strands of hair fell down around her face. She took Link's hand. "In there." She gestured towards what Link assumed was the bedroom.

"Oh no," he said, practically squeaking. "Nope. No, no, no, no."

Darlyn had a firm grip on his hand, and she steered him towards the back of the house. "It'll only take one teeny second," Darlyn said.

Link sputtered and tried to break free, but the woman had an iron grip, and he didn't want to hurt her. One tiny bruise on her snow-white arm, and he was a dead man to the police in Lake Ann. She steered him along until they reached the French doors opening into her and Truly's bedroom.

"No," Link said. There was a moment's silence.

Then Link's tinny voice rose like a shrill apparition. "Holy shit." Then, as always, when all else failed, he quoted Mac-Beth: "Tongue nor heart cannot conceive nor name thee."

13
BEV-LATE MORNING

After Truly left, Bev went into the house. It was sparsely furnished with no lamps, only overhead light fixtures, which were usually off. The house was too quiet. Her beloved guide dog, Spice, died at the age of twelve that winter, and she hadn't replaced him.

She went to her desk and sat down at her computer. She kept a Facebook page even though she never posted any pictures. She posted scraps of poetry or philosophy. Although Bev had a doctorate degree in psychology and a full-time remote job at a think tank, she loved to listen to audiobooks and to write. She had actually written two well reviewed mystery books and recorded them on audio herself.

Bev lost her eyesight in her early twenties, from a rare form of ocular degradation. In high school and college, she prayed medical science would catch up with her, but it never did. Her mother was addicted to drugs, and Bev grew up in foster homes. She was used to hardship, and although her eyesight steadily worsened, she studied hard in school, got her degrees, and then coped with her ensuing disability.

Her position at the think tank had to do with abused and abandoned children. She met Darlyn because there were several calls referring her to child services. Ruby had a perpetual runny nose, diaper rash, and until Truly started staying home tending the child, Darlyn did a lot of screaming, in her house and in public. The first few social workers endured 'that crazy bitch' but they complained so much that the foundation finally asked Bev to take the case in hand.

Bev showed up at Darlyn's door one day dressed in her customary signature color of white. When the door opened, Bev said, "Someone sent me."

Darlyn asked, "You the maid?"

Bev sized up the tone and tenor of Darlyn Ravija. To Darlyn, Bev was a woman of color, and she was wearing white. What else would she be?

"Yes," Bev said.

There were a few seconds of tense silence. "Well, come on in then."

Bev liked a tour of new places before she set foot in them. She prayed that the Ravijas had the same floorplan that she did. Darlyn's house smelled smoky, and when she ran her hand across the foyer table, she felt a thick pad of dust.

"Take your glasses off," Darlyn said. "You're indoors now."

"I'll leave them on," Bev said. "Bright lights bother me. My eyesight isn't very good."

But Darlyn had already lost interest. "You didn't bring cleanin' stuff."

"This is an introductory visit," Bev said. She'd persuaded Darlyn to give her a tour of the house so she could situate the rooms, walkways, and staircases in her mind. She also met Ruby who was wailing, standing up in her crib.

"I watch children too," Bev said. She tripped over some toys the baby had flung on the floor and fell hard against the crib.

"Yeah, watch yourself," Darlyn said with an edge to her voice. Bev felt disorientated until she felt soft little arms around her neck. Steadying herself, she picked the baby up. The child's cheeks were wet, her diaper sodden. Ruby whimpered and clung to Bev.

"That child is of the devil," Darlyn said darkly. Bev took note of the mother's words for the report she would write.

Thinking about it later gave Bev butterflies in her stomach. She began going over to the house in the afternoon instead of eating lunch. Darlyn still assumed she was a maid that Truly hired to help around the house. Bev did little cleaning, though, and spent most of her time with Ruby.

She couldn't see bruises on the child, of course, so she didn't know if Darlyn was actually beating her, but the child's aversion to her mother, and the way the child virtually tried to weld herself to Bev's body was enough of a signal about Darlyn's parenting skills. Bev told herself she would contact the father to complete her report.

Then she met Truly at the neighborhood party. Cherie, made a point of inviting her. Bev suspected this was her one and only social engagement in the Lake Ann suburb, and she really didn't want to go. She didn't know the house, she didn't have her dog, and she hated to use her cane. But she felt it was her duty to represent blind people as competent and socially active. So, she went, put up with Cherie's pandering, *my friend is black and blind*, then made it to a safe pool chair and sat. Which is where Truly found her.

Later, when he walked her home and tried to kiss her in the dark of the common area, she stopped him.

"I don't even know your name," she said.

"Truly. Truly Ravija." He tried to draw her closer, but she put her hands on his chest and pushed.

He stopped. "What?"

"I've been meaning to talk to you," Bev said.

So that first night, those first few hours, Bev brewed some coffee, and they stayed up talking and eating sandwiches. And telling secrets.

Bev told him about the years of foster care, and her brief marriage to a much older man, a colleague, who died after one year. Truly told her about the army. He told her about Jay, who introduced him to Darlyn, after he returned stateside.

"I pretended to believe they were cousins," he said. "But I think Jay is actually her son. There's such a strong resemblance."

"Does Jay know?"

"I don't think so," Truly said. "Not knowing our own mothers has always been something we had in common."

"I can join that club," Bev said. "If you include someone who doesn't want to know."

Truly sighed. "Darlyn came on strong to me. I was kind of passive, at marriage age. Past it, really. She's pretty." He sighed. "We've been together for eight years."

"What made you decide to have a child?" Bev asked. "If that isn't too personal?"

"It was kind of an accident," Truly said. "But I never regretted it, because I got Ruby."

"Yes, "Bev said. "About Ruby. "Have you ever noticed how glad she is to see you when you get home?"

Truly said, "Yes, sure."

"I can't check for bruises obviously," Bev said. "But

something isn't right."

She told him about her work, how she'd been going over to his house to tend to Ruby and to build a report about Darlyn for Child Services.

She reached for his hand. "Are you surprised? Shocked? Truly was silent for a minute. "I guess I just needed to hear someone else say it."

"So, you've seen…evidence?"

Truly's voice was thick. "Once. I've seen black and blue marks. Darlyn told me Ruby fell out of the crib."

"Ah," Bev said, making a mental note.

"I'll quit work," Truly said.

They sat in silence for a moment, their hands intertwined. Finally, he said, "Maybe I was handing you a line earlier. But now I'm not so sure."

Bev said nothing.

He twined his fingers around hers. "You think I do this all the time? No, ma'am. Maybe twice. This is different."

"I feel that way too, "Bev said. Her throat was dry.

Truly said, "Let's get some air."

"Yes," Bev said. She was trembling a little.

"I used to be on a Master's team. Competitive swimming?"

Bev rose. "Come on, then."

She led him by the hand across her living room and pulled the slider back. The smell of chlorine was strong. She stepped onto the deck where the wood was still warm from the day's sunlight. He followed.

"Where's the moon?" Bev asked.

Truly came up behind her and touched her elbows,

turning her toward the slim crescent in the sky. "There it is," he said, pointing, his hand brushing her breast. His other hand drifted lower to the swell of her back.

She spun around and immediately, she was in his arms, her hands tearing at the buttons on his shirt. She heard them go pop, pop, pop as they hit the wooden deck.

With one fluid movement, he lowered the zipper at the back of her dress and pulled it off her shoulders. It spilled to a silken pool to her feet. He put one finger under the elastic of her thong and drew her close as she stepped out of the dress. He held her there while she finished taking off his shirt. Then he moved the elastic aside and touched her between her legs. It felt like the first time anyone had ever touched her.

She broke away and pushed the thong down to her feet. She sensed movement in his direction and assumed he was removing the rest of his clothes. She made her way down the steps of the pool stairs and stood on the second step with the water up to her thighs. In a minute he was beside her, his body hard against hers. He put his hands under her bottom and lifted her. Bev wrapped her legs around him. Her breasts flattened against his chest. She reached down and ran her hands over him. He kissed her, meeting her tongue with his and waded into the pool until the water was up to their waists. Bev arched her back, and she heard him say, "Oh, Bev."

Afterward they clung to each other, standing in the pool, shivering. Then they kissed and it started all over again. Birds were chirping by the time Bev opened her door for Truly to go home. "We'll talk again soon," he said, touching her shoulder.

Bev stood there for a few moments, hearing his footsteps fade away. It was summer, but the morning was cool. She felt a breeze in her doorway. Something blew onto her feet, some dust or pollen. She shook it off.

A year later, Bev smiled, remembering. Soon, she would make her daily visit to Ruby, a little early today because she had a doctor's appointment. She had something to do first.

She crossed the room to her computer and sat down in her desk chair. Her computer was always on, and she used key commands to know where to go. She brought up Facebook, using a screen reader, and displayed Truly's page. Then using a speech synthesizer, she dictated the following message to post:

i want to watch you die.

Humming a little, Bev closed the screen and headed upstairs to get ready.

14
JAY–LATE MORNING

Jay put on his life jacket and stood at the helm of the little boat bobbing in the water. Truly was gone a long time, parking the truck and trailer. When he finally came down the pier, he was staggering a little.

"You okay?" Jay called. He reached out a hand and Truly took it, stepping clumsily from the dock to the vinyl seats in the stern.

"I'm so tired all of a sudden," Truly said.

Unfolding the metal frame of the Bimini top, Jay positioned it over Truly who sat swaying in his seat. "Good thing you're not steering. Hang on," Jay said. He untied the line and flung it onto the deck. It was raining harder now, but looking over the horizon, Jay thought it let up further out into the open waters of the Atlantic Ocean. Still, he hesitated. Rain was probably nothing, especially in the summer in Florida, but then again it suddenly seemed foolish to go out like this in spite of their preparations.

"Hey Truly," Jay said. "Maybe we should take a rain check. Literally."

Truly shook his head and made a 'go on' motion with his hand. Jay felt in his pocket for his amulet, which was gone. Then he turned the key and revved the motor in idle.

Jay centered the wheel before trying to steer and shift gears at the same time. He idled forward. He aimed for the misty horizon, watching the bow. The old man taught Jay long ago to use the engine as the primary way to overcome the environment, to power through adverse situations. The faster the boat moved through the water, the greater the steering force.

If he shifted too soon or turned the wheel too late, he could lose control. He shifted into forward and noted the bow drifting to one side. He made quick, short pulses with the wheel in the opposite direction then re-centered the wheel. The rain was coming down harder. The wind pushed against the boat with gathering strength.

"Sure you wanna do this?" he called over his shoulder to Truly. But when he turned his head, he saw Truly had rolled off the cushions and lay curled up on the deck. Jay felt his gut tighten. There was a slash of lightning and a deafening boom. Jay realized he no longer had the option of turning about. He could not stop the boat in this slanting rain. He was afraid he'd swamp it.

The sky went black, and water was roiling the little boat further and further away from the shore. All visibility was gone in an instant. Like a pilot who loses the horizon and aims the nose toward the ground, Jay didn't know which way to turn around. He was motoring into one of those squalls that set upon boaters out of the clear blue sky. He would have to ride it out. The boat climbed over a particularly large swell, then dropped dramatically. Truly rolled from one side of the deck to the other.

Jay drifted too far from his point on the horizon and overcorrected just as another swell hit the boat with a huge WHOMP. He was knocked from the steering wheel and hit the starboard hard. He thought he heard his arm crack. Meanwhile, the wheel turned on its own, crazily. Using his good arm, Jay managed to get to his feet, and lurch back to the wheel. He centered it with one hand.

Wincing, he let his bad arm hang and threw worried glances back at Truly. In the driving storm, he lost all sense of direction. His skin was already salty from the spray bouncing off the bow. He scanned the dim horizon for other vessels. Then he went forward at top speed into the lashing wind and rain, as he headed out to the open sea.

15

DARLYN- AFTERNOON

A couple of hours passed before Darlyn heard the front door open. Earlier, she thought her sex appeal would seal the deal, but after Link's disappointing reaction to her offer, Darlyn proceeded anyway. She led him, protesting all the way to her bedroom. Once he saw what was on her bed, he cussed and took the Lord's name in vain.

Darlyn grabbed Truly's bathrobe off the hook on the back of the French doors and covered herself, cinching the sash.

"Well?" she asked. "How about some help, hey?"

Link turned to her slowly. "Lady, you need help all right." He started to push past her. Darlyn put out a hand. My hubby will eat you for lunch, he finds out you were here."

"What?" Link squeaked.

"Lookit," Darlyn gestured to the bed. "Y'all must know somethin' about…," she stammered and her cheeks colored a little, "re-cy-cling."

Link's eyes narrowed. "You just figured I'd know something about recycling a bale of marijuana."

Between the white posters of her canopied bed, packed in plastic, on Darlyn's fancy bedspread was at least 100 pounds of gold, green and brown marijuana.

"It is called Gold," Darlyn said carefully. "Worth sixteen thous-sand dolla's for every pound."

Link stopped trying to get past Darlyn. He stared at the bed. "I don't even smoke."

"I can't keep it here," Darlyn said. "Truly would know. I need to, like, bury it ?"

She pointed in the direction of the vacant lot.

Link stared at the bed, and then stared at Darlyn. He was silent for a full minute. "I need money for school. Out of state tuition. And moving expenses."

Darlyn smiled. "Juss break up the pounds and sell ounces of Gold for $1000 per bag. Talkin' one million an a half dolla's. A sixty-thirty cut."

Link said, "Fifty-fifty. Otherwise, the risk isn't even worth it to me."

Darlyn nodded. "Wanna know where I got it?"

"Not particularly," Link said.

"Hubby's daddy died. I took it off his boat."

"How'd you know it was there?"

Darlyn shook a pack of cigarettes out of her robe pocket and flashed her lighter.

"Didn't. Wanted to learn to drive a boat." She exhaled through her nose. "Hubby says no. Figured I'd try it out myself. Found some of this here under the seat."

"All of that sounds questionable," Link said. Your hubby know about this?"

Darlyn smiled. She wasn't sure how much Jay involved Truly in his shenanigans. "If he don't, he will soon." She had poured four Ambien tablets into that pot of oatmeal she fed Truly. He wouldn't awaken for a while.

"You mad at him? What'd the guy do?" Link asked.

Darlyn's gaze darkened as she remembered the neighborhood

party a year ago.

She got home late that night and was surprised to find the sitter still there. She paid and went to bed. She told herself, Truly probly went over someone's house, passed out. But she tossed and turned and finally got up to do some surveillance. Dawn was breaking when she passed Bev's house. Last night, Cherie told her she saw Truly follow that whore home. Although Cherie put it another way, that Truly was a gentleman for escorting poor Bev. Darlyn had snorted. So the harlot had bad eyesight, so what? That was no excuse for what she could do with Darlyn's lawfully wedded husband.

So she hid behind the hedge in the common area, and waited. It wasn't long before Truly appeared in the doorway. He turned to Bev and just the way he touched her shoulder, told Darlyn everything she needed to know about where Truly spent the night.

He took off towards his own house, happy as a puppy with two peckers, towards his own wife and child, thank you very much. Darlyn crossed the street and walked up the driveway to Bev's door. Her maid was still standin' there mooning over another woman's hubby. Smilin.' Didn't even see her.

Someone recently told Darlyn that sprinkling salt across the threshold of a home was bad luck for the person who crossed it. She took the salt shaker she pocketed on her way out of the house and doused Bev's threshold, the way she'd planned to anyway. Bev's feet were covered in salt. She didn't seem to notice.

It was all Darlyn could do not to clobber her. She got close, real close. Then she turned abruptly. By the time she got home, Truly was in bed snoring.

Darlyn was furious ever since. "He slept with my maid," Darlyn said.

"How stereotypical," Link said.

"How…what?"

"Never mind," Link said. "I understand your despair. But how did you get this bale from the boat to your house?"

"Well, my boy Jay, helped me."

Link raised his eyebrows. "That nice-looking young man here earlier?"

Darlyn gave him a look. "He is not into any of that funny-boy stuff." Darlyn ground her cigarette into the wooden bureau and flicked the butt in the trash. "Jay had to move it. So he asked me to help. For 10 percent of the cut. Which means I'm only makin' 40."

"Well," Link said, ignoring that, "likely the boat was used to transport it. I sure as hell hope you're not pissing off some drug cartel. Meanwhile, let's bag this up and take it next door. It should be safe for a while with the house not even sold yet."

Darlyn went to get the kitchen scale, and they got busy breaking up the pound in plastic bags and then stuffing it into her hardside luggage. For the rest she had IKEA plastic bins

That's what she and Link were doing when she heard the front door open. Link looked up, and she put her finger to her lips. It was that goldarn maid, and she's early. The sight of that blasted homewrecker never failed to set Darlyn's blood to boiling. But she continued to employ her because she was good with Ruby. Darlyn was not maternal, and beyond her vanity, she didn't care much about the physical side of her husband's predilections. But she was a practical person, and she did not have education or a work history. With her momma and stepdaddy gone, she inherited the house and a tiny annuity. Besides that, all her momma left her was a cheap blue stone she gave away to Jay. It was the only family thing she had to give him, but it was worth nothing according to EBay.

Without Truly or the old man, she could sink into poverty. She could see Truly moving in with Bev. Leaving her. How was she supposed to continue sending money to the televangelists to pray for her? Bev could jus' wait her turn.

Darlyn drained the old man's savings for years, selling her silence about a certain matter. That's why he died with nothing to show for his life except debt and a crummy little boat. Now she needed a buttload of cash in order to ensure a life beyond Truly. Jay told her about motoring offshore to sell pot to fishermen and college students. He told her he picked it up off the beach two years ago on Duck Key. Someone dumped three bales of Gold over the stern, and it all floated to the remote private beach where Jay was trespassing behind a dune with a Canadian tourist. She was so badly sunburned there wasn't much they could do together physically, so he'd been watching the shoreline, watching the three massive distinct objects roll forward and back, closer and further for an hour. Not the sharpest knife in the drawer, the tourist hadn't even known what Jay found or why he insisted on immediately hauling it up to her Land Rover. He told her it was Chinese herbs. Darlyn's boy literally sat on the beach and watched his fortune come in.

He said a team of welders outfitted the ballast tanks with secret compartments. The first two bales paid off his booze and bolero debt. This last bale was supposed to set him up. Then the old man was hit by lightning. It scared Jay. Having grown up with Darlyn, and the fear of God, he was easily convinced it was time to end the drug profiteering. So, Jay gave Darlyn the Gold. Let her get hit by lightning. Let her get rid of it. He said God wouldn't grudge him 10 percent after the risks he'd already taken.

She was getting rid of it all right and starting a brand new life away from her cheating husband. The house was in her name, and she planned on selling it. She meant to take Ruby with her, too. Truly may not miss her, but he would sure miss Ruby. He was not a decent man to raise her, that was for sure. As if sensing Darlyn's intentions or the maid's presence, Ruby began crying. Link moved towards the French doors as though he were going to leave. Darlyn shook her head. "Bev?" she called. "Ya here?"

"Yes," Bev said in even tones. "I have a doctor's appointment today. That's why I'm early." Ruby's cries escalated. "I'll just go upstairs." Bev hesitated; her foot poised above the step. "Is anyone else here?"

Again, Link looked like he wanted to flee, but Darlyn put a hand over her eyes and shook her head. She pointed at Bev.

"No, ma'am," Darlyn said. "I'm gettin' dressed." With both hands, she closed the twin doors to her bedroom. She switched on the locks on the doorknobs.

"She is here for a couple hours. Let's finish up," she whispered.

Link nodded. Silently, the soon to be runaway housewife and the failed son of a judge and a college professor continued breaking up and packing the illegal flower of the cannabis trade.

16

BEV -AFTERNOON

Bev knew something was up the minute she entered Darlyn and Truly's house. It was a high-ceilinged affair with mirrored walls, window treatments, stained glass, a steep staircase and a kitchen that combined a mud room with a bona fide hearth and iron oven. She thought she heard whispering as she opened the door, which abruptly cut off as she entered the foyer. She heard Darlyn call, "Bev? You here?"

"Yes," Bev said in even tones. "I have a doctor's appointment today. That's why I'm early." Ruby's cries escalated. "I'll just go upstairs." Bev hesitated; her foot poised above the step. "Is anyone else here?"

The tenor of Bev's afternoons at the Ravija house involved her interacting with Ruby and recording dictation on her cell phone. She tidied Ruby's room and ran the dishwasher. Darlyn usually spent her time watching soap operas and maintaining the fiction that Bev was the maid.

Bev paid more attention to her sense of smell since her eyesight failed. She smelled two distinct odors as she took the steps to Ruby's room and passed the foyer leading to the Ravija bedroom. One was the smell of vegetative matter. She suspected it was marijuana based on her experiences in college. And the second odor, overpowering the first, was the strong rank scent of B.O..

Bev climbed to the second floor, holding on to the

handrail. She kept to the perimeters of the house, even though she knew it pretty well now. She felt a lack of confidence in her sense of direction since her dog Spice died. He was her guide, and he was her boy for the past twelve years. He used to yodel at her as though they were having a conversation. She used a cane when she left the neighborhood now, because Spice was irreplaceable to her.

So were Truly and Ruby. If she didn't see them every day, she carried around a strange tightness in her chest, a feeling she hadn't had since her own mother dropped her off at child services and never came back.

The door to Ruby's room was open, and when Bev moved to the side of the crib, she felt the child standing, as usual, with a full diaper. Gently, Bev lifted the child from her crib, speaking softly, and with some difficulty laid her down on the padded changing table. Ruby didn't want to let go.

Bev gathered the baby wipes, a clean diaper, and a plastic bag from the supplies she'd set up along the changing table. "It's okay, sweetie," Bev said, carefully disengaging the child's clasped hands. She smiled and clapped the little hands together. The child laughed. "Bef," she said and Bev felt a kiss on her hand. Bev always missed her sight, but never more than during her time with Ruby.

"I love you baby girl," she said, and lowered her head, so her hair was tickling Ruby's belly. The child laughed and tried to roll over. Quickly, she slid the old diaper out from under the toddler and jammed it in the plastic bag. Then she removed a wipe, lifted the child's feet with her hands, and sponged her down. In a minute Ruby was taped into a clean diaper. Bev felt around for the child's overalls and found them on the side of the crib. Then she took the child in her arms and settled down in the rocking chair. Ruby put her thumb in her mouth.

Bev disengaged it and gave the child a sippy cup of water from top of the bureau. Truly left everything where she could find it. She plucked a book from the top of a pile in a rack by the rocker. "What's this one sweetie?"

"Loff you," Ruby said.

"Love You Forever? Okay. Here goes." Bev began reciting the words from memory. "I'll love you forever, I'll like you for always, as long as I'm living, my baby you'll be." Ruby laid her head on Bev's chest, and Bev could feel the slow inexorable return of the baby's thumb to her mouth. She let her be.

"The baby grew. He grew and he grew and he grew."

Bev read to the child, played patty cake with her, Itsy Bitsy Spider, and Wheels on the Bus. She would have liked to take her outside, but it was too dangerous without someone else there. It concerned her that the child was a year and a half, not potty trained, and had exactly four words in her vocabulary: Bef, Loff, Dada, and you.

It was one o'clock, before Bev took the child in her arms and carefully walked downstairs. She didn't dare leave her alone. She thought of Ruby standing in her crib, crying, stopping to listen if anyone was on the stairs, if Bef was coming. Much as she hated it, she had to leave the child with Darlyn. Ruby would scream when Bev transferred her to Darlyn's arms. But there was no help for it; she had to make this doctor's appointment. It was with her retinologist, a doctor she saw every few years. This visit was particularly important.

Bev stepped off the staircase shifting Ruby's weight to her hip. "Darlyn?" There was no answer, but Bev could hear voices now, muffled, behind the doors of Darlyn and Truly's bedroom.

"Darlyn?"

Bev turned right and stood outside the French doors. She tapped. Immediately the voices were silent. "Darlyn?"

After a few seconds, the door opened a crack, and Bev heard Darlyn's voice say, "What?"

Bev tried to smile. "I have that doctor's appointment I told you about. I have to go." Bev hoped she would feel the breeze of the door opening wide, and Darlyn taking her child from Bev's arms with endearments. Instead, Darlyn said, "Jus' lay her butt down in front a the teevee."

Bev swallowed. "Darlyn, we've had this discussion before. I'm not going to leave Ruby unsupervised. You must take her." She held the child under her arms and extended her to Darlyn. Ruby began to wail.

"Oh, for God's sake," Darlyn said. "Shit and goddamn." The smell of sweat and vegetation was strong with the door open.

Ruby cried, "Bef, Bef."

Bev wished she could call Truly then and there. She knew the minute she walked out the door, Darlyn would plop the child down in front of the TV and go back into the bedroom to whatever it was she was doing. But she had to go. So, she walked out the door with Ruby's screams ringing in her ears and speed dialed a Lyft. She heard the engine of the black Range Rover at the curb by the time she made it home. She knew because the driver stuck his head out the window and said, "Bev?"

She deduced from the gruffness of his voice that he was an older white male. A smoker. She smiled. Even though she couldn't see, she knew what her smile could do to a guy who drove a Lyft. "Hi, she said. "Thanks for getting here so fast."

Sure enough, she felt the air stir and presumed he opened the door for her. She didn't like to carry a purse. She was too easy a target. Instead, she put her credit card and her driver's license in her back pocket along with her phone. She felt her way into the Lyft with some difficulty. She really needed to get another dog or to use her cane. The driver said, "3300 Lake Ann Boulevard? Ma'am?"

"Yes, please." She exhaled sitting in the back seat. In some Ubers and Lyfts, the upholstery felt funny as though it had been reupholstered with cheap seat covers. Bev assumed that occurred because a rider puked in the back seat. But this car seemed in mint condition. She gave the driver a big tip when he let her out in front of the medical plaza where Dr. Dojo, Bev's retinologist, was waiting with the results of her deep eye scan.

Following her instinct and memory, Bev grasped the doorknob of the office and turned it, opening to an air conditioned room and a familiar route to the sign in sheet. Bev scribbled her initials and groped for a seat. Within a minute, she heard the receptionist say, "Miss Cage?"

Bev sighed. The young nurse assistant smelled of bleach and Bev managed to track her scent well enough through the maze of offices to a cold room that smelled antiseptic "It's Kase," she said.

"The doctor will be right with you," the young woman said, probably aware she was telling a lie.

Bev groped her way to a Naugahyde chair and sat there. She had an intuitive grasp of time intervals, more acutely since her disability. According to the clock in her head, it was twenty minutes before the door opened.

"Bev," Dr. Dojo said. "How are you? Good?"

"Still blind, doctor." She felt him take her hand. His was dry, papery.

"Where is Spice? At home, today? Yes?"

"Spice died, doctor." Bev felt tears come to her eyes. She never had a pet when she was sighted. Then when she wasn't, she made do with her cane. But her late husband talked her into getting the guide dog. Her husband was a professor of Ophthalmology, formerly in practice, and all of his blind patients used dogs. She and Olsen had their differences, but he'd been right about Spice. The dog was her friend as well as her guide. They were inseparable for the past decade.

"Oh, so sorry Bev. I liked Spice. I had a treat ready for him."

Dr. Dojo's solicitous bedside manner made Bev's skin itch. It implied they were better acquainted than they were. He met Spice, what, five times? But Olsen recommended Dojo as the best retinologist in the country. He was the reason she stayed in Lake Ann instead of traveling.

She managed a smile although she felt like shivering. The room was so cold. In Florida, every indoor facility cranked the air temperature down to freezing. Bev would prefer to live somewhere else, in a city like New Orleans with culture and more amenities for the handicapped. She used to drive there on break from the University of Florida to see the sights when she still had her sight. She no longer dreamt in images, but sometimes when she woke, she had a faint sense of vision, of color, of the light slowly slipping behind the Piazza D'Italia.

Dr. Dojo was talking to her in his reedy voice, and Bev snapped back to attention.

"What did you say, doctor?"

Dr. Dojo took her hand in his. "I know it is hard for you to believe. But medical science finally caught up with you, yes?"

Bev's throat suddenly felt dry. "Run that by me again, doctor?"

"It is a new technology for restoring vision, a retinal stem cell transplant. The stem cells are taken from your own skin, yes? And genetically reprogrammed. There is a fifty-fifty chance, it will work, especially since you lost your vision so young. Exciting news, yes? Olsen would be pleased?"

Bev thought she had adjusted well to her loss of sight, but she suddenly realized she had not. Not really. A deep yearning gripped her, to see the ocean curl in on itself reflecting the rays of the sun. To run in the sand along the foaming crest of the shore, birds scattering. To match objects to vision. To see the faces of Truly and Ruby. Yes.

"Doctor," she said. "Can you perform the operation?"

"Yes, yes," he said. "I can do it. I can do it, and I will." He squeezed her hand.

For the first time, she imagined what he looked like, Dr. Dojo. She imagined someone stooped with brown skin and thinning black hair. His eyes were dark pools of empathy. He would help her. Bev squeezed his hand back. Hard.

17
LINK- EARLY EVENING

Link helped Darlyn bag up the rest of the Gold. They planned to stash it in his truck until he could think of an easy access place at the construction site. At any rate, it was time to stop. The toddler was banging on the door crying.

"Fixin' to make supper," Darlyn said. "You need to get a move on."

"I haven't had a home cooked meal in quite a while," Link hinted.

They opened the door, and the little girl on the other side collapsed in tears.

Now, I am not abidin' with none of your screeching," Darlyn said. "Link, honey, you tend her while I start cookin.'"

"Me?' Link squeaked.

"Just bring her in the kitchen, and set her in the hearth. And watch her. That child is full of the devil."

Link reached down and lifted the child. She looked small in his arms. He followed Darlyn into the kitchen. "This is some house," he said. He placed the child in the hearth, and she started crying again so he picked her up. She stopped crying. He put her down. She cried.

"I can see you are not any better with her." Darlyn was stirring something on the stove. "You like shrimp n' grits?"

Link nodded though it was hard to hear over the clamor of the child. Actually, he never had the dish before. His mother stuck to salads, lean cuts of meat, baked potatoes or yams. Vitamins, protein, carbs. A well-balanced meal. His mother was disciplined in everything, including her family's diet.

"Your folks living?" he asked Darlyn. She rolled her eyes, set the wooden spoon down by the stove, felt in her bathrobe pocket for her cigarettes, and sat down on the other side of the breakfast bench across from the sweaty construction worker. Grabbing a black plastic ashtray, she said, "Nah." She shook out a cigarette and lit it with a blue lighter she found on the table.

"Mine are," said Link. The child, he was relieved to note, ceased screaming and was now just a disconsolate little heap, knees up, her back against the brick of the hearth, thumb in mouth.

"What's she like?" Darlyn asked, blowing smoke in Link's face. He tried not to mind. "Your momma?"

"She's strict," Link said. "She's a judge." He thought for a minute. "I don't really know her too well to tell you the truth. She was busy when I was growing up."

"How about your daddy?"

When he left home, Link thought his parents would worry about him. His friends complained their parents wouldn't stop texting them stupid shit. But his own parents rarely contacted him. It was understandable, he thought. They were older, Evelyn and Herbert. They were small in stature, lean and agile. They seemed disconcerted by their son's height, his brawn, his sensitive regard for literature. Link always thought he was an accident, evidence of some rare lapse of judgment, proof his parents were not perfect. His father in particular looked at him as …flawed. When he told him that he wanted to become a high school English teacher, his dad curled his lip and said, "What do you want to do that for?" Recalling all this, Link said, "He's a professor. He's pretty busy, too."

Darlyn crushed out her cigarette and took a smaller hand-rolled one out of the pack. "I reckon we should try this shit," Darlyn said, holding the lighter to the twisted tip. She inhaled deeply, blew out a quantity of smoke and began coughing. She passed it to Link. He hesitated, but, shit, if he was going to sell it, he had to confirm it was good. He held the joint to his mouth with his thumb and forefinger, and inhaled. The smoke went down deep into his lungs, and he held it for a minute as he had seen his friends do. He passed the joint back to Darlyn and exhaled a small thin cloud. Immediately, he felt a loosening, as though he'd been freed from some kind of bond. "What did you roll it with?"

Darlyn laughed. "Tampon paper." She inhaled deeply and leaned forward to pass the joint back to Link who took a few puffs. She watched him.

"Lemme," she said gesturing to the joint, her word punctuated by a puff of smoke. Link passed it to her, and she drew the smoke into her lungs, this time without coughing.

"That sure does take the edge off." She exhaled. "You wanna know about me? I grew up with my momma and my stepdaddy. Stepdaddy started messin' with me when I was twelve. I had Jay at sixteen. Never went to school much, which is why I can hardly read. Watched a lot of TV. Beverly Hillbillies. Designing Women."

Link felt disorientated, dizzy. If this was what being high felt like, you could have it. Also, he was starting to have second thoughts about Darlyn. High as he was, she just didn't seem all there to him.

"They died after I had my boy. Momma and step daddy. Wasn't soon enough for me. Anyway, I found a necklace in Momma's closet. And a picture of a tall man with dark hair. The necklace, it's a blue plastic stone with a nickel plated back. There's engraving. A. J. Ravija."

Link tried to think. He had a question for Darlyn. He knew he did.

Darlyn licked the tips of her fingers and crushed the lit part of the joint with her thumb and forefinger." This here pretty good, hey?"

"Yes," Link said. He could not even remember her name or where he was. It would come to him, though.

"Anyway," Darlyn said, "name on the back of the picture? Arthur Jay Ravija."

She looked at Link expectantly. The refrigerator made a loud humming noise, and he jumped. "I found him," Darlyn said. "I found Arthur Ravija. Took fifteen years. And guess how?" Link shook his head.

"From Jay." Darlyn started laughing. "Truly and Jay served together in the army. Truly saved Jay's life or some such." She relit the joint and waved at the smoke.

"The minute I heard Truly's last name, I thought he could be my brother. He said his dad was retired, selling cars. I paid the old man a visit. I told him about me, about Jay. Was Truly my brother? Was Truly Jay's uncle? But the old man said, no, Truly was adopted. And not to tell him, cause he didn't know. I used that information for years and years." Darlyn burst out laughing and then choked a little. " Of course, Truly would not have married me if he knew."

Link let her words wash over him although they didn't make sense.

"The old man told me that my Momma left when she was expectin' me. That he did not know where she went. He told his boy Truly, my husband, that his momma was dead. Truly does not have any real kin that he knows of. "

"Truly... your husband?"

Darlyn scowled at him. "You listening? Truly's adopted. He does not know that."

Her expression changed. "My daddy ... he never did nothin' for me. Beyond what I told him he needed to pay to keep me quiet. Did not even leave me his boat."

"Neither has mine," Link said. He was surprised to hear himself say it. His parents provided all his basic needs. But in the fog of his Gold high, he realized it wasn't true. He interrupted his parent's lives, their relentless climb to the pinnacle of their careers. Actually, he never interrupted it. They glided right over him like a blip on their radar. He couldn't remember ever sitting down with his parents and having their undivided attention. So, screw them and their righteous indifference. He was going to sell the Gold, move to Hawaii, and teach poetry. He tried to think of the Frost poem he loved. "Two roads diverged in a yellow wood..."

Darlyn suddenly sat up straight and glanced at the cheap battery-operated clock on the wall behind the stove. She took a bowl down from the cupboard, ladled something from a stockpot and shoved it at him "I got to get started on dinner. Those boys shoulda been home by now."

Link's head was far from clear, but he could still put two and two together. He dug a tentative spoon into the mush in his bowl and tasted it. He put the spoon down. "How are you going to explain the suitcases full of weed?"

Darlyn was back at the stove, a fresh cigarette dangling from her lips. "Dang. Can you put 'em in your car or somethin'? Til later?"

"Perfect," Link said, his lip curling. The baby on the hearth made a whimpering sound.

"You should tend to your child," he said, and got up to do Darlyn's bidding. He went to the bedroom and lugged the two hardback suitcases out to his truck and put them in the silver toolbox. He looked up and down the street to see if anyone saw him. The streets were deserted. Then, out of nowhere, a police car pulled up at the curb. Link got into his truck, turned the key in the ignition and split.

18
BEV

By the time Bev got home from her appointment with Dr. Dojo, all she craved was peace and quiet. Lost in her own thoughts, she'd spurned conversation with the Lyft driver.

"Where you going, lady?"

Bev could tell, just from his voice, that he was a drinker, a guy with broken purple veins across his nose. She was good at imagining what people looked like.

"Lake Ann," she said. She gave him the address.

"Ritzy area," the driver said. "I'm from Toledo myself. Ever hear of a town…"

Bev interrupted. "I'm sorry," she said. "I just heard I'm going blind. Do you mind?"

"Geez, ma'am, sorry, how was I …" The driver's protests dwindled and sputtered off completely. Bev used this excuse all the time to avoid conversation. It helped that she no longer had to rely on visual cues in social situations. It shielded her from the slights generated by her abrupt mannerisms.

Never had her excuse held more irony than it had today. Because she was blind, and her lack of eyesight may be correctable. She thought about her future with Truly. Then she thought about Ruby, alone in the house with Darlyn, with the unknown presence she had sensed, and alone with a whole bunch of weed from the smell of it.

She planned to call child services for some time, and as

soon as she paid the driver off she rushed in the door to pick up her cell. Then she stood there for a moment tapping one long fingernail against her temple. The hell with child services who would take a week to show up. Child services involved paperwork, a drawn-out process. She would just call the police. The police showing up for suspected child neglect would go down on the record. "And it was," Bev thought, "time for someone to hold Darlyn accountable for her child-rearing skills."

Bev dialed 911, and gave the dispatcher Darlyn's address. She said she was a licensed psychotherapist. There was a child involved. She knew the child, and she could help.

"I can't promise nothing," the dispatcher drawled.

"Why don't you try?" Bev suggested. "We're talking about an eighteen-month-old baby."

"I'll do the best I can do."

Bev walked with quick angry steps to a hard-back chair near the kitchen table. She sat down. Her heart was beating rapidly, and she kept turning over the words Dr. Dojo had said to her. There is a fifty-fifty chance, the operation will work, especially since you lost your vision so young. Exciting news, yes? Olsen would be pleased?"

It was exciting news, but she snorted a little when she thought of Olsen. Olsen, 30 years older, who treated her like a lab rat, not a wife. Bev did not doubt that Olsen could have conducted this 'experimental' operation and the accompanying therapy as the premier ophthalmologist in the country. But he hadn't. Bev knew why.

Their marriage was no accident. He sought her out as a guinea pig for his research. Under his care, her eyesight grew worse until it was entirely gone.

Under the circumstances, she felt entitled to reparations, but Olsen's children, who hated her, didn't see it that way. So she kept some of her late husband's papers.

That was how Dr. Dojo learned of this experimental procedure to restore eyesight using the patient's own stem cells. Bev sent it his way, anonymously. It was Olsen's, he wrote it years ago. Long years when she could have had the gift of sight. But why would her late husband want Bev's eyesight restored, when her blindness was such a potent source of research?

She set up a shell company with an offshore bank account. Olsen also invented a device, which Bev patented in her own name, to assist with the operation, a sliver thin needle to inject stem cells directly into the eye's cornea. It proved to be a lucrative source of income.

So, she had been busy, but in no way neglectful of her promise to Truly to look after Ruby. Right now, with drugs involved, Bev felt strongly that Ruby was in harm's way staying with Darlyn.

When her internal clock told her twenty minutes had passed, she made her way to Darlyn's just as the police arrived. Truly wasn't home, but Darlyn was there, clearly stoned and disorientated.

19
DARLYN-EARLY EVENING

Minutes after Link left, the doorbell rang. Darlyn puffed on her cigarette, walked slowly to the door, and opened it. When she saw who it was, she sputtered and choked a little, as though her three pack a day habit had finally caught up with her. After all, she was still in her bathrobe.

In front of her were two police officers, a man and a woman. Behind them, Bev lurked. Officer Banks spoke first.

"Evening ma'am. May we come in?"

Ruby hurtled into the fray at the door and put up her hands. "Bef," she shrieked. Bev stooped and picked the child up, kissing her neck. She settled into the crook of Bev's arm, her head on her shoulder.

Bev addressed Darlyn, "When I got home, I remembered a roommate I had in college and how our dorm smelled when he was selling weed. A lot of weed. You're endangering Ruby. Where's Truly?"

"Shoulda been home by now," Darlyn said waspishly.

The police nudged their way past Darlyn into the house. She remained in the doorway staring at Bev. "You heard from Truly?"

"You know I can't read texts," Bev said.

Officer Cleary, the woman, materialized next to Darlyn. She held something up. "I found this in the ashtray. Were you smoking marijuana in here, ma'am? Is this your marijuana cigarette?"

Darlyn snatched it away from her, put the fragment into her mouth, and swallowed it. Officer Banks came around the corner from her bedroom. Darlyn caught her breath. How carefully had she and Link cleaned up? Had they left buds or seeds on the floor?"

"Nothing to see there," he said. "But this place smells like an opium den. Ma'am, I'm afraid we have to remand your daughter into the care of Dr. Beverly Kase. At least until your husband gets home."

"I wasn't smoking," Darlyn said. "It was some construction worker next door who was suppose' to fix my pool pump."

Officer Banks took out a pad. "His name ma'am?"

"I do not know his name," Darlyn sulked.

Bev touched her arm. "Let me take Ruby. You call me when Truly gets home.

Darlyn did not curse herself for caving so easily on Link. She was useless as an accomplice. Especially as stoned as she was. She pulled at her lip with her fingers. She turned to Bev. "Hey, do the dishes before you go?"

Bev sighed. "Darlyn, call me when Truly gets home."

The police left a written warning and said they would be back the next day. Bev took Ruby with her. Bev already had Truly. Darlyn had tried to reinterest Truly in her physically, but with no more success than she'd had with Link. What did she have left?

When she was young, Darlyn had no contacts outside the house of her stepfather. When she got pregnant, her momma told her she was a child of the devil, tempting men, and sent her off to the country to some halfway house where sullen pregnant teenagers gestated and gave their babies up to the adoption black market. Just to be contrary, Darlyn insisted on keeping Jay, thinking her parents would never agree. But all her momma said was, "I'm not cleaning up your mess, Darl." In time, everyone maintained the fiction that Jay was Darlyn's cousin.

Darlyn had no idea how to tend a baby. In fact, Jay screamed nonstop with croup the first three months of his life because she didn't know enough to burp him. There were rashes, fevers, and jaundice. Luckily, Jay was a sturdy, healthy baby, not like Ruby at all, quick to talk, able to entertain himself. Later, she couldn't help Jay with his homework because she could barely read herself, but he did well enough on his own.

By the time she was seventeen, she was stealing twenties from her momma's purse and buying cartons of cigarettes. She spent her days sipping Jolt, smoking, and eating Kraft macaroni and cheese, which she could get for thirty nine cents a box in those days. No one noticed. It was a big house. Her momma and stepdaddy were usually too blasted to remember she and Jay were around.

There was a dogged hardiness to Darlyn who retaliated to injustice in petty ways. She'd drop a cup and leave glass on the kitchen floor. She broke knick knacks. Stole her momma's makeup. Put bleach on the seat of her stepdaddy's toilet. Turned all his pants inside out in his drawer.

One day a lady from the Baptist church came knocking on her door. The Baptist woman was tall, young, and had the face of an angel. She handed Darlyn a tract. "Jesus loves you," she said. Darlyn looked at the tract, which was a series of religious cartoons. One was a man hung on the cross. The balloon coming out of his mouth said, "Father forgive them for they know not what they do." The man's suffering seemed familiar to Darlyn. She looked up. The beautiful lady smiled at her. Darlyn smiled back.

The next day, she pushed Jay in a stroller to the church address, located a sweaty hot mile from where she lived. The congregation frowned at the too young mother, and no one said, 'Jesus loves you.'

Still, the image of that angel lady lingered. For months, Darlyn jumped when she thought she heard someone at the door. She would stick her head outside, scanning from side to side, to make sure the beautiful lady hadn't come back. She began watching the televangelists on TV, the men in polyester suits and high pompadours, the women with false eyelashes and hair sprayed as stiff as a Roman helmet. *Are you lost on the path of righteousness? Do you believe you have failed yourself and others? God forgives you.* Though nothing like the angel lady, these slick proprietors of gospel guilt and redemption steadied her, gave her a sense of hope.

She imitated their southern accents, watched their heartfelt prayers. She believed someday the Rapture would come and carry her off to heaven where life would be as it should be. In the meantime, she tended Jay the way a child would tend a doll, paying attention to him now and then, filling his basic needs. There was little demonstrable affection between them.

Her stepfather left her alone after she had Jay. He had another girlfriend by then. Her momma never asked about Jay's father, and had no interest in her grandchild. "He looks like someone. I forget just who," she'd say darkly.

Darlyn knew her momma was married once before. All she knew about her real father was that her momma left him because he was weak, not a real man. Darlyn couldn't see how the stepfather with his gray ponytail, capped teeth, and lascivious intentions was any better.

She was not sorry when her stepfather died with the blood pouring out of his mouth; doctors said his liver just rotted away. Her momma went three days later from a ravaging stomach ache and the same symptoms. Her parents were cremated, but she never picked up their ashes.

She stayed in the big house she grew up in. Since she was the only living relative aside from Jay, she inherited everything, after probate, from her stepdaddy's estate. He was a plumber with a retirement account, and she was next of kin as it turned out. She lived alone with Jay, who joined the army when he was old enough.

Darlyn would never have been able to execute the deductive skills necessary to track Arthur Ravija down on her own. So, it was a real-life miracle, when Jay came home with a war hero. He introduced Darlyn to Truly, in a swoon worthy speech as the man who "saved his life."

Truly's last name was not a common one. And thank the good Lord, Truly, smitten with her, volunteered all kinds of information about his old man. According to Truly, the old man still lived nearby in Lake Ann. He was retired from some federal job. Now he sold cars, Buicks mostly.

Darlyn went to the dealership and pretended she was interested in buying a car, although the old man seemed skeptical of the credit history of a single woman. She noted his hair was dark like hers. He wore a too small red ball cap with his loose gray suit. He did not look her in the eyes, just rambled on about 'weathering treatment.'

Once they were back in his glass walled cubicle with him behind his desk and his computer, Darlyn couldn't wait any longer with her news.

"I think you know my momma," she said.

Arthur looked up from his computer pecking, but he didn't seem interested. "How's that?"

"I said, I think y'all know my momma." Darlyn stood and took the blue amulet out of her purse and dropped it on Arthur's desk. "This look familiar?"

He looked a little dizzy as he picked up the necklace. He looked at it for a long time. Then he turned it over in his large palm and read the inscription. "What do you want?" he said. He didn't look up.

Darlyn leaped to her feet, fists clenched. She wanted to break something. "What do I want? I want everything." He would have to look at her now.

But he never really did. So she took his savings, his son, and soon she was taking his boat. Now it would belong to her, every bit. She would tell Truly so when he got home. But neither he nor Jay showed up. At six, she realized they were late and the casserole with their dinner turned black before she removed it from the cookstove and piled it in the sink with the other dirty dishes. Around eight p.m., she poked around in Jay's room, looking for the number of Jay's whore. She found it in a blue address book under some papers on his desk. S.S.. Sara Shyrock.

Darlyn texted: *Its Darlyn, Jays cousin. He called? I will beat his ass he is not home yet.* There was no return message.

At nine p.m., Bev called, asking if she'd heard from Truly.

"Nope," Darlyn said.

"Should we call the Coast Guard?" Bev asked.

The question troubled Darlyn. She remembered the Ambien she stirred into Truly's oatmeal.

"Nope. The' boys are all right," Darlyn said.

She fell asleep sweaty, worried, troubled. In the middle of the night, she awoke. Someone was stroking her cheek. She could feel the smooth palm on her face, a sensation she thought she ought to know. She opened her eyes. "Angel?"

And there she was, silent and beautiful the way Darlyn liked to remember her. She hadn't seen her since she ordered liquid nicotine off Amazon for a vape, found she didn't like it, and dumped the remaining vial, evenly divided, into her step-daddy's bourbon and her momma's wine.

But here she was again. Her angel. Darlyn felt a sense of a mystery solved, a puzzle completed, a wholeness. She reached her hand out, but the vision disappeared. Darlyn squeezed her eyes shut, water leaking, running down her cheeks, dampening her pillow.

"Angel." She paused. When she finally spoke again, it was a whisper. "Momma."

20
GALVIN-EVENING

At six o'clock, Galvin gathered his jacket and his umbrella and hit the off switch on his office lights. He couldn't resist taking a quick look down the purple hallway to see if Sara was still there. She was, her back to him, seemingly intent on work. He hesitated for a moment trying to decide whether to say good night. Things hadn't been too cordial between them this morning. He decided to walk on.

The light was still on in Danielle's office, and she wore a pair of red plastic reading glasses, staring at the computer screen, its glow a pallor on her face. She glanced up when Galvin rapped lightly on her open door. "Six, already?"
Galvin stood, leaning against the door jamb. "You ready?"

Danielle clicked a few things with her mouse, and Galvin saw the screen go dark. She pushed her chair back, rose, and grabbed her wicker purse with brass fittings. She paused in front of a small square of mirror on the wall and fished in her purse. He watched her outline her lips with red lipstick, press her lips together and blot them with tissue. She tossed the tissue in the wire waste basket, turned to Galvin and smiled as though she were just now seeing him.

"Let's go," she said.

"Are you sure you want to drive?" Galvin was used to Sara's car, which was usually so messy they had to throw out a wealth of fast-food containers and wrappers before they could

119

even sit down.

"Goodness. Of course." Danielle swept past him, and he followed as she shut the door and locked it with a key from a small ring on her keychain. They walked to the elevator and Danielle pushed the down button. "Are you hungry?"

Galvin studied her. She was in her mid-thirties, ripe and ready to settle down. He knew the type, having dated a bit after his divorce. He was drawn to women like Danielle, approaching the peak of their attractiveness, competence, and sexuality. The old biological conundrum. He checked Danielle's right hand and saw no wedding or engagement ring. Someone as attractive as Danielle probably had a man she was serious about, or that she had an eye on. Galvin wondered who it was.

"Yes, a bit," he said and smiled at her. They took the elevator down in compatible silence and walked through the echoing company garage to her car, a convertible Miata classic. "My God," he said.

Danielle eyed him, but he noticed she was smiling. "What?"

"Is this a '93?"

She nodded.

"I have dreamed of driving this car," Galvin said. "But I never thought I would."

Danielle tossed him the keys, which flew over the vinyl roof and neatly into his hand as though they belonged there. "Thanks."

They switched sides. Getting into a '93 Miata was a little like crawling into a spaceship. Galvin bent his knees and settled heavily on the driver's side. He tested the gear shift in neutral, and put the key into the ignition while depressing the clutch.

Danielle, sitting beside him, attached her seatbelt and glanced at the gearshift.

"It's five gears," she said.

"How wonderful." Galvin looked over his right shoulder and shifted into reverse. The engine roared at his touch.

"First," Danielle said. "Shift into first."

Instead, Galvin started in second gear, smoothly, with a little hitch. If Danielle noticed, she said nothing.

Claudio's was as crowded as ever, and Galvin felt his usual irritation at popular restaurants where he had to hold a pager and mill around with other would-be patrons. Sara liked this place too, Galvin remembered. He braked and gave the car keys to the teenage valet and managed to get out of the low car without falling or gripping the kid's arm. "You know how to drive a shift?" he asked.

The kid wore an orange vest and had tattoos of Tweety bird and Taz on his forearms. He grinned. "I been driving since I was thirteen."

That did not exactly reassure Galvin, who pegged the valet as a Florida native with the horrendous driving skills already notorious in the sunshine state. But Danielle was prodding him on so he handed over the keys. Even though it was a weeknight, there was already a long line of people standing on the stone steps staring straight ahead, jostling for advantage.

Danielle marched past them as Galvin watched from the back of the line. He saw her speak to the maitre'd who seemed delighted to see her. He summoned a waiter who grabbed two menus. Danielle beckoned to him. Galvin bounded up the steps.

The waiter handed him two menus. "Well, hello sir," he said.

Galvin cleared his throat. "Hello," he said. This was the same waiter who often attended Sara and Galvin at the height of their romance. He felt a pang of missing her wild red hairdo, her pale lithe body, her youthful energy. He considered the discount factor that went along with Sara-the impulsiveness, lack of judgment, the quick temper. Danielle took his arm.

"Deep thoughts?" she asked.

Galvin shook his head as though to clear it. He patted her hand. They followed the waiter to a discreet table on the north side with a view of a pier and a lake. Motor boats were pulling up and cadres of passengers in brightly colored summer garb spilled onto the docks, some with drinks in hand. Galvin pulled out Danielle's chair, a perfunctory courtesy that Sara had seemed unfamiliar with. Danielle sat right down as Galvin glided the seat closer to the table.

"Thanks," she said. taking out her phone. Sara did that too, but after a brief scan, Danielle put the phone away. "Have you been here before?"

Galvin sat down on the opposite side of the table across an expense of white linen, a flickering candle, and a single pink rose drooping from a ceramic vase. "Oh," he said. "Once or twice." He pretended to study the menu even though he knew it pretty well. In fact, he already knew he would order the chicken picatta. A glance into the kitchen as they passed showed him the chef tonight was Jimmy. He liked Jimmy.

"What do you recommend?" Danielle asked.

Galvin looked up from his menu. It was strange seeing Danielle in this setting instead of in the office. It all happened so quickly. Outside, the motorboat roared away from the dock.

"Hmm," he said, folding the menu and placing it next to

his silverware. He looked up again and saw that Danielle's gaze was still upon him. "Try the spaghetti and meatballs. It's basic, but it's really good."

"That's settled, "she said and put her menu aside too. A fork clattered to the floor and Galvin bent down to retrieve it. When he straightened up, he rolled the utensil in his napkin.

"Sorry." Danielle clasped her hands and leaned in. Galvin involuntarily shrank back a little and took a sip of water.

"Have I told you I'm a sensitive?" she asked.

"A what?" Galvin liked women who made eye contact, but there was something hypnotic about Danielle's gaze.

"I'm a sensitive," she said, touching the locket at her throat. "Did you ever watch that show that used to be on, *Medium*?"

"Um," Galvin said.

Well, I'm a little like Allison DuBois."

Galvin had to clear his throat numerous times. "A psychic?"

Danielle smiled and unfolded her napkin. "Do you think that's odd?"

Yes, he thought. "No," said Galvin. "No, not at all."

Fortunately, the waiter showed up. He was an old man with gray hair, the stub of a pencil tucked behind his ear. "Good to see you again, sir."

Galvin gave Danielle a weak smile and ordered for both of them. "And an ice tea," she added, and Galvin said, "Make that two." No alcohol. Well, it was clear this was a business dinner.

Then it was just the two of them again, and Galvin regained his game face. "So. Why are you telling me this stuff?" he asked. "Do you have a prediction?"

"I know who will win the presidential election in 2020," she said.

"You ought to sell that info," Galvin said. "Who wins?"

"Actually," she said, "I'd rather talk about a dream I had the other night." Her face in the flickering candlelight reminded him of when he'd surveyed her at her computer. She looked exactly the same as someone conveying information from a data spreadsheet." It was about you."

"Do tell," Galvin said, although he immediately wished he hadn't.

"You were alone in a room full of people, "Danielle said. "They were all, you know, talking. and laughing."

Galvin didn't know what to say. He hated rooms full of people.

"And then," Danielle continued, "a child ran into the room. A little girl, I think. She ran to you, and you picked her up and swung her in the air." Danielle looked at Galvin expectantly. "Has anything like that happened to you?"

Galvin opened his mouth and shut it. Then he said, "My ex-wife called today. She's getting married and having a baby."

Danielle smiled. "And that's why you want to go to Alaska."

"Well, yes," Galvin said. He leaned forward and told her about his marriage, his divorce, his past, his present, his hopes for the future. The waiter discreetly served their food, refilled their glasses, removed their plates. More than an hour sped by. The waiter brought the check.

"On me," Galvin said, and he noticed Danielle didn't argue as Sara would have as he signed. Either one of them could have used their American Express business cards, but they hadn't discussed business. "I feel guilty," Galvin said. "We didn't talk about you. We didn't talk about Alaska."

"Let me leave the tip," Danielle said, tucking two fives under the linen napkin. Then she reached across the table and took his hand. "And the evening doesn't have to be over." She smiled. "I can read your tarot cards."

Inexplicably, Galvin found himself twining his fingers through hers. His chest felt tight. "All right."

Danielle stopped to talk to the maitre'd, and Galvin walked outside. He took a deep breath of the humid air, which fogged up his contact lens. He stopped wearing glasses when he was dating Sara in order to look younger. He looked across the parking lot, and there was a car under an oak tree, an old Saturn, that looked exactly like Sara's car. But he had to stop thinking about her. He turned as Danielle opened the door. After the 6:00 rush, the restaurant was having a lull on a weeknight. The steps were deserted.

Danielle reached out her hand, and he took it. She drew him into the shadows of the eave, half hidden by a pygmy palm. He thought of Sara with Jay. Pulling her close, he bent his head to Danielle's and lifted her chin. Their first kiss was a long one. It was all Galvin could do to restrain himself from lifting the hem of her gauzy skirt.

"I'll take that tarot reading now," Galvin said, brushing her hair from her face.

Danielle laughed. Hand in hand they walked back to the valet who roared to the curb with her sporty little car, stripping the gears. Galvin noted the old Saturn under the oak tree was gone.

Galvin put the top down on the Miata for the ride to Danielle's home. She settled into the passenger seat and turned to him. "By the way. It's Donald Trump," she said. "He gets re-elected."

"Is that so?" Galvin said, barely listening. Something about this car made him feel decades younger. In every way.

21
SARA-EVENING

After getting off the call with Meryl, Sara was able to concentrate on her new training session. She worked at her desk straight through lunch until six p.m. She intended to stop by and say hi to Galvin, to indicate there were no hard feelings and to fish for an invitation to his ex-wife's wedding. After all, Galvin usually worked late. But when she glanced down the purple hallway, she saw his door was closed and the lights were out. "Oh, well," she thought, "I can catch him tomorrow." She checked her messages and saw Jay hadn't texted her either, although he was surely back by now.

Sara stretched, leaning back in her swivel chair. She thought she may as well go eat dinner by herself at Claudio's. She was starving, and it was too late to call anyone. And who knew? Maybe Galvin would be there. She hated eating by herself.

Sara worked for another two hours, and by the time she pulled up in Claudio's parking lot, it was almost dark, and Galvin's car wasn't there. She parked under an old live oak in the shadows of the parking lot facing the restaurant. She couldn't decide if she wanted to go in.

Then she sat up because she saw someone coming out of the lighted restaurant, a man of Galvin's height, wearing a business suit. Sara noted his distinctive long stride, and she almost opened the car door to call to him. Then her hand fell away from the door handle.

Behind Galvin was his dinner companion, a woman in a flowing dress. Sara squinted. What the…wasn't that Ms. Biggs, head of the training department? Her boss?

Apparently, it was, because the woman seemed to take charge, pulling Galvin into the shadows of the shrubbery under an overhanging eave. It was dark, but Sara saw the two silhouettes become one. For a long time. She shrank down in her seat and peered over the top of the steering wheel. Her phone made a chirping noise, which meant she had a message.

Please. Please let it be Jay.

But when she held her phone up, she saw that it was from an unfamiliar number. *Its Darlyn*, she read, *Jays cousin. He called? I will beat his ass he is not home yet.*

Sara threw the phone into the passenger seat. So Jay hadn't gone home. He was probably with his real girlfriend. *Maybe I should get a cat.* Sara turned the key in the ignition and put the car into reverse.

22
DANIELLE-EVENING

Danielle gave Galvin directions to her home, a gated townhouse on the fashionable side of Winter Cove, even though in Central Florida they were at least an hour's drive from any body of water other than a retention pond. There was a big one in her complex with a fountain, of all things, that gurgled and spewed water day and night.

Galvin pulled up in front of the gates and the call box. "Code?"

Danielle gave it to him without hesitation: 1028, the month and day of her birthday. But he didn't know that about her, or that this fall she would be forty years old. She looked into his personnel file, and she was five years older than him. Well, so what. All night long, she rode a wave of sensory perception relating to Galvin. She had always been attracted to him and even told her girlfriends if he was free, she would jump on him. Now, at long last, her intuition paid off.

Galvin punched in the code, and the gate lifted. He followed her directions to her address, a two-story brick building attached to a townhouse on both sides. The landscaping surrounding the building was lush, sodded, and bordered with flowering hibiscus and azalea bushes. From a distance, he could hear the fountain in the retention pond.

"This is nice," Galvin said.

Danielle seldom entertained, so she tried to look at her

neighborhood through his eyes. He was right. The road curved and street lamps glowed in front of snug two-story buildings. They were a mile away from the nearest road, so it was quiet. A house light gleamed from Danielle's porch. Flowering milkweed overflowed from a clay pot by the door.

"Home sweet home," Danielle said and hoisted herself out of the tiny car.

"I would have opened the door," Galvin said, "except standing up takes me a minute."

Danielle laughed. Galvin skirted the hood and walked to her side of the car. "Shall we go in?" he asked.

She took his hand, and they walked together up the brick path. Danielle found the key in her purse without fumbling, fitted it into the brass lock, turned it, and opened the door. Her foyer was narrow with cream-colored walls. An antique cuckoo clock hung above silver framed photographs displayed on a Turkish chest. Galvin stopped to look at them.

"Who's this?" he asked, picking up the picture of her and Denny.

"My twin brother," Danielle said.

"I did not know you had a twin. Does it run in your family?"

"I wouldn't know," Danielle said. "My mother gave us up to child services when we were six years old. We had no relatives. Denny and I were fraternal twins. Obviously." She laughed. "There's not supposed to be any connection." She was in the kitchen already rummaging through the fridge. "Aah, here we go." She pulled out a pitcher of iced tea.

Galvin hesitated. "Is your brother...sensitive too?"

"He wasn't," Danielle said.

"Wasn't?"

Danielle poured the tea into two water tumblers. "It's unsweetened," she said, holding out a glass.

Galvin draped his jacket and umbrella on the back of a straight wooden chair. He sipped. "This is good," he said. His gaze lighted on her shelf of herbs. "What are these?"

Danielle bought a white-painted wooden shelf online from Wayfair and put it up herself. There was a row of tiny clay and ceramic glazed pots, each sprouting healthy green growth. "Oh," Danielle shrugged, "basil, sage, oregano. Ginseng. I have more outside."

Danielle led him into the living room. She sat down on a beige divan and patted the seat next to her. Galvin put his glass on a wooden coaster and sat down about three feet away. He was tall, his knees grazed the glass coffee table.

Danielle looked up and saw that Galvin was gazing at her. "Denny was in a boating accident," she said briskly. "And his neck was broken." She leaned back and switched on an overhead lamp, then lifted a small gilt box off the table. She opened the lid and took out her tarot cards. "Water skiing accident. And, no, I'm not sure he was sensitive. But we were close."

"I'm sorry," Galvin said.

Danielle shuffled the cards a few times and cut the deck. "It was hard. I started drinking." She smiled briefly. "A lot. It cost me a marriage." She glanced up. "Do you want to ask me a question? Before I read your cards?"

Galvin moved a little closer. "I noticed you don't drink. How did you stop?"

Danielle laughed. "Is that what you want to ask me?" She got up and opened a lower cabinet on a wooden bookshelf and punched a few buttons. The sound of a solo saxophone flowed from the speakers. "Kenny G," she said.

"No," Galvin said. "How did you get over your brother's death? A divorce? A drinking problem?"

Danielle looked into his eyes. "I joined Alcoholics Anonymous. I got a sponsor. I promised never to touch alcohol again. That was three years ago."

Galvin said, covered her hand with his. "I admire that."

'That's not all you admire,' Danielle thought. She leaned in to kiss him and, when he met her halfway, the kiss just went on and on. That would be the effect of the tinge of powder she slipped into his water glass when he bent to pick up the fork she'd deliberately dropped. She'd made it herself from the Williams Pomona aphrodisiac 'click and grow' herbs she grew in her backyard. The restaurant was dark, and he didn't notice.

The effect of his lips on hers swept away any doubts as to its potency. Her mouth opened a little and their tongues touched. Galvin put his hands on her waist and started to move in closer. Danielle broke away and picked up the tarot cards.

"Okay," she said. "Question." She let her breath out slowly, flaring her nostrils a little.

Galvin shifted closer, slid his arm around her, and played with the zipper on the side of her dress, close to the curve of her breast. He put his other hand on her knee. Almost imperceptibly, he pushed some of the fabric back.

He said, "I don't know what's gotten into me." His hand slid under her dress, stroking her leg. "My question is." He stopped, laughed, and then soldiered on. "How about I spend the night?"

Danielle felt his breath on her face, his hand on her leg as it inched up the tender inside of her thigh. She sat forward, not quite dislodging him. "Let's see what the cards say," she whispered.

"Okay." Galvin released her and leaned back. She still felt the trace of his touch as she shuffled the cards and laid out ten of the brightly colored cards, face up.

To steady herself, she said, "This, the Rider Waite, tarot deck includes seventy eight cards divided into two groups, the major and minor arcana. It's almost like a deck of cards, divided into four suits: wands, swords, pentacles, and cups. These are like clubs, spades, diamonds and hearts in a regular deck. It's possible to do a reading with just a deck of regular cards."

She paused studying the card layout. "This is the Celtic Cross formation, one of the most common. Each position in the cross indicates the past, present and future."

Galvin resumed stroking her thigh.

Danielle frowned. "Regarding your question, not sure. Mostly minor arcadia. A lot of wands and swords, which relate to challenges and work. And this guy." She pointed to a leering figure of the Devil in the tenth position. "Lust."

Galvin leaned forward, picked up his glass, and took a long pull of iced tea. "Is that good? Bad? Should I pack it in and go home?"

Danielle rose and held out her hand. "Not at all. The cards can change."

She led him into a snug room with double doors adjacent to the living room. A Tiffany lamp illuminated a nightstand piled with magazines, mostly industry related, and a clock radio. Danielle moved to turn the lamp off.

Galvin took her hand to stop her. "Don't," he said.

Danielle shook her head, feeling her heart speed up. Instead of arguing, Galvin pulled her close and ran his hands up and down her back. Then her hips. Kissing her, he pulled the side zipper on her dress down. "Let's take this off," he whispered. He pulled up the flowing skirt of her dress and lifted it over her head.

"Galvin," she said. She moved to turn off the lamp again, and again he caught her hand. He released it, unknotting his tie and unbuttoning his shirt. He quickly shed his upper garments and took her in his arms, lowering his face to hers. He kissed her until they were both breathless. Reaching up, he pulled the straps of her bra down revealing the deep well of her cleavage. He dipped his fingers inside the lingerie. Danielle tried to turn away, but he held her shoulders. " You're beautiful," he said. "But I'll stop if you say so."

His words seemed to set something loose in Danielle, something freeing and tremendously exciting. She put her thumbs in the sides of her underwear and flipped it to the floor, stepping out of them. She reached behind her back and unclasped her bra, pulling the straps over her shoulders. Now she wore nothing except her locket, which she touched once for luck.

Then she fumbled with his belt buckle, which was not complicated at all, but haste made it difficult to successfully un-clasp. She pulled at the gabardine of his pants until they slid down his thighs, along with his boxer shorts. Galvin, Danielle saw, had concealed a lean finely muscled physique inside his Brooks Brothers suits. And that wasn't all.

"My word," Danielle said. She didn't socialize with the young trainers who gossiped about their boyfriends. Still, she was surprised Sara had been so discreet. She put both hands flat on Galvin's chest, which was hard and covered with curling dark hair, and pushed him onto her bed.

They made love for hours, resting, starting up again. At some point, they both fell asleep. Danielle awoke as Galvin nudged her on her side, lifted her leg, and entered her, sliding his hands up to her breasts.

She waited a moment until she heard his breathing steady and rumble into a slight snore. Reaching between their bodies, she eased away from Galvin as she ran her hand up and down until she found the condom, somewhat wilted, but still attached. She plucked it off. Lifting his arm, Danielle slid out from underneath still holding the crumpled condom. Tiptoeing into the kitchen, she did not turn on the lights. Instead, she rummaged in her cupboard and withdrew a Yeti cup. She placed the condom in the cup and sealed it. Then she hid the cup in the deepest recess of her freezer. She washed her hands at the sink.

A few minutes later, she turned off the bedroom light, lifted Galvin's arm once again and slid in next to him. She whispered, "Thank you," and was finally asleep for good.

23
JAY-EVENING

Jay couldn't outrun the storm. The speed of the boat, combined with the speed of the storm, along with the steepness and intensity of the ocean, could only add up to disaster. And disaster struck, in the midst of the storm, in the midst of lashing rain, deafening thunder and jolts of lightning. The tiny boat climbed to the top of an immense wave. It seemed to Jay the *Early Byrd* hovered, which gave him a nanosecond of hope. Then it slid downwards in an uneven trajectory and at a speed that flipped him overboard.

For a few seconds, he was dragged along beneath the boat after his bad arm became entangled in a rope he'd tied to his waist. Somehow, he managed to break free. He wore a limp life jacket, and the whitecaps kept crashing over his head, driving him further and further underwater for longer and longer. His visibility was only a relentless restless waterfall. A storm at sea is noisy and it is cold. The waves kept crashing, and Jay kept gulping sea water. Soon, he found he could barely keep his face above cresting swells.

His life didn't flash before his eyes, only his regrets. His biggest regret was that he hadn't saved Truly. His mentor would slip from sleeping off some bender to sleeping with the fishes without, Jay fervently prayed, regaining consciousness. It was a terrible defeat for Jay who had sworn to protect Truly with his life.

24
TRULY–LATE MORNING

Truly was tired, so tired, he couldn't keep his eyes open. He closed them. And dreamed.

He was carried down a street. His head bobbed as he looked over someone's shoulder. The afternoon light was soft, golden, filtered through the leaves, making grotesque patterns on the buckled sidewalks. Tree roots emerged here and there. The air was heavy. He looked down, and the sidewalk seemed close. He looked up, and the houses and trees towered over his head. The wires hanging from utility poles were sagging and tangled. Black wrought iron fencing molded like corn stalks ran along the outer rim of the sidewalk. The sound of hurried footsteps went thwack, thwack, thwack.

In his dream, he expected someone to catch up with him. Instead, he was caught in a grip like a vise and flung into the back seat of a car. He rolled to the floor and lost consciousness.

Then, in the manner of dreams, he was back, a grown man. He was sitting across the table from a woman in her sixties. She wore a purple turban. She leaned across the table and took both his hands. In his dream, she was crying. She stood up and tried to hug him. Her tears were wet and salty. Truly could taste them, and the flavor was like the sea.

He opened his eyes. He was lying on the deck of the boat bearing the brunt of drenching rain. The Bimini top was gone. There were several inches of water on the deck. Sitting up almost caused him to pitch forward.

"Jay?" The wind shrieked around him. The boat keeled, and he slammed hard against the console. Soaking wet, staggering, slipping on the deck, he caught the steering wheel and centered it. The tiny boat still roiled, but it wasn't going to capsize. Truly shook his head and tried to clear it. Never had he wished so much for land, even a glimpse of it.

A dot of red on the control panel indicated the bilge pump was running. Water was pouring onto the deck of the boat. The wind slammed rain into his face, hard little droplets. The ship pressed upward on waves at forty-five degrees, and then crashed down, jarring Truly's bones. Then the waves spun the vessel sideways. He held tightly onto the wheel, the gear shift, anything. It was difficult to hang on. A bolt of lightning struck nearby.

"Don't you care we're going to die?" Truly screamed at the sky.

There was no mercy in that wind, no grace in the waves, only wrath and tempest. The air was thick with a briny mist, the deck awash with waves. There was no staying still, and Truly picked himself up repeatedly from the deck where gravity flung him. The boat climbed a wave and seemed to hover there almost to the tipping point. Truly was lashed back and forth as he hung onto the wheel. The boat crashed down into the sea and Truly was stunned that the boat stayed upright and in one piece. His biggest problem right now was avoiding getting swept out to sea. With sodden, chilled, water-soaked fingers, he unbuckled his belt and lashed one end of it to the wheel and the other end doubled around his arm. In every direction, the gray blue tempest, laced with white, blended into a horizon of the same hue. There was no rescue from land, sea, or air.

"Jay," Truly called into the watery inferno. "Jay!"

Only the wind screamed in his ears.

25
JAY

Jay swallowed more sea water. His mind wanted to panic, wanted him to thrash, wanted him driven deeper and deeper under water until there was no return. He wanted it to be over. But his body had other ideas, kicking, grasping, reaching. Then his mind clicked into gear.

Jay, the Juice.

There was a trick he heard of from a former Navy Seal during a night of drinking in a far-off foreign bar. Taking a deep breath, Jay unclasped his belt and let it slip out of his hands, wincing at the pain in his arm. He kicked off his shoes. A wave overtook him, and he struggled for a full minute to emerge from the furious ocean. Once his head bobbed above water, he struggled to take off his jeans. They were wet and heavy. He was shivering with cold. Still, he got them off and managed to tie a square knot with numb fingers at the end of the legs and to pull up the fly. He was so cold he could barely feel the pain in his arm. Or maybe it was shock.

Another enormous swell knocked him several feet under water, but he held onto his jeans and swam furiously upward, the heavy wet denim slapping at his arms and legs. Once he was above the wave, he treaded water while he drained the jeans, then inflated them by pulling the heavy denim over water and swinging them over his head to get air inside. Every time he did this, he sank, but he managed to close the waist of the pants until he emerged. Pull, swing, sink. Pull, swing, sink.

The whole time he was tossed and turned like a minuscular piece of flotsam on an incorrigible sea. Eventually, though, he managed to put his head through the ring formed by the inflated pant legs while holding the waist closed and underwater. The self-devised life jacket rested atop the standard orange one he was wearing and buoyed him higher out of the water. He was still swamped with swells, but he seemed to emerge from them faster. Eventually the squall passed. Ten hours later, as the sun set, Jay was still a bobbing fleck in the vast ocean with a flat coral ridge just out of sight. He was barely conscious.

26
SARA-THE DAY AFTER

Sara found Jay's amulet the next morning as she groped her way in the dark towards the toilet. Her foot hit the piece of jewelry, and it skittered into a corner. She flicked the on switch and squinted at the fluorescent glare. Getting down on her hands and knees, she scrabbled her hands along the cold tiles. She felt something behind the toilet and drew it out.

It was a blue stone, probably aquamarine, mounted on silver, hung on a silver chain. She turned it around in her hand. There was writing on the back. Initials in a curly script.

A.J. Ravija
10-31-1972

Sara grasped the necklace in her hand and descended the stairs to the kitchen, feeling her way in the dark down the banister. She switched on the overhead light and sank into a chair at the round table. She wasn't thinking clearly yet, but the only person who was in her bathroom recently was Jay. Her heart felt a little lighter. He hadn't texted, but now she knew he had to get in touch with her again. For all she knew, he left the jewelry here for that express purpose.

Humming a little, she dropped the necklace into the blue ceramic centerpiece and got up to fix herself some coffee. What she needed was a little feminine feedback. She knew just the woman to go to.

She poured coffee into a thermos and left it on the

counter. Then she went upstairs to shower and get ready for work. She would stop at her grandmother's house on the way there.

Her grandmother lived in an old-fashioned Florida suburb, the kind with soaring oak, palm, and pine trees that came crashing down on everyone's parked cars during hurricane season. No one put their car in the garage because the houses had few closets and a tiny attic. Everyone's garage was full of junk.

Gran Rain had lived there forever. She kept her old Buick in the garage. The septuagenarian just took Lyfts when she had to go anywhere. Sara pulled up in the driveway next to a gray Lincoln. Why on this of all mornings did Gran have company. And this early?

She grabbed her coffee thermos and headed up the walk. A white and gray cat, half grown, emerged from under the jasmine bush, startling both of them. The cat raised its back, hissed at her, and darted off into the neighbor's yard.

Sara felt free to barge in on Gran whenever she felt like it. She was practically her only living relative, and she'd lived there most of her life. She unlocked the door with her own key, and stepped into the cool foyer. It smelled of burnt wax. Usually, her grandmother was in the kitchen baking or in the family room reading. Occasionally, she'd be swimming in the pool, but it was too early for that wasn't it?

"Gran?"

There was no answer, only the strident whir of the silver refrigerator in the kitchen. Sara huffed because she didn't have much time before work. She walked into the living room. The window rods were hung with sheer white curtains, and the blinds were open. Sara looked out at the pool. She squinted.

Then she lifted her hand to her mouth.

She saw her grandma's head emerge from the water, tossing back her long wet hair. A second later another head emerged. This head also had long wet hair, but it belonged to a man. Apparently, Gran Rain knew him well enough because she caught him on the shoulders and leaned in for a kiss. Sara had the strong impression that neither of these senior citizens wore any clothes.

Quickly she backed towards the door. Without turning, she slid outside, shutting the door after her. She stood there a moment tapping her toe. Then she stabbed the doorbell button with a tapered nail. She resisted the urge to tap it over and over. After about three minutes, the door opened, and Gran Rain stood there in her peach bathrobe with her damp hair streaming over her shoulders. She looked surprisingly young without her chignon and cardigan. "Sara, my angel," she said and hugged the young woman who pulled away and jerked a thumb towards the house. "Who is that you have in there?"

Gran Rain ran a hand through her wet hair. "Don't use that tone with me, Sara Shyrock."

"Since when are you dating?"

"Don't be so nosy."

"But you never did before."

"Well, I was busy. And you're the one with problems. Which I presume is the reason for the early morning stop over."

"Is he sleeping here, Gran?" Sara's voice squeaked a little as she said this.

"Oh, for God's sake, Sara," Gran Rain said, raising her voice. "Do you want to meet him?"

Sara sniffed. "I have to get to work, Gran."

Gran Rain dug her hands into her terry-cloth pockets. "Did you eat breakfast?"

Sara shook her head, and her vision blurred with tears. "You know I never eat breakfast. Listen, let's do this another time."

Her grandma reached behind her and closed the door. "What is it?" she asked.

Sara sniffed. "It's embarrassing." She wiped her nose with the back of her hand. "I've been seeing someone new. He's incredibly good looking. But we only get together during the week. He's always busy on the weekends."

Gran frowned. "Some men are what I'd call too good looking. They go after every woman that moves. If she doesn't move, he shakes her."

"It's the other way around with Jay. Women throw themselves at him. I threw myself at him." She paused. "I have feelings for him."

"Oh, Sara. You don't have to fall in love with everyone you're attracted to." Gran sighed. "I liked Galvin."

Sara stiffened. "He's dating someone else."

"Well." Gran straightened up. "I find it hard to believe it's serious. I saw the way Galvin looked at you. I thought to myself, 'Oh now it's over.'"

"Galvin took his ex-wife to the wedding of a close friend."

"An error," Gran Rain said. "But one that could perhaps be exonerated after sufficient contrition."

Sara was digging in her bag for a tissue. "What?"

Gran took a packet of tissues from the pocket of her bathrobe and pressed them in Sara's hand. She hugged her again. "Not everyone is as perfect as you are."

Sara started to speak and stopped. "Okay," she said. "And who the hell is that in there again?" She gestured towards the closed door.

Gran smiled. "So good to see you sweetheart. Come again soon." She paused. "And call first."

Sara stared at Gran for a minute. Then she shook her head, waved goodbye, got in her car, waved again, and backed out bumping hard over the curb. She saw the gray and white cat peep through the slats in the neighbor's fence. Then she drove through the familiar streets to the highway where she cut cars off aggressively to make it to work.

After winking and bypassing the initial sign in for Roosevelt, Sara sauntered past Jackie's reception desk.

"Is Mr. Montana in yet? We had a meet." There was no 'meet.' Sara just liked to pretend she was friendly with the boss when she was late. She wondered if Jackie fell for it. If she had to guess, she would say no.

Jackie didn't even bother to call his desk. "Haven't seen him." She bent her head with its helmet-like hair toward her laptop screen. She looked up briefly, her glasses making her eyes look owlish. "Have you?"

Sara laughed. "That's what I asked you."

She waved and walked down the hall towards her cubicle. Then she turned and veered sharply to the right. She walked down two rows of cubicles and paused outside a pink panel.

"Knock, knock," she said.

A woman with white-blonde hair looked up and smiled with perfectly defined red lips.

Sara entered the cubicle, moved some manuals and

binders off the spare swivel chair and plopped down. "Gabby." Sara dug her toe into the carpet and inched the chair around to face her colleague. "Have a minute?"

Gabby and Sara were in the habit of commiserating. There were few intimate details the young women spared each other. A lot of these revelations were confided at bars and accompanied by alcohol and loud laughter. Commiserating at work was rare. Yet Sara didn't feel she had a choice after Gran's ignominious defection.

"Keep your voice down," Gabby whispered. "I stole that chair out of Danielle's office." She was a pale girl with skin so white her veins were visibly blue in her wrists and ankles. Her signature color was black. Sara noted the snug Prada suit and the Jimmy Choo stilettos that lengthened Gabby's legs. She, on the other hand, barely brushed her hair this morning.

Sara swallowed. "It's Jay."

Gabby nodded. "Of course."

"I think... Jay." She stopped and her eyes filled with tears. "Men are such assholes."

Gabby leaned forward and clasped Sara's wrist. "Of course, you're upset."

Sara withdrew her arm. Gabby was so touchy feely. "How would you know?"

Gabby rolled her swivel chair away from the desktop computer, so Sara could see the screen. Sara scanned it and turned white.

On the screen was a US NEWS picture of Jay and a middle-aged man Sara assumed was Truly. There was a separate picture of a smiling woman, probably Darlyn. And there was the headline:

Missing Men in Florida Never Returned From Fishing Trip.

"I think I feel a little woozy," Sara said. She leaned heavily on the arm of the chair, which fell to the floor. Sara toppled head first onto the carpet in a dead faint.

27
GALVIN -MORNING

Galvin woke up in his own bed, shaken, dizzy and with an erection. He just lay there and listened to his alarm blare the classic rock station anthem, "Hotel California." He was sure to hear the 'living it up' lyrics stream through his head the rest of the day. The events of the previous night began to filter through his memory like acts from a play. Leaving work. Driving the Miata. Claudio's. Danielle's house. The sex. Lots and lots of sex.

He shivered. Then he tossed the covers and staggered out of bed. Naked, he made it to the bathroom and switched on the too bright overhead light. In the mirror, he looked gaunt and pale. He looked down and groaned. Abruptly, he turned off the light and shoved the shower curtain aside. Twisting the shower knob to scalding hot, he stepped into the stall and took deep steamy breaths.

Of course, it was understandable he would be off kilter after the news from Meryl that she was getting married and expecting a child. But that didn't explain his outrageous familiarity and sexually provocative behavior with Danielle. He never behaved like that in his life. And although the titillation was still with him, obviously, (here he glanced down again) the sense that all was right in his world wasn't.

True, Danielle was an exciting woman, but there was a baseline to his own behavior that sat uncomfortably with him. Danielle was a colleague, entitled to his respect. He worked with her, for God's sake. And he was not in love with her, how could he be? They spent one evening together.

Galvin turned off the hot water with a sharp twist to the knob and stepped out of the shower grabbing a white towel off the rack that he wrapped around his waist. The truth was that much as he liked Danielle, and it was fair to say after last night he liked her a lot, he didn't have that budding sense of elation he felt when he started dating Meryl. Or Sara. Plus, the sensitive/ psychic conversation freaked him out. Did she speak to her dead twin brother?

Galvin was a pragmatist. The tarot cards alone should have sent him packing. What had gotten into him?

He shaved and got dressed, yanking his suit off the wire dry cleaner hangers. Not even bothering with breakfast, he grabbed his umbrella, looked at it for a minute, and then flung it to the floor. It wasn't going to rain, and who cared if it did?

Getting into his own sensible Buick sedan, he flashed back to driving Danielle's Miata the previous evening, and his expression softened a little. He kept his own MGB in the garage because he rarely drove it without having to call AAA for a tow. But the Miata ran like a dream. However, he reminded himself, there were some men who could be tempted into a relationship by a classic convertible sports car, but he was not one of them.

At work, Jackie greeted him at the InterTech reception desk with a nod. "Mr. Steele."

Something in her expression made him pause. "What?"

She glanced toward his office. "You have company."

Galvin groaned inwardly. There was no one, no one, he felt like seeing right now. He hoped it wasn't Danielle wanting to pick up where they left off after she drove him to InterTech at

3 a.m. to pick up his car. If they hadn't been in her Miata...well, who knows what would have happened? The Miata, for all its merits, would require gumby like contortionists to accommodate sex in such a confined space.

He breathed in sharply and marched down the purple carpeted corridor to his office. The door was open. He was tempted to yell down the aisle to Jackie, "Don't open my office when I'm not there." Storming into his domain, intending to get rid of whoever had the bad taste to begin his day with their unwelcome presence, he stopped short.

The chairs in front of his desk were occupied by two young women. One was a petite blonde he vaguely recognized as one of the trainers. The other was Sara. His heart leaped.

"Good morning," he said shortly and moved to sit behind his desk. Then he took a look at Sara and lowered himself slowly into his chair. Her eyes were red, swollen, there was a prominent bump on her forehead where her hairline met her brow.

"What happened?" he asked.

Sara burst into tears. He saw she already appropriated his box of Kleenex and a half dozen wadded up tissues lay on the floor surrounding her chair.

He looked at the other woman.

"I'm Gabby." she said. "I work with Sara?" She smiled, and then her smile faded. She drew a deep breath. "Something terrible has happened."

Sara emitted a loud sob.

For a minute Galvin wondered if it had anything to do with news leaking about his sexual foray with Danielle the night before. "Ridiculous," he thought, involuntarily looking down.

This was a place of business and surely Sara wouldn't enlist a coworker to unveil an office liaison. Galvin leaned his hands on the desk. "What is it?" He addressed Sara directly. "What happened to your head?"

Sara just buried her face in her hands.

"I borrowed a chair from Danielle's office?" Gabby said. "The arm of the chair fell off, and she hit her head when she fainted. She's lucky she didn't break her neck like Hillary Swank did in *Million Dollar Baby*. Did you see it? I love boxing movies."

Galvin took a deep breath. "Why did she faint?" He hated to confer directly with Gabby, but there was no help for it.

"Well," Gabby said, "you hadn't heard?"

Galvin was a patient man, but in one minute he was going to throw his plaque for InterTech employee of the year at the wall. He cleared his throat. "No."

Gabby opened her mouth, but Sara chose this moment to leap to her feet, fists clenched.

"He said he knew the water. He knew the boat. He knew what to do, for sure."

Galvin stood as well. He glared at Sara. "Who then? Who for God's sake?"

Sara collapsed in her chair and covered her face.

"It's Jay," Gabby said conversationally. "In IT? He went on a fishing trip or something…"

"To help his cousin scatter his father's ashes," Sara said. Her voice was muffled.

"Wait a minute," Galvin said. "Jay? Who works here?"

"Yes," Gabby said with great weight. "He's lost at sea."

"Well," Galvin said, "can't they find him?" He didn't know the young man intimately, but he did not like to think of an InterTech employee floating around in the Gulf Stream.

Sara gave a loud sob and sank further into her chair. Gabby fiddled with her phone for a minute. "It's on TV," she said. She turned the volume of the news report up:

A desperate search of the Atlantic continues for two men lost at sea. The U.S. Coast Guard has searched an estimated 24,000 square miles after Truly Ravija, a local businessman, and Jay Hicks, an InterTech employee, were reported missing early Friday morning. They were last seen in the Early Byrd, a twenty four foot center-console boat with a white hull and black T-top.

"Jesus," Galvin said. Sara blew her nose and began a fresh round of crying. Galvin rose. Perhaps he could comfort her. Perhaps he could do it so well that by the time they found Jay she would no longer be interested. Perhaps...Galvin stepped from behind his desk.

Danielle appeared in the doorway. "Did someone take my chair?" She took one look at Sara and glanced at Galvin. He stopped his advance towards Sara, sat back down, and fiddled with a pencil on his desk.

Danielle put a hand on Sara's shoulder. "You poor thing." Sara rose and flung herself into Danielle's arms, weeping on her shoulder. Danielle patted her back. "There, there," she said.

"You can go home," Galvin offered, desperate to provide some solace.

"I'll take her," Gabby said, rising. "She's too upset to be driving on her own."

Danielle transferred Sara from her shoulder to Gabby's. Sara looked up for a minute, her bloodshot eyes searching out Galvin's. "The ponies are gone," she said.

"What?" Galvin turned and looked out his office window. Sure enough the pasture was empty except for trees and grass. When he looked back, Gabby and Sara were limping towards the elevator. "I'll call you," he shouted after Sara, but she did not turn around.

Danielle shut his door. "Don't we have something to finish from last night?" she asked. She touched the locket at her throat and began unbuttoning her blouse. "I have a condom," she said.

Galvin exhaled sharply at the sight of her in a lacy bra. "It's almost like you have some kind of power over me," he said, laughing a little. He turned to close the curtains.

"Leave them open," Danielle said, smiling. "No one can see. Except us."

Galvin cleared his desk.

28
SARA

Leaving her own car in the parking lot, Sara allowed Gabby to drive her home. She intended to lie down, and then call Gran, maybe go over there and stay for a few days. She couldn't believe Jay was missing, perhaps dead. Her pique with him from the day before vanished. She imagined a reunion on the beach as the Coast Guard towed him in, running so hard the sand flew, then melting into his arms as he set foot on land.

Gabby followed her into the house and then up the stairs to her bedroom. When Sara flopped onto her unmade bed, Gabby kicked off her shoes and lay beside her. Then she leaned over and picked her purse up off the floor. Opening it, she extracted a pillbox and pried the lid off. She extracted two capsules. She dry swallowed one and extended her palm with the remaining capsule to Sara.

"What is it?" Sara asked dully, staring at the ceiling.

"Xanax," Gabby said. "It's for anxiety. I take it before I have to teach a class."

If Sara had been herself, she would have laughed. She felt more alive in front of a classroom than she did anywhere else. Instead, she took the proffered pill and choked it down.

"You don't need to stay," Sara said, but the words were no sooner out of her mouth than grief and exhaustion overcame her, and she fell asleep.

She awoke hours later with a dry mouth, a headache,

and the uncomfortable sensation of sleeping in her clothes. She swung her legs over the side of the bed and rose. Gabby was still sleeping beside her, a gentle snore emitting from her open mouth. Tiptoeing into the bathroom, Sara shed her clothes on the floor, sat on the toilet, flushed it, turned on the shower, and stepped into the stall. Fresh tears mingled with the shower water as she recalled that just the day before Jay stood where she was, whole, healthy, alive.

She was still under the effect of the sedative Gabby gave her, and so lost in her thoughts, it took a moment or two to register that she was not alone in the bathroom. The sound of the curtain sliding open caught her unaware.

It was not a big shower. Gabby, shorter than Sara, stood naked right under her nose. Sara frowned. "What are you doing here?" It seemed to her that her voice came from far away and echoed slightly.

"I'm here to wash your back," Gabby said. "After what you've been through, you shouldn't be alone."

Sara furrowed her brow, but Gabby was already soaping up a green washcloth with Sara's expensive exfoliate. She sighed, turned around, and leaned forward, bracing her arms on the shower wall. She was so logy, it took more than a few minutes for her to realize that something wasn't quite conventional about Gabby soaping her back with a few up and down strokes. Gabby extended the reach of her hand lower, to Sara's buttocks and then, astonishingly, dipping between her legs. Sara dropped her hands and reached around batting at Gabby's caresses. "What are you doing?"

Gabby hesitated then hugged her, speaking into the wet tendrils of Sara's hair. "Oh. You're so pretty. I'm sorry, I just…"

Here she trailed off and reached around covering Sara's breasts with her hands. She rasped her palm across the nipples. "See," Gabby said. "You like it, too."

"Oh, for God's sake, Gabby." Still, Sara did not move her friend's hands, which continued to rove over her breasts and belly.

Gabby hummed in her ear. "Do you want me to wash you all over?" Still wielding the green washcloth, she trailed it down the flat of Sara's belly to the triangular fiery patch of hair. Sara's arms broke out in gooseflesh despite the warmth of Gabby's body and the warm water cascading over them. Gabby dropped the cloth with a wet plop, and twined her fingers in Sara's wet pubic curls.

"Gabby…" Sara turned, and Gabby kissed her. It wasn't the first kiss she'd ever had with a woman. But somehow nothing ever proceeded beyond a kiss. This was different. Sara opened her mouth and Gabby's tongue darted in touching the tip to Sara's. Sara lifted one leg and wrapped it around Gabby's thigh drawing her closer, as close as they could get. Gabby extricated herself and sank slowly to her knees. Gabby kissed Sara's navel and then kissed lower. Sara put both hands on Gabby's head and pushed her closer.

Gabby abruptly straightened up, reached past Sara, and turned the water off. She stood a little apart from her friend and traced a rivulet of water culminating at the tip of Sara's nipple.

"I don't want you to be mad at me," Gabby said.

"Well," Sara said, gasping a little, "I'm not. You're distracting me."

Gabby took her hand. "Let's towel off and go back to bed," she said. Sara shivered and allowed herself to be led out of the shower, dried, and taken back to bed under the skillful machinations of her friend. Later, she didn't like to admit that it was hours before she thought of Jay again. She wondered what that meant.

29
LINK

Link didn't wear a watch to work, but the sun was not high over his head when the police pulled up at the curb of Darlyn's house. The two officers, a man and a woman, got out and instead of walking up the driveway to Darlyn's door, they walked over to the construction site and stood there watching. Link kept an eye on his work, digging the foundation of the house, and passed a bandana over his brow, which was moist with sweat.

The cops branched off, speaking quietly to individual workers. Eventually both of them converged on Link who, as it happened, was the only black laborer in the gang. Officers Banks and Cleary. One male, one female. Both white. "But this was Lake Ann after all," Link thought. "What do I expect?"

He leaned his hand on his shovel, balancing it, looked at the law enforcement officers, and lifted his eyebrows. "Can I help you?"

"Yeah," Officer Cleary said. She jerked her thumb in the direction of Darlyn's house.

"We found some marijuana in that lady's home yesterday. She said it wasn't hers. She said someone came by to check her pool pump. Someone with a pool business. That's you, right?"

Link chose his words carefully. "The lady asked me to look at her pool pump. I did, and it seemed all right."

Officer Banks said, "You know, I checked it myself before I left, and it seemed all right to me too. Brand new, in fact."

"Mind if we search your truck?" Officer Cleary asked. She had a small earnest face with a sprinkle of freckles on her nose.

"Don't you need a warrant or something?" Link asked.

"Let me handle this," Officer Banks said to his partner. She frowned and took a step back. "Look," he said to Link who suddenly noticed Officer Banks had hazel eyes and the kind of wide curvy mouth that invariably supported a cleft chin. Officer Banks broke off briefly under Link's gaze. He turned away, and Link saw his Adam's Apple bob. "Let us search your car," he said. "If we find nothing, this all goes away."

"No big thing," Officer Cleary chimed in. The men ignored her. Finally, Officer Banks reinstated eye contact. "Well?"

Link shrugged. "Okay. I don't care."

"Keys?" Officer Banks held out his hand. Link dug into his pocket and dropped the keys into the officer's palm with a flourish. Their hands briefly touched. "There you go."

Officer Banks inspected the key chain. "State? I went there, too."

Link smiled. "Lame campus."

"I'll say!" Officer Banks matched Link's smile, but it quickly faded. "Let's go," he said to Officer Cleary who scurried to his side.

Link leaned on his shovel, heart pounding, and watched the two of them search his car. They looked at the cab first, going through the glove compartment, sweeping under the seats, lifting floor mats. Then they unlatched the tailgate and climbed up into the flatbed. Officer Banks tried to lift the lid of the silver tool box. "Is this a separate key?" he asked.

In answer, Link climbed into the truck bed himself, reached into his pocket and dropped a smaller set of keys into the officer's open palm. "Try that," Link said.

Officer Banks turned and fitted the keys into the small exterior lock face on the side of the tool box. The lock clicked. Officer Banks glanced at Link briefly and tossed him the keys, which Link caught one-handed. Then he lifted the lid.

Officer Cleary crowded in to see. She stood up. "There's nothing there."

Link spread his hands, palms up. "See?"

"Maybe, "Officer Cleary began, but Banks cut her off.

"Nothing to see here," he said, rising and slamming the lid back on the toolbox. "See you around," he added as he stepped down from the bed of the truck. He extended his hand to Officer Cleary who jumped to the curb on her own. Link moved forward and latched the tailgate.

"Til we meet again," he said to Officer Banks, who started to say something, and then thought better of it. Instead, the police officer shook his head and followed Officer Cleary to the police car. She opened the driver's side, got in, and slammed the door with unusual force for such a small woman. Officer Banks opened the passenger side, got in, the car started, and streaked forward leaving tire tracks in the road. Only then did Link realize Officer Banks still had his keys.

He would have to come back. Later. Probably after he got off work.

One of the construction workers approached Link, yellow hard hat on his head, beer in hand. "Dude. I gotta take a leak."

Link gestured toward the two Port O'Potties perched in the front of the construction site. "Rusty's in one of 'em," the worker complained. "T'other is locked. You have the key?"

Link shook his head. The guy in the yellow hard hat tilted his head back and drained the rest of his beer from the can. Then he shrugged his shoulders, stepped behind the pile driving machine, unzipped his fly, and squirted a stream of urine into the flattened earth.

Link worried how a crew of a half dozen men would make it through the next few days with only one Porta Potty.

30
DARLYN

Darlyn woke up before dawn to the ringing of her cell phone, charging on the nightstand beside her bed. She pressed the button at the base, and said, "Wha."

It was Bev, and Darlyn heard Ruby clamoring in the background. "Did Truly come home last night?" Bev asked. "Because he's not answering his phone."

Darlyn glanced at her bed, but the answer couldn't be found there. Truly slept in the spare room or on the couch, usually. "Not here," she said.

"I'll watch Ruby," Bev said. "You should call the Coast Guard." She hung up.

Darlyn looked at her phone for a minute, then put it back on the charger. She walked across the hall to the guest room, but the bed was made and hadn't been slept in. She walked into the living room, half expecting to see Truly's tall frame draped over the couch in a tussle of blankets. But he wasn't there either.

"Jay!" Darlyn called. Her voice echoed in the big room. She clattered down the back stairs and wrenched open the door to the closet-size converted laundry room. The first glimmers of dawn peeked from behind the brown valance over his bed, which had not been slept in. Jay kept up his army habits, and his blue blanket was tucked into sharp corners, the pillowcase facing south.

"Wha the…" Darlyn stomped up the stairs to her bedroom, sat down on her bed, lit a cigarette and smoked for a minute, swinging her feet, which didn't quite reach the floor. She checked the boating conditions for yesterday and came up with a special marine warning. After a while, she picked up her phone and said, "Hey Siri. Connect to the Coast Guard."

Immediately, a big red button appeared on her phone screen. It said, 'Press for Emergency.' Darlyn glanced at the clock radio on her nightstand. 7 a.m. Truly and Jay had been gone twenty hours. Darlyn pressed the big red button on her screen.

After that, things happened fast. Describing the failure of her cousin and her husband to return home last night, she was transferred to Petty Officer Duke Clayborn, who sprang into action. A Coast Guard search plane and two patrol boats were readied. The police picked her up, and Darlyn found herself on the beach at Jetson Park. A woman with a weathered face and a thousand dollars' worth of sportswear on her back made her way through law enforcement officers and approached Darlyn.

"I'm Jenny Zinn. What can I do to help?" She clutched at Darlyn's hand as she gestured to a substantial crowd of earnest looking peers, hatted, with dabs of zinc oxide on their noses, standing along the sea oats. "I have dozens of private citizens just waiting to search the beach."

In spite of, or perhaps because of, the isolated life she led, the idea of organizing a search electrified Darlyn. Everyone was looking at her, waiting for her to speak. Usually, no one paid attention to her. Certainly, Truly never did.

She said, "I want every square inch of beach covered." The crowd nodded and continued to look at her expectantly. "And I want prayer walks, too. " The group broke into polite applause.

"Is the Catholic lit, okay?" Jenny asked Darlyn, who stared at her blankly. The woman nodded and bustled back.

Darlyn called after her, "Keep eyes out for anythin' they might have tossed over."

Jenny gave her a thumbs up and began speaking and pointing out parts of the beach to the volunteers. Slowly, they began to separate into twos and threes. Their voices rose in prayer. "Lord God, heavenly king…"

Darlyn smiled. A police officer approached and said, "Maam? The Coast Guard has committed to six full days of search."

Darlyn's smile brightened. "Six days?"

"I'm sure it won't take that long," the officer said, removing his cap and wiping his brow with a tissue, which stuck to the sweat on his face. "They plan to cover 20,000 miles of coast." He looked at her face. "If necessary."

"Take your time," Darlyn said, nodding. "This is a very devastatin' time, but I need everthin' possible done, not a doubt in my mind about that." She gave him such a dazzling smile, he furrowed his brow.

The rest of the afternoon passed in a daze. People plied Darlyn with water, soda, and sandwiches. They hugged her, deferred to her, stopped talking when she spoke. Jenny gave her a full pill box of Seconal for nighttime, if she had trouble sleeping. The casual transfer of narcotics between women was not uncommon, raised as they were watching ads for pharmaceutical companies in league with the medical infrastructure.

At one point, Truly's tackle bag was found, floating off the coast of St. Augustine. Officer Clayborne handed it to

Darlyn ceremoniously, and she screamed and clutched it to her chest.

"It's just a lil ray of sunshine, like a lil wink from God. They are out there still," she said.

"Well," Officer Clayborn said.

"What?" Darlyn asked.

"How did Jay and Truly get along? Any tension there?"

"My Lord, no," Darlyn said.

Officer Clayborn, scratched his crewcut, displacing his coast guard hat. "They serve together?"

"Truly, he is a Purple Heart," Darlyn said. "He never shared the ex-act story with me cause he wasn't one to give himself credit.

"Sometimes things go wrong in war," Officer Clayborn said, looking out to sea.

"Huh?" Darlyn was distracted by a pair of new volunteers. They were getting the lowdown from Jenny.

"You know anything about the threats Truly was getting on social media?" Clayborne fixed a steely gaze on her. Darlyn swallowed.

"Course not! What is that talk about?"

"Death threats," Officer Clayborne said darkly. "Had to be someone close to him, close enough to know his password. Anyone mad at him, you know of?"

Darlyn smiled. She shook her head.

Officer Clayborne trod off through the sand. Darlyn watched him. The sun beat down, causing perspiration to dampen her long hair, making it stick to her neck. Jenny got her a red ball cap from somewhere. The women walked the beach, Jenny supporting Darlyn with an arm around her waist.

Around three p.m., a local broadcast news anchor, Cade McCarthy, approached Darlyn and stuck a mike in her face for the six o'clock news broadcast. Jenny followed and stood by her side, shading her eyes from the sun. The rest of the volunteers shuffled back and milled around that one section of the beach.

Cade began the news clip, "Surrounded by volunteers, Darlyn Ravija, the wife of a local businessman and cousin of an InterTech employee, calls for prayers and positivity as they search the shoreline at Jetson Park in Fort Canaveral."

Here Cade gestured vaguely. "Farther out to sea, the U.S. Coast Guard is joined by over a dozen private boaters and other agencies, scouring a section of the Atlantic to find the two men missing after leaving Fort Canaveral, Thursday. They are saturating the area. If caught in the current, the two men could be drifting north toward Jacksonville, authorities report. If they were blown towards the intercoastal waterway, they could wind up in south Florida."

Cade stuck the mike in Darlyn's face. "How are you holding up, ma'am?"

Darlyn smiled and blushed. "I have an army that is just bathing me in prayer," she said. Jenny squeezed Darlyn's hand. "Holdin' prayer vigils, we're gonna be up all night."

"Anyone with information is urged to contact the Coast Guard Central Command Center." Cade stopped, his smile vanishing. "Cut." He saw someone on the other end of the crowd, "Officer Clayborn," and ran off spewing little clouds of sand with his Berlutti leather slip ons.

Dozens of people fanned out searching for clues that

may have washed ashore. Two of them, the blonde and the redhead that Jenny briefed, stood a little apart from the crowd, holding hands.

Darlyn shouted, "I'm callin' on all my prayer warriors. We serve a big God who holds these men in His holy hand and will guide them to us. I covet y'alls prayers for peace and comfort." She began to sing:

> *Jesus my revival*
> *I canna delay*
> *I gonna feed on ya*
> *Ya fill my fate.*

Eagerly, the volunteers, even the two young women on the perimeter, took up Darlyn's song: Jesus my revival...Darlyn sang as the sun beat down and people everywhere beamed down on her. Personally, she never felt so alive in her whole life.

31
DANIELLE

Sex with Galvin was raw, unbridled, exciting. Danielle reckoned the herbal Viagra was still assisting Galvin's libido. Afterwards, she helped him clean up his desk items, which were all on the floor. She picked up a piece of paper and looked at it.

"Transfer to Alaska?"

Galvin nodded. "Printed out and ready to go. I'd appreciate your recommendation."

Danielle nodded and bent to remove the sodden condom he'd flung in the trash near his desk. "We don't want the janitor seeing this," she said, holding it away from her gingerly. "I'll take care of it."

Galvin nodded, shuffling forms back into folders. "Do you think they'll find Jay?"

Danielle said, "I bet Gabby and Sara took the day off to help with the search. I don't know Jay very well, or I'd be down there myself."

Danielle could tell Galvin wasn't listening. She tried on a smile. "I'll be going back to my office."

"Okay." Galvin didn't look up.

Danielle said. "Talk later?"

"Sure." Galvin continued shuffling papers. Danielle let herself out and closed his office door.

Danielle reached her office, and closed the door, leaning against it from the inside. Unlike Galvin, she did not have a window. Her walls were bare. There were no family photos on the work desk that housed her computer. She had no family.

She and her brother were everything to each other. Denny had the looks of what was called Black Irish with dark hair, light skin, blue eyes, and the perfect features of a movie star.

"Muffin," he would say, whenever he greeted her. "I love the hair, the dress, you've got it going on!" He would hoist her in the air, and they would hug. There was a kind of telepathy between them; they finished each other's sentences. With Denny there was a sense of lightness when they were together, of grace as if in being twins, they reflected one another. They were going to conquer the world.

Instead, Denny died in a water ski accident at Waki Weetchee where he worked as a merman. Danielle hadn't liked him having the job. Denny was accident prone; he attracted disaster wherever he went, car accidents, sport injuries, identity theft. But he was an avid athlete, competing in the Gold River Classic, an annual race.

A cigarette boat had sped by, churning up a wake. The driver of Denny's ski boat lifted his arm, indicating he was de-accelerating and to prepare for waves. Denny hit a small wave, and his ski flipped into the air. He fell heavily to his right side and cartwheeled along the water. His helmet came off, and he died the next day of catastrophic head and neck injuries. A freak accident.

She buried him with their blue baby quilt, full of holes, the satin bunting frayed where Denny used to rub it between his fingers. Afterwards, Danielle went to a bar and had her first hard drink, club soda and vodka, mostly vodka. After a while, she was drinking straight vodka for breakfast.

Danielle touched the heart shaped locket at her throat. On the other side was thin spidery script: From your twin bro. Forever together. 10-28-89. She blinked a few times and said, "Love you, Denny." She never removed the locket.

Now, a decade later, Danielle was forty years old. She loved her profession, she loved InterTech, but she had been so busy building her career and getting sober that she had no personal life after her brief failed marriage. Galvin had given her hope, but after she saw his transfer application to Alaska, she realized he was not serious about her. Some good times. Nothing permanent.

Danielle realized that she was still holding the slimy condom she'd fished out of Galvin's trash can. Slowly she walked to her desk, and opened the Yeti cup she'd stashed there that morning. She unscrewed the lid and dropped the condom, hearing a wet plop. Then she sealed the cup. Tonight, a turkey baster would transfer the contents of the condom to her uterus as it had with the filled condom she'd stored in the freezer the night before and thawed before going to bed. She would lie on her bed with her knees raised for 30 minutes. It was a full moon and she was ovulating; of that she was sure. She wasn't a sensitive for nothing.

She felt a twinge of remorse for tricking Galvin whom she was sure was a good person. But he would never know. And she would take such good care of the child, love it, provide for it, and be a good role model. She knew nothing about her own genetic background. In fact, she was a little afraid to know. But her child's father had to be perfect. And Galvin, for sure, had good genes. She needed them.

32
SARA

Sara picked up a ceramic frog perched on the brick cladding of her house and retrieved her key from underneath its glassy green bottom. Her key turned the lock. She opened the door to her home, and she and Gabby trudged into her living room. They were sandy, and Sara was sunburned. "Let's take a shower together," Gabby said, squeezing Sara's hand. Sara squeezed back, and they were taking the stairs two steps at a time when the doorbell rang.

"Shoot," Sara said. She turned around and stomped down the stairs, turned the knob, yanked the front door open. On the doorstep stood Gran Rain. "Oh Sara," she said. "I just saw it on the news. Poor Jay." She stepped forward and enveloped Sara in a hug. Then she stepped back, brushing at her shirt. "Did you just get back from the beach?"

"Who is it?" Gabby called from the stairs.

Gran said, "Company?"

"It's my Gran!" Sara shouted up the stairs. "Come on in," she said to Gran in a normal tone. Gran followed her into the tiny foyer, into the smell of potpourri meant to disguise mildew, and the chill of air conditioning. "Sit," Sara said, gesturing at the couch. "Can I get you something?"

Usually, Gran said no or asked for water, but this time she said, "A cup of coffee if you've got it." She moved the towels the girls had flung on the couch, pushed three pairs of shoes under the coffee table. She sat down gingerly on the threadbare cushion of the couch Sara dragged in from a neighbor's curb a year ago.

"Sure," Sara said, suddenly at a loss. Because of the strange design of the house, she would be separate from Gran in a whole other room while she made coffee.

Gabby chose this moment to emerge from the stairwell. She wore nothing but a salmon-colored thong bikini with a sheer net cover up. She stepped forward with her hand extended. "I'm Gabby," she said.

"Gabby and I work together," Sara said.

"Hello, Gabby," Gran said, taking her hand and half standing. "I'm Felicia Rain. It's nice to meet you." She disengaged her hand with some difficulty and sank back down.

"Nice to meet you," Gabby said, her voice a tad too loud.

"Gabby," Sara said. "Could you do me a big favor and go in the kitchen and make us all some coffee? The beans are next to the coffeemaker. The grinder is next to the sink. There's Evian water in the fridge."

"Sure," Gabby said. She put her arm around Sara's waist and kissed her on the lips.

"Coffee coming right up," she said.

When she left the room, Gran looked at Sara with her eyebrows raised. Sara sat on the couch and stared at her knees. "What?"

Gran cleared her throat. "You're asking a guest in your house to attend to you and your grandmother? To grind the beans, brew the coffee, serve it? I raised you better than that.

Sara hid a smile. "I thought you were shocked because… of Gabby."

"Oh for God's sake, Sara." Gran lifted her hands and let

them fall in her lap. "I was at Woodstock. I was young once, too."

Sara stared at Gran, her brow furrowed. "Did you ever..."

"You're a lot like I was, you know," Gran said. "But don't put a label on yourself . You have years and years to figure that out."

"Oh," Sara said. "I think I'm really in love this time."

Gran stared straight ahead. Sara could tell she was trying hard not to roll her eyes.

"Seriously," Sara said. "Gabby and I know each other."

"What about Jay?" Gran asked. "The man you were crying over this morning?

"Oh," Sara said. Her eyes filled with tears. "I feel terrible about Jay."

Gran got up and moved over to Sara and put her arm around her. "There, there," she said. "Everything will be all right."

"You always say that," Sara said in a muffled voice. Her face was buried in Gran's neck who smelled like peaches. Gran took her granddaughter's face in her hands and kissed her wet cheeks. "I know things haven't been easy for you. And I'm proud of you. Very proud. But why do you keep forming these strong attachments so quickly?"

"I don't know," Sara mumbled.

Gran got up and resettled in her original spot on the couch. "Galvin, Jay, and now Gabby." She ticked them off on her hands. "Before that, there were three others. And before that three others." Gran leaned forward. "Why do you need to be in love all the time?"

Sara shrugged. "Abandonment issues?"

"That's too easy," Gran said. "Mimi does the best she

can."

"Oh Gran," Sara said. "You always defend her." The last time she saw her mother, Mimi was living in a halfway house that belonged to a minister. She had a small pallet in the corner of a living room, populated with people trying to get off drugs or who needed an address for probation. Or both.

"She hasn't had your opportunities," Gran said. "A single mother, poor… "

"I know the story," Sara said, loudly. "And I hope you're not still giving her money."

"No, of course not," Gran said a little too quickly. They were both silent for a moment. Sara wiped her cheeks with the back of her hand.

"Look," Gran said. "Mimi self-medicates with drugs. You do it with people. All I'm saying is that at some point you have to face your fears. Otherwise, you never stop." They heard Gabby drop a cup in the kitchen and then heard her say "Shit," loudly.

"What are you afraid of Sara?" Gran asked.

Sara squeezed her eyes shut so she wouldn't cry again. "You know she used to leave me."

She didn't remember much about her childhood before Gran, but she would never forget the fear when Mimi dropped her off at a stranger's house. She stayed there for weeks at a time, sometimes wearing nothing but a diaper and one of her mother's old t-shirts. One day, this older woman with long blonde hair came to see her, picked her up, and held her close. When the woman tried to put her down, Sara screamed and held on to her neck as tight as she could. She remembered that. She remembered the scent of peaches and the woman's small pearl earrings. Similar to the ones she wore today.

"I'm afraid of being alone," Sara said. She thought of Jay lost and shipwrecked. She drew a deep shuddering breath.

Gran swallowed. "Well," she said.

"What should I do, Gran?" Sara leaned forward and grabbed a tissue out of the box of Kleenex on her coffee table. She blew her nose loudly.

"You won't like it," Gran said.

"What, already?" Sara asked. She aimed the tissue at a waste basket in the corner. She missed.

"Pay attention, Sara."

Sara grimaced and turned her gaze to her grandmother.

"I lived alone after Gramp died," Gran said. "I was afraid, too. But I had my own interests, my own home, and a career. If I hadn't spent time with myself, and learned what I could do for myself, I would not be able to give such good advice to you." She laughed.

Sara sniffed. "I'm afraid I'm like Mimi. Do I have an addictive personality?"

Gran smiled.

"Huh," Sara said. "I'm too unorganized to be an addict." She was silent for a moment.

Gran said. "Can you tell me, honestly, who you are really in love with. Galvin, Jay, or Gabby?"

"Oh, Gran," Sara said. "You know I don't know."

"Well, there you go," Gran said.

Gabby took this moment to arrive with coffee cups, spoons, milk, sugar, and a silver urn on a tray.

"Where did you find all that?" Sara asked.

"You have to know where to look," Gabby said archly.

She put the tray down, distributed the cups and began pouring.

"I drink it black," Gran said and picked up her cup and tasted it. "This is good." Gabby smiled at her, and Gran smiled back.

Sara sipped her own cup after adding plenty of milk and sugar. "I can make coffee, too."

"Not like this," Gran said. "Gabby, you're an honorary Rain. You may call me Gran."

"All right!" Gabby said. "Gran!"

"Ha," Sara said. She smiled, and some of her worry about Jay abated a bit. How bad could things be when her grandmother was around?

"By the way," Gran said, sipping from her cup. "I brought you something."

Sara and Gabby looked up. Gran set down her cup, walked to the front door and opened it. On the front stoop was a plastic beige box with a grate. Gran lifted the rod out of the hold that fastened the grate shut. There was a feline yelp and a gray and white creature streaked into the house, dislodging the Welcome mat.

Sara stood. "What the heck was that?"

As if on cue, a cat peered from behind the floor to ceiling drapes, which hung from the picture window.

"Meet Tiger," Gran said. "She's part Siamese, so she's a talker."

"Yow," Tiger said.

"She looks feral," Sara said.

"I'm allergic," Gabby said.

Gran sat back down, picked up her cup and took another sip. "I have a cat box, litter, some food out in the car. You can keep the kitty case. She was a stray hanging around my house. I had to trap her." She smiled at Gabby and Sara who were staring at her and then staring at Tiger. The cat began to crawl up the drapes. Sara could hear the fabric ripping.

"Benadryl should help," Gran said.

"For Gabby or the cat?" Sara said.

Gran sipped her coffee.

33
BEV

After Officer Cleary's discovery of Darlyn's marijuana roach, she issued a written warning, and Bev, with Darlyn's permission, got to take Ruby home with her. The police fussed about a blind woman watching a toddler, but it was too late to call child services. They said they'd be back in the morning. Bev was certain, with her impressive educational credentials, she could convince them to let Ruby stay with her temporarily. It was tricky minding a toddler without sight. But Ruby wasn't big enough to open doors or to climb out of her crib. So, Officers Banks and Cleary drove Bev and Ruby the block and a half to her house.

Bev could tell Ruby was sucking her thumb by the slurping sounds she made. She settled the child in her high chair and pulled fish sticks, apple sauce, and frozen carrots from the freezer. She wasn't one of those childless women who thought she had to do everything perfectly or the kid would implode. Kids ate disgusting food, like fish sticks, but they had to eat something and with a sippy cup full of milk it could be worse.

She piled the defrosted food on a plate and sat with Ruby. The little girl hummed to herself as she ate, and Bev managed to get a few spoonfuls of apple sauce into her mouth. The child drained her cup of milk. Then Bev picked her up and carried her upstairs.

She didn't want to risk a bath without someone else there, so she just sponged the child off with a washcloth. She found a new toothbrush from her dentist in a plastic bag under the sink. She gently brushed Ruby's teeth and got her to rinse with a paper cup. Then she buttoned her into a clean diaper and onesie pajamas and bundled her into her travel crib with a clean blankie.

Hanging over the crib, using gestures, she sang, "The Wheels on the Bus," and she had to trust Ruby followed along judging by her chortling sounds. Then she kissed the child good night. As usual, Ruby whimpered and clung to her neck when Bev tried to leave. So, she stayed, pulling up a chair from her office and holding Ruby's hand through the bars of the crib. Eventually, the child's whimpering trailed off to even breathing, and Bev extricated her hand.

The clock in her head said 9:00. She called Darlyn. "Have you heard from Truly?"

"Nope," Darlyn said.

Bev waited to see if Darlyn would ask about Ruby. She didn't. Finally, Bev asked,

"Should we call the Coast Guard?"

"They're all right," Darlyn said. She yawned.

Bev hung up and fell into her own bed wearing her clothes, without washing her face or brushing her teeth. As tired as she was, it took a while for her heart to slow down, and her breathing to become deeper. Exhausted, she dreamed of Spice. He was lost, and she couldn't find him. Bev still dreamt in pictures, but she only knew her dog from scent, feel, and sound. She kept getting close to him, reaching out her arms and finding only air.

She woke suddenly, abruptly. Her face felt warm from the sunlight; she forgot to draw the curtains last night. The sounds of Spice crying in her dream were the sounds of Ruby stirring in her crib. Quickly, Bev sat up and reached for her cell phone on her night table. She called Truly, then Darlyn, who took a while to answer.

"Did Truly come home last night? Bev asked. "Because he's not answering his phone."

There was a pause. "I do not see him," Darlyn said.

"I'll watch Ruby," Bev said. "You should call the Coast Guard." She hung up. She lay there for a minute thinking of Truly because the thought of him calmed her and gave her purpose. She fell back asleep; her phone clutched in her hand.

Gradually, she became aware of the doorbell ringing. She sat up and just like that she was suddenly wide awake. She clattered downstairs and flung the door open.

"Finally," said a male voice. That would be Officer Banks, she thought. She felt a little breeze as he passed her and stood in her foyer. "Are you here too, Officer Cleary?" Bev asked.

"Yes, ma'am." Bev felt another little breeze as the woman joined her partner on the threshold. Bev sensed a third person join them, and she held out her hand. "I haven't had the pleasure?" She could imagine how she looked, in her rumpled clothes, her hair wild.

"Dr. Kase? I'm Ms. Pederson," said a brisk voice. "I understand we're colleagues more or less. I'm a local social worker with child services."

Bev relaxed a little. "Of course."

"I'd like to see the child now if you don't mind. Ruby Ravija, is it?"

"Follow me," Bev said. She heard someone follow her up the stairs. "I'd like to keep her until her father gets home," Bev said over her shoulder.

"That would be hard to do," the social worker said. They stood together at the top of the stairs.

"Why is that?" Bev asked.

"Well," Ms. Pederson said. "No one seems to know where her father is." Her voice was young, reedy, and a little shaky.

"What?" Bev tried to make sure she was facing her.

"He never came back from a boat trip. The Coast Guard is searching ninety miles of coast line."

"That's horrible," Bev said.

"Yes. This is where she sleeps?"

"Yes," Bev said, pushing ahead of her. She walked over to the crib and reached down.

"Ruby?"

"Crib's empty," Ms. Pederson said.

Bev thought she could literally feel her heart lurch into her throat. She tried not to look or sound wild as she turned around. "Is she in the room?"

"No," said Ms. Pederson.

Bev, who couldn't see, hadn't known Ruby was big enough to climb out of her crib. And if she was big enough to do that...the doors...

"The back door," Bev gasped. She pushed past the social worker and half ran, half fell down the stairs. Careening wildly around the rail, she felt arms catch her shoulders. One of the cops. She shrugged him off. "Please!"

"Where's the fire?" Officer Banks asked. Violently, she wrenched herself free and made for the back door. Flinging back the curtains, she froze for a second as she felt for the slider.

It was open.

With an anguished cry, she slid the glass door all the way and burst onto the deck. "Ruby!" she called. "Ruby, Ruby, Ruby!" Holding her hands out in front of her, she found the steps to the pool and waded into the deep end. She thrashed wildly. "Ruby, Ruby, Ruby!"

Chlorine water got into her mouth, and she choked and gagged. She dived underwater into the deep end, checking the bottom of the pool with wide swept arms. Panic consumed her, a black void of reason, and she almost lost consciousness, swallowing water. Someone was pulling her up. She fought the arms that grabbed her from behind and pinned her own arms to her waist.

"Dr. Kase, please!" She went limp as Officer Banks dragged her to the steps and up onto the deck. She rolled on her side and vomited water. She wished with all her heart to die.

"Bef?"

Bev sat up and reached out her arms. Ruby screamed. Bev got to her feet and followed the sound of the hysterical child being borne off into the distance.

"Where is she?" Bev asked.

Officer Banks put a hand on Bev's arm. "Calm down. She was wandering around the yard. She's fine. Ms. Pederson is taking her into child services."

"Why?" Bev sloshed towards the house; she was soaking wet, her usual self-assured stride vanished.

Officer Banks sighed. "Her mother is at the beach searching for dad. Let's face it, you can't take care of a toddler. Not without help."

Bev nodded, tears streaming down her face. He was

right. Ruby's screams rang in her ears. "Will I be able to see her?"

The policeman's tone was gentle. "No, ma'am. Not unless you're related."

Bev clawed her way back into the house and sat in the swivel chair by her desk, water dripping onto the floor. She bowed her head.

Officer Banks put his hand on her shoulder for a second. Then Bev heard him at the door murmuring to Officer Cleary. They let themselves out and a minute later, Bev heard the cars back out of the driveway. She leapt to her feet and sprinted towards the door, flung it open, and stood there. Never in her life had she wanted to see as much as she did at that moment. To see Ruby's face. To smile in reassurance. She waved, hoping it helped.

"Oh, Truly", she thought. "I'm sorry. So, so, so, so sorry." Nothing was turning out as they'd planned.

34
DARLYN- SIX WEEKS LATER

Jenny Zinn was an unbelievable prayer warrior, and she was probably the first friend Darlyn ever had. They spent hours together each day, praying, and offering testimony to the Lord. Jenny wore Lilly Pulitzer, a different outfit every day, and she showed up one day with a paper bag of discards that she presented to Darlyn. After that, the women coordinated their outfits by text and wore their hot pink shorts in a paisley design with their neon yellow tops. Or vice versa. After all, they were photographed every day.

It was Jenny who told Darlyn to stop smiling during interviews, and to dab her eyes with a Kleenex on occasion even if her eyes were dry. The older woman was also generous about dishing out Seconal to Darlyn during the long hot month after Truly and Jay disappeared in the *Early Byrd.* Neither the men nor the boat was recovered, only Truly's blue tackle bag, which held the box of Arthur Ravija's ashes. They were returned to Darlyn, who, when she returned home that night, unceremoniously dumped them down the toilet and threw the box in the trash.

So, after a long day of parading up and down the beach with Jenny and her entourage for the TV cameras, after meetings with the local police who were still interested in the death threats on Truly's Facebook page, after giving her daily Jenny inspired quote to the newspapers, *We are burdened with glorious purpose*, she really was hyped beyond measure.

Then the Coast Guard decided to call off the search. "It's an extremely tough decision with this level of community involvement, and when you have a constituent out there that you just can't find," said Officer Clayborn into Cade Mc Carthy's mike for the 6:00 news. Within two hours, the overhead helicopters and the motor lifeboats were gone.

Private craft still trolled up and down the coast line, and Darlyn and her army of prayer warriors continued to march up and down the beach. Jenny told her to start thinking about a funeral service, and Darlyn imagined how she would look in mourning. It was too bad she couldn't wear white, though. Darlyn's hair had lightened a shade from the sun, and she was tanned to a butternut brown.

With all the unaccustomed activity, and all the things she had to do, Darlyn had trouble settling down at night. That's where Jenny's Seconal came in. At first, just one or two of the red pills would send Darlyn into a dreamless slumber. Three or four worked even better. Jenny had just given her a bottle with 100 of the red "dolls." She couldn't imagine going to sleep without them at this point. Sometimes she took five or six to get the same effect she used to get from one or two.

Sometimes she went to sleep in her own bed and woke up in the spare bedroom or Ruby's nursery. How did she get there?

Everything seemed so unreal. Her own daughter was in Child Services, in a foster home, and her own neighbor Bev Kase, was suing her for guardianship. What with driving to Jetson Park every day, organizing the prayer walks, speaking to the press, she just had not had time to hire a lawyer and address

Bev's allegations.

For Darlyn, everything had changed. Since Truly was gone, she had no need to flee with all their money. And she would get Ruby back when this was over. She had the name and number of an attorney from New Orleans that Jenny's family used for generations. Link was holding onto their bale of Gold, somewhat impatiently, which was another issue she would deal with when she was officially a widow.

Now she knelt beside her bed, clasped her hands, and lifted her eyes to the ceiling. "Oh Lord," she intoned, "if it is Your will, after his many sins on earth, may Your humble servant Truly, my husband, only suffer third degree burns in his afterlife of holy hellfire." She paused to light a cigarette and placed an ashtray between her elbows on the bedspread. She took a deep drag, let out a thin stream of smoke, and continued her conversation with God.

"An' Lord? Please don't blame my boy, my Jaybird, for goin' off with Truly and leavin' me to my own devices. Please except him into your heavenly kingdom." Darlyn felt she embodied the right forgiving tone in this leg of her prayer. She moved on.

"An' Lord? Please bless that bitch Bev with a long life, so she can suffer without my husband, which she stole." Darlyn took another deep drag at this point. "Lord, please take the devil outta Ruby, so she is a normal child and not some scared coughin' zombie."

Here Darlyn crushed out the butt of her cigarette and placed the ashtray under the bed. She heaved herself to her feet, staggering a little. She popped a few more Seconal, just to make sure she could sleep. Her chest felt tight all of a sudden, as though there were a weight on it. With some difficulty, she turned off her lamp and got into bed huddling between the sheets.

As her eyes adjusted to the dark, she saw a shadow emerge from the floor to ceiling curtains and walk towards her bed. Darlyn felt as though she were in a dream, the kind of dream where you want to scream and can't make a sound. She prayed with all her heart the shadow wasn't Truly, here to rebuke her for her fake sorrow, her private glee he had gotten what he deserved.

But the shade began to glow as it got closer, and Darlyn saw to her relief that it wasn't Truly at all, but her Angel. She reached out her hand and Angel took it, moving closer to stroke her cheek. Darlyn closed her eyes. The Angel's glow seemed to shine behind her closed eyelids, shine with increasing veracity and warmth. "It is the Lord's holy aura," Darlyn thought. "Its sacred cleansing fire."

The Angel continued to stroke her cheek. Darlyn slept. At five in the morning, she arose, her eyes glassy and somnambulistic. Instead of wandering around the house, as she was prone to do during her Seconal sleep walking, this time she went into the bathroom. Her hairdryer was lying next to the sink, still plugged in.

Perhaps she had been dreaming about Truly, about his watery bed at the bottom of the ocean. She switched the hair dryer on and aimed it at her long brunette tresses, lifting the hair with her fingers to spread it out as though it were really wet. Then she dropped her arm, still gripping the hair dryer.

Darlyn broke out in a cold sweat. She gripped the edge of the sink with her free hand. Then she took a deep breath and struggled to take another one. It didn't come. She toppled over as though she'd been struck by lightning. She landed on her side with her eyes wide open, her lips parted. The hairdryer landed, still running, with the dryer nozzle pointed right at her head.

Heat transfer by thermal convection is found in a hair dryer. The source is a coil, which heats the surrounding air. In order for warm air to reach the hair, a fan creates an airflow instantly heating the moisture in both hair and scalp. There is water inside hair follicles, even in dry hair, which can turn to steam. And a hair dryer pointed at a scalp for hours can create superheated steam with so much energy stored that it can start a fire.

As Darlyn lay motionless on the carpeted floor just outside her master bathroom, the hair dryer droned on relentlessly, it's arid stream of air drying all latent moisture in her scalp, until, after a while, the hair follicles just curled up, singed, crinkled, became as dry as kindling.

Then, spontaneously, her scalp burst into flames.

Within the house the fire spread with ease, turning the once pretty floor and stairs into a maze of flame. The shrill scream of the smoke detector was cut off when it melted.

35
LINK

Link didn't like to bother Darlyn, but the Gold situation was becoming untenable.

As the construction foreman, Link carried the key to the Porta Potty with the bale of Gold locked inside. So, the men doubled up on the one remaining outhouse. They drank a lot of beer. They were just putting the finishing touches on the newly constructed house. The sod had gone in over the weekend. But the whole lot smelled like a sewer.

"Why, it appears no other thing to me than a foul and pestilent congregation of vapors," Link kept muttering.

"What?" the man working beside him would ask. "Did you say something?"

Link would shake his head. More and more his dream of going to a Hawaiian university and teaching on one of the islands, seemed to separate from his plot with Darlyn. He wanted out.

Link tried to be patient about the Gold. He felt badly for Darlyn. Losing a husband and a son in one day had to suck. Darlyn told him some bitch on the same block was having an affair with her husband and suing for custody of the little girl. So that was a lot to handle.

But the construction job was just about finished. Any day, the company would come by to pick up their portable sewage systems. The Gold had to move. Today. Not "tomorrow and tomorrow and tomorrow." Today.

Link wished he had never gotten involved. The whole scheme was too complicated. He found out, too late, he was embarrassed to deal drugs. He wanted to move the Gold back to Darlyn's house and be done with it.

A lot of that came from a family council meeting he'd attended the night before. Link wondered what he had done to invoke this mandatory parental summons. What transpired was even stranger than he imagined.

"I'm home," he'd squeaked, using his key to get in the door. Usually, his parents were in different parts of the house, and it took a while to round them up. But this time, they both came running at the sound of his voice. "It's Link," he heard his mother say.

He walked in the direction of her voice and bumped into his father in the kitchen. His father pumped his hand, and said, "We're proud of you son." His dad reached up to put one hand on Link's massive shoulder and held the graduation invitation the state college had mailed in the other. "You worked hard and kept up with your studies."

"Oh," Link said, "it's no big deal." He certainly didn't have the academic credentials of his parents.

Link's mother approached from the other side of the kitchen and nodded at her son who stood awkwardly near the dishwasher. She and Link approached each other and just as quickly stepped back. His mother cleared her throat. "Perhaps we don't say it enough," she said. "But we love...the way you rose to this challenge."

"I have to admit," his dad said, "when we cut you off, I thought you'd work a bunch of minimum wage jobs and give up on college."

"But," his mom said, "you didn't give up. You worked, supported yourself, and went to school."

"Just like we did," his Dad said.

"We had to give you the incentive," his mom said.

Link shifted uncomfortably. They didn't know what he promised to do for Darlyn. He lost the thread of the conversation and tuned back in to hear his dad say, "We just need to talk more. What's this thing I keep hearing about, Zoom?"

Link said. "It's a computer program for online face to face meetings."

"Well, why don't you show it to me?" Link's dad headed towards his office.

Link shrugged. "What for? We live a few miles away."

"Yes, well," his dad said. "About that."

It was his mother who broke the news; his mother with her hair pulled back so tight it looked like it hurt; his mother whose voice was as harsh as a metal file on steel; his mother who missed all his small triumphs as an adolescent, his winning football games, his awards, because she was always, always working. His mother whom he could never please.

"We'll give you the tuition for the University of Hawaii," she said. "That's where you want to go, isn't it? And we'll pay your rent for a year."

Mother and son stared at each other. Slowly, Link reached out a hand. His mother took it in both of hers and solemnly shook it.

"I'm gay," Link said. "I thought I may as well get that out of the way."

His mother actually smiled. "You think I'm stupid, don't

you?"

It was late when he got home. He'd sat on the edge of his bed, thinking. All he needed to wreck this new alliance with his parents was to get busted for a bale of Gold.

It was still dark the next day when Link pulled up to the curb in front of the three-story house he'd spent two months constructing. He leaned forward and unlocked the passenger door. A minute later it opened, someone got in, and the door closed.

"Hello Officer," Link said, and passed a Styrofoam cup to his visitor.

"Thanks," Officer Banks said, and sipped the hot liquid.

Link and Matt Banks were in the habit of meeting for coffee every morning around five a.m., the end of Matt's shift and the beginning of Link's.

"Are you okay, man?" Officer Banks asked. "You look kind of down."

"In sooth, I know not why I am so sad," Link said. "Especially since my parents offered to finance my last two years of college. Out of state."

"Wow," Officer Banks said. He held his cup aloft and touched it with Link's.

"I know," Link said. "And guess what? "His voice veered into a higher range. "They already knew I was gay. How did they know? Do you think it was my earring?" Link tugged at his right earlobe where a gold stud festered.

"I guess we'll never know," Officer Banks said.

A minute passed. "Matt?" Link said.

"Yeah?"

"Will you come visit me in Hawaii?"

"Would you like me to?"

"Would I have asked?

Officer Banks smiled, but it didn't reach his eyes. "Sure, but that don't mean it'll happen."

Link drew a deep breath. "Have you ever met someone? And felt like you'd met them before? It's what they call karma."

"No, no," Officer Banks said. "That's déjà vu."

"Well, whatever it is," Link said. "It's a meeting that brings results, good or bad."

"So?" Officer Banks sipped his coffee and avoided Link's eyes. "I don't act on that stuff."

"But, we have karma, right? Link asked.

Link saw Officer Banks open his mouth to answer, but his attention was diverted by something beyond the curb. "Holy shit." Officer Banks dropped his coffee, which spilled all over Link's console. He fumbled with the passenger door. The inside of the car was suddenly bright as day.

Officer Banks fumbled with the door handle, gave up, and dove out of the open car window. Flames were licking their way across the fresh green grass. There was an explosion next door at Darlyn's house, a window blew out, and flames shot out in a hail of hot glass and debris.

"Are you okay?" Link shouted out the window. Officer Banks waved him away and said, "Go! Go!"

Link jammed the key in the ignition, took off around the block, where he parked willy nilly at the curb of an embankment. He was a big man wearing work boots, but he ran towards the fire, ran as hard as he could.

He found Officer Banks across the street from the spreading flames, speaking into his phone. "Yes sir. Overlin and

County Road. Lake Ann. Hurry." He ended the call, and Link stared at him and then at the pre-dawn inferno lighting up the sky in a hellish landscape. Darlyn's house was in flames and the fire was burning the grass on the newly constructed house on the corner lot. Neighbors were starting to open their doors, to step out into the driveway.

"I called the fire department," Officer Banks shouted at the exact moment Link, following the line of flames, saw the Porta Potties explode.

Link got a 'B' in high-school chemistry, and he knew that polyurethane, a light-weight plastic petroleum-based compound, was the main component of a Porta Potty. The chemical toilet contains a blue dye mixing formaldehyde and bleach. All of these materials are highly flammable. A pump and holding tank form the portable sewage system. These items are fastened with an assortment of screws, nails, rivets, bolts, and hinges.

Link watched as the blue outhouses made a burping sound. Then, like a volcano, they erupted, spewing hot pieces of metal far and wide. The actual containers quickly melted down to puddles of blue goop. Formaldehyde irritates the eyes, ears, skin, nose, and throat, in addition to vapor inhalation. Link, Officer Banks and the neighbors, now lining the street, began to cough, liquid running out of their eyes like faucets. There was another smell too, a smell almost like incense, only grittier. Link recognized it immediately as 8,000 ounces of Gold going up in smoke. That, and two months worth of excrement.

The toxic fumes permeating the neighborhood included a great billowing cloud of the finest marihuana this side of South America. Greasy black smoke billowed and eddied around the small crowd huddled across the street. It formed curls in the breeze, illuminated by the street lights. Everyone breathed it in.

Officer Banks had never been high in his life and his knees buckled. Link caught him, under his armpits. The policeman opened his eyes, righted himself, swaying. Link feeling dizzy, released him, brushed off his shoulders, which were covered with ash. He heard the fire truck in the distance, sirens wailing around the bypass.

A gray haired man in a bathrobe was standing beside them. "Watch him," he said to the neighbor gesturing to the stoned law enforcement officer. Officer Banks said, "Hey," stumbled and sagged against the slight older man. Link ran across the street and gestured to the fire fighters as they pulled up.

"Someone lives there," he screamed, pointing to Darlyn's house. The firemen looked at each other with the expressions men make of a desperate cause. They shook their heads.

"The best we can do is stop the spread," the chief shouted to Link. "Do you have a gas mask?"

The air smelled of burning, an acrid, chemical infused burning. Choking, Link could barely speak. His eyes moved from face to face in the gathering crowd. Most of the neighbors were out now. Like a Greek chorus in their nightclothes, they stood in the grass, their bare feet wet with dew. A few of them, down the block, climbed on top of their cars.

The uniformed men dug into their supplies. Link shrieked, "Throw me one," and one of the firefighters obliged, sending it over the side of the truck. Link caught it one handed and put it on adjusting the straps on the black rubber front piece, which covered his face and extended into a rubber respirator. An ambulance pulled up, lights flashing. Then another police car arrived and set up a barrier, pushing back the neighbors who crept closer and closer like moths to a flame. Link saw Officer Banks sink to his knees, get up and lurch to the driver's side of the patrol car, speaking to the officer.

Later, Link had no explanation for what happened next, except that he, like everyone else at the scene, including the fire-fighters, was high as a kite. Link thought of Darlyn inside the house. He shuddered.

He could just go see. The fire started on the ground floor. Maybe Darlyn was upstairs. He started towards the house, walking, then running. Thick black smoke engulfed him as he closed in. The firefighters shouted. The neighbors stood on their car hoods to get a better look.

Link ran into the house. The floor beams were on fire, the stairs, and the drapes. The white carpet was a black smoldering lava pit. The heat was intense. Link screamed," DARLYN" into the mouthpiece of his mask. But all he could hear was the fire as it ate through different substances, like the couch, the chairs, fabric and wood, all expanding and contracting, releasing gasses, making popping and crackling noises to the pitch of lightning.

"DARLYN." From the corner of his eye Link could see Darlyn's iron stove, glowing red hot in the kitchen as the picnic table and the benches burned. The hearth roared. He turned and saw the entrance sealed off by a ring of flame. He edged closer to the far wall. The bookcase was still standing. Link grabbed a book at random and clutched it to his chest. He thought, "O, who can hold a fire in his hand." He backed into a corner. Then the roof fell in.

36
GALVIN

Galvin was shopping at ERE, Entertainment Recreational Equipment. He was looking for waterproof boots, but he was sidetracked by the tents, the backpacks, and the ice cutters. He was reading books and watching YouTube videos about Alaska; The Last Frontier. Jackie Moates said Nick Montana approved his transfer to Anchorage. Nick promoted Danielle to take over Galvin's job at the Lake Ann office for a bigger title and a higher salary.

He and Danielle saw each other weekly. She cooked him dinner at her house, and then they spent the weekend in bed. She seemed perfectly okay with his imminent departure from the Lake Ann office. It was a companionable relationship, one he easily slipped into, and one he could easily slip out of.

Moving to the northernmost part of the country was no easy task. There was so much to do. Instead of hearing a persistent tune in his head, he now heard buzzing. In fact, he likened the sensation to a feeling of bees in his head, because he couldn't pay close attention to any one thing.

He was going to sell his condo in Lake Ann and buy a concrete block house near the Anchorage Town Square. It was walking distance to the shops, bars, and museums, in the summer anyway. He suspected everyone stocked up in the summer and stayed indoors in the winter. The first year, he would work from home. He planned to read Proust in front of the fireplace during the long dark evenings.

He was going to sell his car, the five-year-old beige Buick with 20,000 miles on it. He sold the MGB on Facebook marketing for a song to a Lake Ann guy who loved cars. He thought about buying a snowmobile. Galvin whistled and tried on some insulated mittens. He glimpsed his watch. He swore at the time. He was supposed to meet Sara at three for coffee in the mall food court. He had five minutes.

Well, there was no help for it, he'd have to come back for his purchases later. The glass doors opened automatically, and Galvin hummed a show tune as he walked into the asphalt parking lot. Heat waves shimmered above the black tar, packed with back-to-school shoppers. His heart sped up as he crossed to the walk lane and headed for the Lake Ann Town Center. He hated being late.

The mall was built in the sixties, in a boxy modernist style, all one level, looking like a long, insulated train station with shops instead of stops. He pushed through the turnstile entrance and emerged in the food court, a horseshoe shaped enclave of fast food counters overseeing an oval pavilion crammed with square aluminum table tops and molded stainless steel chairs. Above was a sunroof with a few birds perched in the rafters.

Galvin's gaze followed a toddler, scampering madly away from the outstretched arms of his grinning father. The man scooped the child up and slung him over his shoulder as the child shrieked with laughter. When the man passed, Galvin saw Sara sitting against a cushioned booth backed against a towering plant atrium. It provided a modicum of privacy. For the first time, Galvin's pleasant anticipation of seeing Sara turned to unease.

He waved. She waved back. She stood as he approached her, and they exchanged a quick hug even though her cubicle was in his direct line of vision from his office, and he saw her every day. "You look good," Sara said. "Happy."

"You do, too," Galvin said sitting down opposite her. It was a lie. Sara had lost weight, there were dark circles under her eyes and a few blemishes on her forehead. Her nails were un-manicured and bitten down to the quick. There was a long red scratch on her arm. Galvin gestured toward it. "How did that happen?"

"Oh," Sara laughed a little. "I have a new cat. She's hav-ing a little trouble adjusting."

Galvin smiled politely. He was a dog person, although Meryl had custody of their pooch, Walter, an overgrown stan-dard poodle, whose most violent outburst entailed sustained licking. "Should we get our coffee?"

"I already ordered it," Sara said. "You like a tall latte, extra expresso, right?"

As if on cue, an employee from Volcano Mocha set pa-per cups of latte in front of them. Galvin started to pull out his wallet, but Sara waved it away. "On me."

Knowing from past experience how Sara felt about pay-ing her own way, Galvin put his wallet back. "Well, this is nice." What would have been nicer was his lunchtime peanut butter and jelly sandwich. But it was still nice.

Sara nodded. "I know we haven't talked much since Jay…" her voice trailed off and for a minute Galvin thought her easy tears were sure to follow. But she swallowed and continued. "I wanted to say goodbye."

"That's nice, Sara," Galvin said, leaning forward. "I'm sorry about Jay."

She nodded absently and blew on her coffee. "They called the search off the other day."

Galvin took the lid off his cup and inspected his latte. He hated drinking through a plastic hole, and he wanted to check that the latte had a frothy crown of milk. He took a sip.

"Actually," Sara said, "I asked you here for another reason. Besides just saying goodbye." She dug into her Coach purse and came up with an envelope. She handed it to Galvin. "I got this in the office mail."

Galvin knew what the cream-colored envelope was about without even opening it. But he did anyway, and withdrew the single piece of cotton cardstock engraved with gold script.

> *Ms. Meryl Smith Steele and Mr. James Roy Beckel*
> *request the pleasure of your company*
> *at their marriage ceremony*
> *on November 3rd, 2019*
> *at Lew Gardens Chapel in Winter City*

"Are you going?" Sara asked.

"I don't know," Galvin said. He took another sip of coffee. It was too hot.

"I wonder why she invited me," Sara said. "Are you taking anyone?"

It dawned on Galvin that Sara had invited him for coffee not to say goodbye, but to finagle an escort to Meryl's wedding. He wondered why.

"I'm not sure I'm going," Galvin said, although he was, in fact, sure he wasn't. He remembered Sara's fury when he took his ex-wife to a friend's wedding. What would Danielle say if he took Sara to Meryl's wedding instead of her? Probably nothing, but he had learned his lesson. "I'm leaving the next day. It would be too much."

"Oh," Sara said. She picked the invitation up and dropped it back into her purse.

"Why don't you take Gabby?" Galvin asked. The two had been inseparable since Jay disappeared.

Sara gave him a half smile. "She broke up with me."

"I'm sorry," Galvin said. "You've had some bad luck lately."

"Yes," Sara said. "It's awkward that Gabby and I still work together."

"We still work together," Galvin said. "Or at least we will for another month."

"That's different," Sara said. "You're different." She looked off. They were silent for a minute.

"Look," Galvin said. "I'm moving to Anchorage to put some distance between me and my past. That includes Meryl and her new life, although, God knows, I wish her well."

Sara bit at a loose fingernail, and then put her hands in her lap. "I bet that includes me as well."

"Well," said Galvin. "It sort of does."

Sara nodded and looked down. "It makes me sad to think we'll never see each other again."

"Yes," Galvin said. "Me, too." His heart sped up, and he almost reached out and touched her hand. He was so close. It would change everything, he knew.

Sara looked at him from under her eyelashes and

seemed to come to some sort of decision. "Thanks for meeting me." She gave him a tiny smile. Then she gathered up her phone, her purse, her coffee cup. "Goodbye, Galvin." She stood and held out her arms. "Do I get a hug?"

He stood up, stepped forward, and took her in his arms. She was several inches shorter than he was, and she felt small and fragile. He kissed the top of her head and stepped back. "I'll still see you at work," he said.

"I'm taking a leave of absence," Sara said. "By the time I come back, you'll be gone."

"What for?" Galvin asked.

"Oh," Sara said. "I'm taking my vacation to move. To a nicer neighborhood. You know."

Galvin knew Sara had been promoted to Lead Trainer. Danielle must have given her a nice raise. "That's great," he said.

Sara hesitated. "You have my email."

"And your text number," Galvin said.

"Goodbye, then." She gave him a little wave.

Galvin waved back. And then she was gone. He watched her walk away. The food court buzzed with private conversations, kids yelling, the clang of serving dishes, and muted soft jazz over the speakers. Why was he still sitting here? Was he hoping she'd come back? Galvin chugged his coffee. It was lukewarm now and had an unpleasant aftertaste. He stood up, almost overturning his chair.

He should have felt closure; he should have felt relief. He strode out of the food court quickly, his eyes shiny, wishing for five more seconds with Sara, which was all it would have taken to set things right. He took a deep breath, put his hand on his chest, and quickly dropped it, as though the bees in his head had found a new location.

37
BEV

The bus was stuffy and hot. Few of the cracked seats were taken, and passengers dozed or stared straight ahead. There wasn't much to see. Landscapes of brittle brown fields streamed past windows that wouldn't open. The driver listened to a ball game on the radio where large crowds of people cheered intermittently. Bev held Ruby in her lap and patted her little palms together. *Clap your handies, one, two, three, clap your handies just for me.*

The little girl chortled with laughter. Ruby's face was still new to Bev. Her eyesight was weak, and she had to wear dark glasses. But she could see the child's round gray eyes, the fluff of black hair that stood up on her head. Looking at Ruby made her heart flutter.

After Dr. Dojo operated on her eyes, she spent a week in anxious anticipation. And when he ceremoniously removed the bandages during an office visit, Bev found it somewhat anticlimactic. True, she could make out some forms, but everything was blurry and too bright. Dr. Dojo told her that her sight would most likely continue to improve. Or it could weaken. Since the procedure was so new, there was no way of knowing.

The first thing Bev did was look up Truly's Facebook page. Even though he was paired with Darlyn, he looked familiar, as though the year of close physical contact imprinted an image she had come to expect. Unlike her own visage. Bev spent literal hours in front of a mirror staring at her own reflection.

The last time she had sight, she was a young girl. Now, she was a middle-aged woman. She studied herself from the front, sides, and back. What she saw had no relation to the self she had carried in her mind's eye. She was unrecognizable.

She sketched Truly's face and showed it to Ruby to see if she recognized the likeness to her father. But the child had no interest in the drawing, just touched it briefly with the stuffed tiger she carried everywhere, and then drew back eying Bev to get her reaction. The child was timid, but there was hope for her. She planned to enroll Ruby in a Montessori school as soon as possible.

Bev hadn't counted on raising Ruby without Truly. Her sight was better, but she could never drive. At some point, she might see well enough to read large print books, to see distinct features of faces, to recognize road signs, to watch a sunrise, a sunset without squinting. In fact, it had been an emotional event just seeing her own home for the first time.

Her home was for sale, though. She was moving to a city with public transportation, culture, and theater. Sales of her latest book, *The Pathology of Childhood Neglect and Abandonment*, were surprisingly high. In fact, it was a scholarly and popular literary triumph. Copies were literally flying off the shelves.

The success of her book, her professional reputation, her returned eyesight, all helped in her effort to win temporary custody of Ruby. She was aware she wouldn't have a chance, if it weren't for Olsen's legacy, and Dr. Dojo vouching for her. Darlyn could still contest Bev's temporary custody, but she made no move to do so.

She resigned her position with the think tank. She would make enough money on the house to move anywhere she wanted. She had savings. She had royalties. It was time for a new life. She had counted on sharing a new life with Truly. The hole in her heart regarding her missing lover registered daily on a painful basis, more so since she took care of his daughter.

Bev gathered the child in her arms and kissed the top of her head. Nothing had gone according to plan. She had no idea where Truly was.

Bev and Truly prepared together for their new life. Truly didn't want to divorce Darlyn. He said she was too unstable. It would have entailed time where Darlyn leveraged access to Ruby based on her whims. Both Bev and Truly could attest Darlyn had difficulty meeting the child's needs. That she seemed to have little affection or interest in her child. Still, the courts would insist on some maternal access to Ruby, and Truly told Bev he had no doubt Darlyn would take it for spite if nothing else. Truly and Bev wanted to cut through the red tape.

The motion of the bus rocked Ruby to and fro until the child's eyes were heavy, and she drowsed finally, her head resting on Bev's shoulder.

Bev reflected that the plan she and Truly concocted seemed cold blooded. Illegal. But effective. Foolproof. And best for everyone in the long run. It was also creative. She liked to use her intellect to find unconventional solutions. And Truly, she discovered, was her partner in arms. It all began when his father, the old man, died, and left Truly the boat.

When Truly checked out the old man's boat, he found the bale of Gold stuffed in the ballast portal. Since Jay was the old man's crew on recent ocean excursions, Truly asked him what he knew about it. Apparently, Jay knew all about it. He had been using the old man's boat to sell the square groupers. Now he was down to the last bale of illegally marketed cannabis. But the old man's death gave Jay second thoughts. Coinciding with the old man's electrified exit from the earthly realm, and after a horrific bender, Jay joined AA and sobered up.

Jay told Truly he dumped the Gold, which Truly doubted, but he didn't argue. He told Jay they were going out to sea one last time to scatter the old man's ashes. The truth was he asked Jay because he needed a witness for his own disappearance.

Truly had been mulling the idea of faking his own death for a long time. He didn't want anything from Darlyn, and he didn't want to hurt her. His disappearance would allow her to save face. He knew how much appearances meant to her. And he wanted to start over for reasons of his own. For so long, he felt as though he were living another man's life, walking around in alien skin. He told Bev all this at her kitchen table, clutching a coffee cup with both hands.

"But you have Ruby," Bev supplied.

Truly nodded mutely. His eyes shone, and he put a hand up his brow briefly. "I have to get out of this mess with Darlyn."

It was Bev who came up with the rest of the plan. If the men left from Fort Canaveral, at 11 a.m., it would take an hour to get out far enough to legally scatter the old man's remains. Truly planned to toast Arthur with cans of beer. In spite of his newfound sobriety, Jay would go along with the toast if Truly asked him to.

At the right moment, Truly would simply dive over the side of the boat and stay underwater long enough to put on his goggles and equip the ExtraLung, a handheld device with an integrated air source inflator. Then he would head to shore. With luck, Jay might not notice he was gone long enough for Truly to make headway. Bev obsessed over the details. It was an audacious plan, and it could have worked.

Eventually, the death threats on Facebook would surface. People would suspect foul play. Truly would be presumed dead. Jay would come under suspicion, but there would never be any real proof to convict him. The suspicion would serve him right, in Truly's eyes. Sucking up to the old man, running dope on his boat. That was the thanks Truly got after saving Jay's life in the middle east. Well, this was pay back.

At any rate, there would be no body, no real crime. Darlyn could file a death certificate after a few years. Truly would have a new identity. Bev would wait until he contacted her, she hoped sooner rather than later. She would nag Darlyn into calling the Coast Guard or maybe Jay would do it. The sticky point was how to get Ruby.

Bev was diligent in keeping an online journal on Darlyn. Quotes, times, and dates when she called Ruby a devil. The times Bev found Ruby wide awake standing in her crib with a soiled diaper. She could prove Ruby was developmentally behind in language. And, thanks to her quick thinking, there was now a police record of Darlyn caught with marijuana contraband. Darlyn would probably quietly give up custody of Ruby rather than go through the public embarrassment of a custody fight. But none of that was certain. All of it promised a long time in court.

Bev was a childless woman. She'd never conceived even once. In a few years, she would go through menopause. Truly and Ruby were her last chance for a family. Still, it wasn't hard, with Bev's connections and her educational status, to convince some of the powers that be to 'lose' Ruby in the system. It happened all the time. The case files were full of missing children. Darlyn didn't check on Ruby. By the time anyone noticed the child was lost, Bev would be long gone.

But where? Truly never showed up; Bev feared he drowned. Jay never returned from the boat trip, either. The boat didn't surface. Towards the end of the search, Bev was able to watch the hazy images on TV of Darlyn and her prayer warriors stalking the beach for Truly and Jay. She shook her head, but she didn't have any idea where to go.

Until she did. That was why she was on her way, via Greyhound, to Fort Canaveral. She intended to walk to the dock where the men departed. She planned on questioning everyone she saw. She had to know if the men left together, if there was anything peculiar about their departure. Then maybe she could fill in the blanks.

There was one person in particular she was eager to meet up with. She shifted the child in her lap and checked her purse to ensure the envelope with the wad of greenbacks was intact in the zippered compartment. It was.

An hour later, the bus pulled alongside the curb, banked by grass and white as a bone in the scorching sunlight. Holding the child in her arms, Bev stood and slung her purse over her shoulder. Stepping carefully, she descended the stairs on the bus to suffocating heat. A huge cheer from the radio broadcast accompanied her descent.

She hadn't taken two steps, when a truck pulled up beside her. The driver was wearing a turban, and she powered down the window, leaned into the passenger seat, and said, "Hop in."

Bev barely inclined her head. "I don't have a baby seat. Meet me at that yellow a-frame store? The Water's Edge? At a picnic table." She trudged on, until she came to a nest of dying palm trees and picked a picnic table that was not white with bird shit. She put Ruby down and reached into her purse for a juice box. She stabbed the straw into the carton and passed it to the flushed child who sat down obediently and began sipping.

Bev watched the truck pull up in the adjacent parking lot. The driver's door opened, and a brown stick of a woman wearing Lily Pulitzer emerged. The turban was covered with rhinestones that glittered in the sunlight, sending little laser-like flashes challenging Bev's fledgling vision. The woman hoisted a bag that even Bev, with her poor eyesight, guessed was a Louis Vuitton. The woman walked through the grass to the picnic table and put her bag down with such a bang that Ruby jumped.

"Hello, Dr. Kase," the woman said.

Bev had never laid eyes on her before, but here was one person who looked exactly the way she imagined.

"Hello, Jenny," she said. "I brought your money."

38
SARA

Sara pulled her blue Saturn into the driveway and slammed the car door as she got out. She walked up the driveway and groped for the key under the ceramic frog on her ledge. It wasn't there, so she dug in her purse to find her spare. She did that all the time. Used the key and left it in the house. It was time for her to grow up, to become responsible. To put away childish things. Her fingers closed around the key chain, and she separated the pink key and fit it into the lock. She opened the door and walked into her empty house.

The stacked boxes were lined up against the wall, all forty-two of them. Basically, she just emptied drawers into the open boxes as though she were feeding a cardboard maw, feeding it with tangled sweaters, half empty tubes of lotions, nylon stockings, and socks without mates. Her old life was a mess, a confusing assortment of objects and memories. She didn't want to throw any of it away. She would sort it all out later.

She called "Tiger," and the gimlet-eyed feline peeped from around the wall. "Are you hungry?" she asked the cat, keeping her distance. Emptying the house had not helped the cat's temperament. Sometimes, when she least expected it, Tiger would fly into a rage and attach herself to Sara's calf with her teeth. The scratch on her arm was the result of trying to pick her up.

Living in constant fear of attack sharpened Sara's survival instincts. When she called Gran Rain to complain, her grandmother laughed. "It's hard to tame a feral cat," she said. "When you need to take her to the vet, just throw her in a pillowcase and dump her in the carrier. So, how's Gabby?"

Sara didn't want to tell Gran she and Gabby broke up, nor did she want to explain the circumstances. "She says hi."

"Tell her I say hi, too," said Gran. Sara grimaced. Gabby was more or less living at Sara's until about two weeks ago. That was when Sara woke up one morning feeling ill and proceeded down the stairs to make coffee only to throw up in the sink.

It was weird, but she didn't think about it until a few days later when it happened again. This time Gabby was in the kitchen too, and she started gagging along with Sara. She bolted for the bathroom, and Sara finished retching and turned on the faucet and the garbage disposal. She was just wiping her flushed cheeks with a wet paper towel, when Gabby emerged looking pale. "What the hell?" she asked.

"I don't know," Sara said leaning against the counter. "It's the second time I've felt sick lately. Maybe it's a virus." She picked up an aerosol air freshener and started spraying it.

"Hmm," Gabby said, sinking into a kitchen chair. She wrinkled her nose. "Could you be pregnant?"

Sara, putting bread in the toaster, suddenly froze. "Why would you say that?"

"Why would I say that? I was kidding. Why would you say that?"

Sara said nothing.

"Is it possible?"

"Is what possible?"

"You know." Gabby made a rocking motion with her

arms.

Sara laughed shortly. "Of course not. Except…"

"Except!" Gabby stood up.

"Oh well. You know. Condoms aren't foolproof."

"No, they're not." Gabby's tone was suddenly steely. "Have you had sex without a condom?"

Sara said nothing, but her cheeks flamed.

Gabby slammed her palm down on the table. "Of course, you did. You are sloppy with everything else. Why not birth control?" Gabby griped about Sara's clothes on the floor, Tiger's litter box, and no T.P. in the bathroom.

Stung, Sara shouted, "It was only once." On the kitchen table with Jay. That night with Galvin in the hot tub at his condo shortly before they broke up. "Or twice."

There was a moment of intense silence between the two women. Then Gabby said, "That's all it takes, girlfriend." Without another word, Gabby dressed and got into her car.

When she got back, she shoved a pregnancy test into Sara's hand. "Here. Go find out if you're knocked up."

It turned out she was. Knocked up. The positive blue line materialized on the wet little swab. She showed it to Gabby, covering her mouth with her palm so in awe of the catastrophe befallen her. At the same time there was a tiny little flame of pride, knowing her body actually worked the way it was supposed to.

Gabby gaped at the proof of Sara's pregnancy. "I didn't want to believe it."

"Oh, Gabby." Sara began to embrace her, so grateful to have someone beside her during this difficult time.

Gabby pushed her away. "What are you going to do?"

"Do?" Sara had no idea. She'd never even held a baby before. She never babysat. A baby was definitely a foreign element to her. She had seen college friends transformed into haggard unkempt zombies during the infancy of their children. She had been glad about her independence from all that. Now she was one of them.

Gabby was saying something. "Are you going to have it?"

Sara was aware that Gabby definitely did not sound on board with that idea. "Jeez Gab, I just found out." She put a hand to her forehead. "I could use a little support here."

"You may be going ahead with this pregnancy."

Gabby was very deadpan as she said it. "Kind of robotic," Sara thought.

"I said I just found out," Sara said.

"Definitely a career killer," Gabby said. "Do you expect me to support you or something?"

"That's it, Gabs," Sara said. "Sure." It occurred to her that Gabby really didn't know her at all.

"Well," Gabby said, apparently immune to sarcasm, "I didn't sign up for this." She flung Sara's positive pregnancy wand at the wall. It bounced off and fell on the carpet.

"Sign up for what?" Sara's face got a little red. "We're not married, are we? Or even engaged. Or even exclusive! So, what is 'this?'"

"This is that," Gabby said, pointing vaguely towards Sara's uterus.

"The first thing that goes wrong and you're like this," Sara said. "Good to know."

"The first thing? The first thing?" Gabby looked as if she

were straining to contain her vital organs, so they didn't spontaneously explode. "This is kind of a big thing, you know!"

"If you don't like it, you know what you can do," Sara said between clenched teeth.

All of Gabby's neck muscles were visible. And just like that, she began packing. Gabby made sure she got her toothbrush, toothpaste, nightgowns, massage oil, and underwear crammed into a paper bag in less than fifteen minutes.

"I can't handle this," she said, clattering down the stairs.

Sara walked over to the balcony. "Don't tell anyone at work. Not yet."

Gabby looked up at her with an expression that actually made Sara recoil. Then her girlfriend was gone with a firm slam of the front door. As though Sara had done this on purpose.

So here Sara was. With the big raise that went along with her job promotion, she impulsively bought a brand new condo in a high rise near downtown Lake Ann. With practically no money down, she was soon heavily mortgaged on the tenth floor of a one bedroom, 900 square foot living space. She had a balcony, and she could just see the fountain in the lake if she leaned out a little and craned her neck. The rest of her view consisted of construction workers putting up an almost identical high rise across the street, which would soon block out any cursory view of nature.

She would miss the awkward architecture of her frame house and the live oaks visible from every window. But the house sold within a week. Soon she would downgrade to the white walls and sterile gray carpet of her new flat. But she didn't plan on being there much. Her job would demand a lot of office time.

Sara found the best way to cope with the complications in her life was to ignore them. She could go to bed, and in the morning little would have changed. As far as her pregnancy was concerned, it was impossible for Sara to become a mother since she didn't feel like a mother. It was easy to assume that nature miscalculated and would soon correct its mistake. All she focused on was getting out of her house, moving, and furnishing her condo.

This was hard to do as she had to pee all the time, and she continued having regular bouts of morning sickness. She felt ill and lost weight. She asked Danielle for a month off, ostensibly to move and resettle. She'd worked there two years and had never taken a vacation or a single sick day. Danielle readily agreed. In spite of her boss's monopolization of Galvin, Sara had to admit she was fair.

So, Sara was closing on the condo, ordering the inspectors, switching services off and switching services on, and booking the movers. Still in the packing stage, she kept finding mementos of the past few turbulent months. Things of Gabby's, things of Jay's. Most of it she just flung into a box. She took Jay's amulet to work and held it in her palm sometimes, staring at it, wondering what it meant to him. But it was the reminder of Galvin that stopped her cold.

Tucked into the corner of her mirror with a million other mementos, she almost threw the square engraved card away. It was the invitation to Meryl's wedding.

She placed the invitation in her purse instead of a box. She began to wonder. Jay was gone, but Galvin had made no secret of his expectation to be a parent someday. "Stuff I'll tell my grandchildren," he'd often remark, watching the news. Once, she found a box with some old roller blades in a corner of his closet. She asked him if he still skated. "No," he'd said. "Just something for my kids to laugh at some day."

Sara kept her condition a secret from Gran Rain, but she knew what her grandmother would say. Just as she'd advised Sara to always pay her own way, she would insist it was only fair for Sara to tell Galvin about the possibility she was carrying his child.

Which Sara intended to do when she suggested they meet for coffee. But Galvin was on the brink of a great adventure, and she hated to spoil it for him. And he never indicated in look, word, or tone he wanted her back. He said he wasn't going to Meryl's wedding. So that was that. And now she was alone in her echoing empty condo except for some boxes and a feral cat who hated her. Tiger was rubbing her face on the corner of the wall when a box toppled over. They both heard it. Tiger took off, disappearing in an instant.

"What the..." Sara threw her keys on the counter and rounded the corner into the living room. "Tiger," she called. There was a rushing sound, then someone grabbed her roughly around the waist and put a hand over her mouth, so she couldn't scream. Sara froze. The voice was a whisper, it tickled her ear. "Don't make a sound," the voice said. "I need you to be very very quiet."

39
LINK

Link opened his eyes. He woke as if it was an emergency, as if sleeping was a dangerous thing. His eyes opened wide, ready for anything.

It was white, white everywhere, and he squinted. Wherever he was, he clearly slept too long.

A voice said, "You're awake."

Link cut his gaze to the left and to the right. The raspiness in the voice indicated some lens or filter to his situation he had missed out on. Tubes ran up each of his nostrils, IVs ran into his arms. The room smelled simultaneously of disinfectant and urine. Near the door, were dispensers for rubber gloves, hand sanitizer, and soap. Separating his bed from a window, a curtain hung limply on a chrome railing. An old TV was stanchioned to the wall. On either side of his bed were two chairs. The chair on his right contained a tiny older woman.

She wore an intense expression, and her eyes were red and puffy. Link tried to say something, and the woman put a hand on his bandaged arm. "Don't talk," she said. Then in a louder voice, she called, "Nurse."

A woman in green scrubs entered the room. She turned to wash her hands at the sink. The older woman pointed at Link and said, "He's awake."

The nurse came over to the bed and put cool fingers on Link's wrist. He wanted to jerk his hand away. He wanted to ask what was going on. He found he couldn't move without intense pain. He couldn't speak either. His tongue felt swollen and bandages covered his entire face.

"It's the drugs," the older woman said as if she were reading his mind. "You have second degree burns and smoke inhalation. A beam fell on your back, and they had to put you under to operate." He looked at her, not comprehending.

"Oh, Link," she said. "You're a hero."

The events of the past five hours did not return to Link. He remembered running into a burning house. Everything was blank after that. And before that too.

"You need to rest," the nurse said, taking his temperature. She scribbled something on a chart and propped it in a plastic bin by the bed. She turned to the older woman. "It's good he's awake," she said. She left the room.

"I need to tell your father you're conscious," the old woman said. She put a hand on his bandaged forehead and missed his wince. Then she was gone.

"What the fuck had happened to him? More importantly, where was he? For that matter, who the fuck was he?"

He had heard of amnesia, although of course he couldn't remember how or where. His only memory was of running into a burning building. He was obviously burned after being in a fire. He was in a freaking hospital, so there was only one conclusion he could make. He was a fireman.

Link wondered if he was married, if he had kids. Did he own a Dalmatian? The old woman said he was a hero. What had he done to deserve that?

There was a rap on his partially open door. A man in a wheelchair rolled into the room. Like Link, his face was bandaged with slits cut out for eyes. He rolled up to the foot of the bed and stared across the length of the blanket at Link. Link wondered if he was a fellow firefighter. Perhaps they worked side by side for years. He envisioned savage flames of ghastly orange tearing through verdant woodland. Unfettered infernos, licking, twisting, and swaying in a dance without rhythm. Fire burning like a temper, its tendrils everywhere. Soon the air would be too smoky to breathe, too hot to inhale. That's when they would make a run for it.

Link was so wrapped up in his daydream, he hadn't noticed the occupant of the wheelchair pulled up right next to his bed. The man took out a cell phone and typed something in it. He passed it to Link who handled it clumsily with his bandaged hands. He read, *Link, u OK, man?*

He shrugged his shoulders and handed the phone back. The patient got busy texting again. This time, when he passed the phone back, Link read, *They're saying you a hero. Me too. Although we didn't save anyone.*

Link cocked his head to one side and passed the phone back. This time, the patient texted for quite a long time. When he passed the phone to Link, he texted. *I hope this don't upset you, bro.* Link read, You were under a burning bookcase when I found you. The ceiling caved in and a beam cracked us both on the back. We're lucky to be alive. But the woman you went in to help? Darlyn? She's gone. Burned up. Along with the Gold you hid in the Porta Potty.

Link handed the phone back slowly. He had no idea what this patient was talking about. He was a firefighter, and who was this guy? Where was his wife and where were his children? Shouldn't they be standing vigil over him?

He looked up as a woman in a police uniform entered the white room. At last. Was this his beautiful wife?

The policewoman stood for a moment. Then she said, "Is this the thanks I get for saving your miserable lives?"

The patient in the wheelchair opened his arms to the police officer who gave him a brief hug. Link cocked his head to the side. The patient in the wheelchair grabbed his phone, texted and passed it to Link.

Link read, *It's Officer Cleary. Remember her? She saved our lives.*

Link looked at her again. A glimmer of memory, a vignette flashed, in the logy synapses of his brain. This was not his beautiful wife. This was a woman of superhuman strength, a woman in a hazmat suit, who'd lifted the burning beams off the men and dragged them through the flames to safety. How?

As if she had heard his unspoken question, Officer Cleary said, "Adrenaline, I guess." She slung an arm around the patient in the wheelchair. "Had to save my fiancé and his buddy."

Link and the patient stared at each other through the small opening in the bandages that covered their faces. And suddenly, slowly, Link started to remember.

40
JAY-SIX WEEKS AGO

The fire coral was agony. His face actually dipped into the water, so the coral outcrop on the projecting part of the reef probably saved his life. He woke up suddenly, and lifted his head, gasping for air. His face burned and stung. He could already feel it swelling up, the salt water invading the newly opened crevices in his face, heightening his agony. The tidal current was strong, and he bobbed to and fro, screaming, clawing at his face.

"Whoa, Bub, whoa." A man in a Jon boat motored up to Jay, and dropped an anchor regardless of the coral reef. He was a weathered man with ashy blonde hair under his Miami Dolphins ball cap. He crouched in the tiny vessel and extended his arm over the side of the boat. "Here, Bub, take a hand up."

Jay tightened his grip around the old man's skinny wrist, heaved himself up with his last ounce of strength and fell face first onto the plywood floor of the boat. He lay motionless for a few seconds. In spite of the agony in his face, it was the first time Jay was on a dry surface for eighteen hours. Reflexively, he touched his side where the amulet used to be.

"Where am I?"

The old man took off his cap and scratched his head.

"What's that?"

Jay managed to turn himself over from his stomach to his back. His skin and what was left of his clothes were encrusted with salt crystals. The orange life vest and his denim survival vest were still wrapped around his body. The old man passed Jay a bottle of water, and Jay sat up by gripping the center bench seat. The water that passed between his lips tasted cold. After contemplating his own death for so many hours, it was jarring to realize he may survive. "Where am I?" he asked again through clenched teeth.

The old man hoisted the anchor and the rope into an untidy heap on the deck. He stooped and tinkered with the engine. "Less see, can I get this mother to run." He turned his head. "This here is Hens and Chickens. You in the Hawk channel just off Plantation Key."

The engine roared to life suddenly, and Jay jumped, shielding his raw battered face from the sun with the V of his hand. The old man sat on the bench seat closest to the engine.

"Name's Captain Tom," he yelled over the roar, steering around the bobbing waves.

Closer to shore instead of out to sea, Jay would have caught the Gulf Stream. He suspected the massive squall in the Atlantic threw him south. Jay hesitated. If he gave his real name, someone could link him to the guy missing from Fort Canaveral. If he was going to live after all, he wanted no part of his old life. "You can just call me Bub," he said.

"You as red as the side of a barn, Bub," the Captain said. "Can't feel pretty." He pulled a flask out of a side pocket and thrust it in Jay's face. "Take a swig of this, boy. Then brace yourself. Only thing that takes that sting away is piss."

His face was on fire. Jay unscrewed the cap and sniffed. The flask contained brandy. He had been sober for exactly ten months. But surely this was a special circumstance. After all, there was no way to get in touch with his sponsor. Tom stared at him steadily, swaying a little as he motored over the waves. Jay debated; his face was so painful tears leaked from his eyes. Finally, he inclined his chin and tilted the contents of the flask into his open mouth, swallowing as the alcohol burned its way down his throat. He emptied the flask and threw it on the floor.

"Lie flat as you can," Captain Tom said. "With your head facing up."

Jay scooted forward and closed his eyes, so he didn't have to see. He heard the boat idle. He heard Captain Tom unbuckle his belt and fumble with his zipper. There was the sound of water streaming over the side of the boat.

"Here," Captain Tom said, handing him a bilge rag that smelled of diesel and urine. Pat this on your face. Should take away some o' the sting. Jay patted the rank cloth on his wounded face. The crude remedy did make his wounds feel a little bit better. Then he passed out.

It turned out Captain Tom had little interest in who Jay was and where he came from. He ran a poor as shit fishing line for local restaurants, and he needed help on the open waters to eke out a living. He let Jay share a bunk in an old fishing shack in a deserted harbor. After a week, Jay's rash faded a bit to an ugly reddish scrim. He began accompanying Captain Tom out into the bay.

The job wasn't much money. Mostly it kept Jay in beer, whiskey and cigarettes. He fell hard off the wagon, so hard that, even squinting, his sobriety was too far into the distance to see clearly. After all, he floated miles in the open sea and survived. Obviously, he was living on borrowed time.

Every morning he emerged from the shack, hung over, gulls screeching on the white splattered dock. He would hop into the boat, untie the lines, start the motor, and drink a beer with Captain Tom on the way out to the reef. Captain Tom had a few choice spots for yellowtail, snapper, and mahi mahi. They would fish all day and while they fished, they drank. A lot. Jay wondered how the Captain made out before he showed up.

"What were you doing out here the day we met, Tom?" Jay asked. "Fishing?"

Captain Tom lit a cigarette and inhaled deeply. With the same hand, he finished a beer, smacked his lips, and threw the can into the plastic tub they kept for recyclables. He threw the cigarette butt in the water and recast his line without answering.

Jay said, "No, really. What?"

Captain Tom rubbed his wrinkled face with a spotted hand. "I woulda thunk you'd a figgered that out by now, Bub."

Jay opened another beer. He always thought he would love to live in the southernmost islands, but it was summer and the Keys reeked of rotten fish. He was still uneasy out on the water, but Captain Tom rarely lost sight of land. He wondered why he put so much faith in Captain Tom's judgment. As far as he knew, the old man never even listened for small craft advisory warnings on the radio. Perhaps it was because Captain Tom reminded him a little of Arthur, Truly's old man. Perhaps it was because Captain Tom, like Truly, saved his life.

But now Jay was a pothead and an alcoholic. Maybe it would have been better to die than to live and to become what he'd become. He touched his side pocket briefly, missing, as always, his lucky amulet. Not that his life was worth much.

Maybe he and Captain Tom had that in common. He looked up and observed the captain through narrowed eyes. He was an old man bobbing on an ocean in a boat, not knowing when death would finally sever the rope that bound him to shore.

"What's my name, Captain?"

"Name's Bub," Captain Tom said. "I'm Captain Tom." The old salt lit a cigarette from the stub of his last one and passed it to Jay. "I call everbody Bub," he said.

The old man lifted his head as if he were sniffing the air. There was a pregnant silence. Finally, he said, "My dad had whatchu call it. Couldn't remember his own dang name at the end."

Jay laid his fishing rod across his knees. When it was calm, it was quiet out on the water except for the gulls screeching and the water lapping the hull of the boat. "Your father... couldn't remember things? Like names?"

The old man nodded. "I can't be like that."

Jay leaned forward and put a hand on the old man's skinny shoulder. "You've got a while. I've heard it goes slow."

Captain Tom nodded. "Glass still half full. But I got a plan b'fore it's empty."

"Good to have a plan."

The old man turned around, faced Jay, and looked him in the eyes. The captain's eyes were blue, like the blue inside a glacier, reflecting the ocean. He hoisted a foot in Jay's direction.

"Gotta rope. Gotta anchor. When I ferget my own name, I'm gonna tie that rope around my ankle, tie the other end to anchor, motor out to Hens and Chickens, and let her fly."

Jay thought for a minute. "Is that what you were planning on doing when you found me?"

Captain Tom shook his head with the tiniest of smiles. "Truth tell, Bub, I can't even remember."

"That's good," said Jay. "Because chances are the rope will break. After it breaks your leg. Or pulls it out of its socket. But hey. Pain is something you remember."

The old man stared blankly as if he'd lost the train of conversation. "I've already saved his life," Jay thought. "Once." It was a relief to know that in this instance at least, he discharged some of his debt.

41
DANIELLE

It turned out Galvin's imminent departure to Anchorage was a career boost for Danielle. She managed to convince Jackie Moats to tell Nick Montana, the CEO of InterTech, she could handle her department and Galvin's for a promotion to vice presidency. It entailed a huge jump in salary. A staff. Galvin's office with the view of the pasture.

Danielle thought it was only fair to spread the wealth, so she made Sara her lead trainer. She did this partly as compensation for poaching Galvin's attention, but mostly because Sara was the best damn trainer on the floor.

Still, she had to wonder what Galvin and Sara would say if they knew what she was up to, standing in her bathroom, staring down at the pregnancy test stick laying on her vanity counter. She knew the test was checking for the presence of the pregnancy hormone in her urine, which her body would begin to produce after she conceived. It was the first day of her missed period. If it was positive, it was probably about two weeks since she conceived. She waited for the plus or minus symbol.

She felt like a sniper, in a prone position, ready to fire. Her neck muscles were taut as she maintained her watchful gaze, her eyes never leaving the small strip as if that could determine the outcome. She was forty years old, and she wanted her life settled. She didn't have time to woo Galvin into marriage, nor, if she were honest, did she want to anymore. He was a nice guy, handsome, good in bed. He would make a great dad. But not with her. He was too conventional. Also, she never felt she had his undivided attention. The fact he was so eager to leave the firm, to leave the state, was evidence of his lack of commitment. Their connection was casual. Although if Danielle had her way, Galvin would leave a permanent imprint.

She planned to say she went to a sperm bank. It was not so unusual for women of a certain age to get pregnant on their own. Of course, if Galvin got wind of it, he would almost certainly propose. That would be messy. The last thing she wanted was a marriage of convenience. She wanted to be with someone who got her, who shared her interests. She would rather stay single than settle.

Of course, Galvin had a right to know if he was going to be a father; on the other hand, how would it hurt him not to? What would he lose? Besides, she never really believed her plan would work. Briefly, she touched the locket around her neck.

She could almost hear Denny's voice, a distinct sound. *Easy Danny*. She looked around. Everything was the same. The vines on the wall paper. The granite vanity of black with veins of gold and green. Even the scent from the plugged-in wall flower, a vanilla aroma, the only kind she ever got. "'Denny," she thought, "wish you were here." The need for him to be with her at this pivotal moment of her life was like longing for a drink. *It's okay*, she imagined him saying. *I'm here. I'm always here. That's what twins are for.*

Denny always maintained they had gotten lost in the system, and their mother couldn't find them. It never occurred to either one of them their mother could be dead. Did that make a difference? Would she have rescued them if she lived?

There was a loud clatter in the shower stall. The plastic scraper, which hung on a plastic hook, fell onto the shower tiles. Distracted, she looked away just as something began to emerge on the stick, a blurry symbol beginning to appear. In two seconds, it was distinct. Danielle felt her throat close and tears come to her eyes. Her cell dinged. She picked it up.

Got a new tent! It's up in the living room. Come on over and try it out.

Danielle smiled through her tears. This was crazy stuff for Galvin. He must be excited about his upcoming move.

Hope it's for the summer! Can't come, work. You know how it is.

Galvin texted her a sad faced emoji. But Danielle was smiling. She patted her stomach as though it were her baby's back. For all she knew, it probably was. She replaced the scraper, which she used to wipe down the glass doors after her shower. There was no reason for it to come off the hook. *Denny*, she thought.

42
BEV

"She's dead," Jenny said, sitting down next to Ruby. "Darlyn's dead." Bev and Ruby looked at her.

Jenny said, "As of this morning. House burned up."

Ruby put her thumb in her mouth and scooted closer to Bev. "Don't be ridiculous," Bev said. She hated to smoke around Ruby, but if there was ever a time to do it, the time was now. Her hand shook as she withdrew a pack of Kools from her purse.

Jenny fished in her purse for a Kleenex, releasing an odor of face powder. She dabbed at her face. "I was actually starting to like the little moron."

Bev felt her sense of panic flare up a notch. Had the neighborhood burned as well? Her house? No. Jenny would have said. She lit her cigarette and inhaled. When she spoke, her words were punctuated by little puffs of smoke. "She probably fell asleep with a lit cigarette."

"That may be," Jenny said, her hatchet shaped face turned in Bev's direction. "These two firemen ran into the burning house. Someone had to save them." She laughed a little.

"The news said a bale of weed in the Porta Potty on the property next door, melted down. Everyone in the neighborhood was high."

Bev remembered the smell of pot in Darlyn's house. "Did they stop the fire?"

"Oh yeah. The new house next door went, and Darlyn's

house of course. And Darlyn. Did you bring the money?"

Bev reached into her purse, removed the envelope and passed it to Jenny. Jenny opened the envelope and counted the bills. Several times, like an OCD patient in full swing. But when she looked up the lines in her weather-beaten face eased a little.

"Well, there's that. Do you need me for anything else?"

Jenny, whose background was a mystery, emerged from the internet in the past year, soliciting discreet services. Lately, she took on the role of the evangelist, Jenny Zinn, offering prayer, comfort, and drugs to a bereaved wife. Bev supplied the prescriptions and planned to report Darlyn for misuse of prescription drugs. The new governor was pretty strict about opioid use.

Bev tossed her cigarette in the sand and ran the heel of her sandal over it. She drew Ruby into her lap and hugged her. She hadn't heard a word from Truly. Darlyn had retrieved Truly's truck, but Jay's Regal was still baking in the heat of the parking lot, its tires flat. Jenny was the last person to see the men alive. She told Bev she'd pulled up in her truck and watched them depart.

"Are you sure Jay and Truly left on the day and at the time you said they did?"

"Sure as shit," Jenny said. "The sky was getting dark and the good lookin' one looked a little rattled." She paused for a minute and thought. "Truly looked half asleep."

"What do you mean?" He looked okay the last time Bev saw him. It seemed like an eon since they kissed in her driveway and talked about the future.

"He was yawning. Looked ready to pass out."

Bev mulled over her words. Ready to pass out. What if

Truly fainted and drowned in the ensuing squall? She felt actual pain in her chest considering this outcome. She assumed, until now, hoped, he was laying low. She grew more and more uneasy. Surely, Truly would have found some way to contact her. If he were still alive. Bev realized Jenny was asking her something. "Sorry," she said.

"Do you get to keep the kid, now?" Jenny eyed Ruby and reached for her hand. Ruby shrank back and put her fingers in her mouth.

Bev considered. Her forehead was damp. She ran the back of her hand over it. "No living relatives," she said. "Probably." Ruby was all she had now.

"I gotta get goin'," Jenny said with a sour smile. She stood and pocketed the white envelope. She eyed Bev and Ruby the way a hawk eyes prey.

"Hold on," Bev said. "As a matter of fact, there is one more thing you can do for me."

43
SARA

Sara froze. Not that she had much choice. The hand over her mouth and the arm around her waist did not allow for much movement. She smelled cigarette smoke and a faint odor of fish. Again, the voice whispered, breath tickling her ear. "Don't make a sound. D'ya hear me?"

Heart pounding, Sara moved her head up and down. The man's grip did not yield. She was trapped. Her eyes darted around the room looking for escape, a weapon. She heard a loud ripping sound behind her, the cat on the curtain, and the intruder's grip momentarily loosened. Sara wound an ankle around his and jerked hard, bringing him to one knee. Then she reared back and kicked as hard as she could on the back of his other kneecap. He fell flat on his face. Sara was onto him in an instant, straddling his back and pulling his wrist up, twisting his arm behind his back. She leaned on his elbow.

The man yelled, "Stop, Sara, for God's sake. Stop!"

Sara paused, but did not relent on the pressure.

"It's me," the man screamed. "It's me! Jay."

In one fluid movement, Sara released her painful grip and stood up. The man on the floor slowly, painfully got to his feet. Then he turned around.

Sara felt the blood drain from her face. "You're not Jay."

The man who faced her was not the handsome boyfriend she was so taken with two months ago she'd had sex with him on her kitchen table. With no protection.

The man facing her had a beer gut, and he smelled. His face and legs were scarred, and his long greasy hair came down to his shoulders. He was dressed in tattered cutoffs and a T-shirt that bore the logo, *Got Crabs?*

"I am, though." His voice was the same, she realized, though a little hoarser. A little coarser.

"Jay?" In other circumstances, she would have run into his arms, crying with joy. Now she just stared. "What happened to you?"

Jay raised his arms, palms out. "Do you have anything to drink around here? Or eat?"

Three minutes ago, Sara was afraid this man would take her life. Mechanically, she walked past him, into the kitchen. She opened the refrigerator. "Water?' her voice shook a little.

Jay shuffled into the kitchen and sat down heavily on a chair. "Do you have a beer?"

Sara reached far back into the fridge and came up with a single amber bottle of beer. She handed it to him. Jay bit off the cap and spit it on the floor. He took a long slug. He belched.

The shock was beginning to recede, but Sara's hands still trembled. "Cheese sandwich, all right? I don't have much in the fridge."

Jay wiped his mouth with the back of his hand. "That would be great."

Sara handed him a napkin, which he crumpled up in one fist. It was silent for a moment as Sara transferred the bread, cheese, and mayo to the counter.

"So you're moving," Jay said.

Sara nodded, her back turned to him. "I bought a condo

downtown." She set the plate with the sandwich in front of him so hard the plate clattered. Jay picked up the food and tore into it. Sara sat down opposite him. "Where have you been?"

Jay chewed and spoke around the remnants of his food. "The Keys."

Sara took a deep breath. "Jay. You've been gone for two months. You've been missing. The guy you went with is missing. The boat was never found." She spread her hands. "We've all been worried sick."

"Sorry." Jay shoved the empty plate back to her. "Would you mind making me another?"

Sara got up and then sat back down. "Not until you tell me where you've been."

Jay told her how he and Truly planned to scatter the old man's ashes. How Truly seemed drugged, comatose by the time they boarded the *Early Byrd*. How it was raining when they left, but instead of letting up, the rain became a full-fledged squall. Jay was swept overboard and floated in the Atlantic all night on a flimsy orange life jacket and his jeans, inflated into a life preserver. He told her about floating onto the reef with the fire coral. He told her about living in the fishing shack with Captain Tom.

"Didn't you know people were looking for you?" Sara asked.

"Um, no," Jay said. "There was no TV or radio where we slept. We went out to the bars, but the TVs there are always on the sports or weather channels. I hadn't any phone, no computer."

"Why, Jay? Why? What about your cousins?" Sara could not fathom the kind of life Jay said he'd been leading. Unless…

"Listen," Sara said. "Is there anything you want to tell me?"

"What do you mean?"

"I mean…you got along okay with your cousin, right?" Jay stood up so abruptly the table rocked. "I loved Truly," he said, hoarsely. "Like a father." He broke down in tears suddenly, sinking into the chair, and holding his head with both hands. "I lost him. And I lost her, too."

For a minute Sara thought Jay meant her, their lost romance. "Go on."

Jay cried for a minute, and Sara rose impulsively. She stood behind him and put her hand on his shoulder. Jay gripped it tightly and then he turned, and he was in her arms, his tears wetting her sleeve.

"There, there," she said. Was this what it was like to soothe a child? Her face felt flushed suddenly, as she fought against the urge to tell him about her condition. Now was not the time. It may never be the time. Then because she felt she should be saying something, anything, she said, "My Gran always says whatever is bothering me now won't matter as much in ten years."

Jay broke away from her and sat up, wiping his nose on his arm. Sara got up and went into the bathroom. She came out with a roll of toilet paper. "Here," she said.

"Thanks," Jay said, tearing off several sheets, holding them to his nose and honking loudly. "The thing is, I think I'm still going to feel bad ten years from now."

"Why Jay?" Sara sat down across from him again.

"You hadn't heard? Watched the news?"

"Heard what? My TV is packed, and I met a friend for

lunch."

Jay ran his hand through his hair, which no longer looked adorably tousled as it had when he did that in the past. "I couldn't think past Truly being dead. I knew he was dead, knew it in my soul, as though a light went out. All he wanted was to give the old man a decent burial at sea and come home. I couldn't save him. He saved my life, and I couldn't save his."

His eyes started leaking tears again. It was as though he'd come back from the sea, but he carried this ocean of grief inside him.

"Oh," Sara said. She grasped his hand.

Jay bowed his head. "I started thinking, I know this is crazy, if I had my lucky amulet none of this would have happened. Everything started going to shit when I lost it. So, I leave the old guy I was staying with and come home. I hitched rides from the Keys, and if you think hitchhiking on the eighteen-mile stretch is easy, you got another think coming. It took days, me dozing in the passenger seat or the flatbeds of trucks. I arrive this morning a block or so away from my house. I smell smoke." Jay gripped Sara's hand so hard she winced.

"Smoke?"

"Darlyn's house burned down early this morning."

"Oh my God, Jay." Sara's hands flew to her mouth, covering it. She felt ill.

"I think Darlyn's gone. I feel it. I don't know about Ruby. I hope not. I hope I have some kin left."

"Oh, Jay." For the first time in her life, she considered what someone else was feeling before she reacted. Her own feelings always seemed so important, especially to Gran who was there to listen. Because Gran was always there, Sara seldom needed her. But Jay had no one.

Jay tried to pull himself together, to sit up, dry his face, and smile. Sara saw a glimpse of the old handsome Jay, a part of him that would never die, but would, she suspected, never fully be resurrected. "The thing is," he said, "I'd really like my amulet back. I know I left it here."

Sara never suspected the stone held magical properties, but she had found it soothing to hold it in her hand and think of Jay. "It's at work," she said. "Why don't you help me finish moving this weekend, and I'll take you with me to the office on Monday."

Jay looked at the ceiling and then at the floor. "Is that a good idea?"

"Yes," Sara said firmly. "I want you to talk to Danielle, too. Remember her? She's my boss, but she's very caring. She'll know what to do about Darlyn, Ruby, and the house. She's super capable."

"That good looking older woman? Okay," Jay said. He tried to sit up straight.

Sara got up and walked around to the counter. She began making another sandwich. Out of nowhere, Tiger bounded into the room and leaped into Jay's lap. Jay petted her back. "Nice kitty."

Sara stared her hands on her hips. She heard purring.

"Her name's Tiger. She's anything but nice."

"Whatever you say," Jay said. They grinned at each other.

Sara turned back to her sandwich making, somewhat heartened. Their romance was clearly over. But they were still friends.

44
DANIELLE-MONDAY MORNING

Danielle worried about facing Galvin at the office. The secret she carried was hard to keep. For one thing, she was smiling all the time. She wondered if people could guess her condition by her appearance, although at this point, she had no morning sickness or any physical changes. The fetus was still an embryo about the size of a peanut, but she kept putting her hand over her stomach and humming.

By this time next year, she'd have a baby, who would be sitting up and smiling at her. Would her baby look like her and Denny? Even if it looked like Galvin, by that time people would forget the connection. She hoped.

She got to the office early, wishing there was someone she could tell about her good news. Although she was closer to Sara since giving her the promotion, she certainly couldn't confide in her about her pregnancy. Sara was young and carefree, and babies were probably the furthest thing from her mind. Plus, she might guess who the father was.

Danielle was still humming as she stacked pencils, tore off a calendar page, and readied her desk for a day of work. Gabby in Training had scheduled a presentation later this morning. She wondered what that was about.

There was a tap on her open door. She looked up. Galvin stood in the doorway, smiling at her. For a fraught moment, Danielle thought maybe he sensed her condition. But, no. Galvin was one of the least intuitive men she ever dated.

"Hello, there," he said. "You."

"Galvin, "she said. He was smug, practical, so literal, so everything she didn't need in a soulmate.

"I missed you this weekend," he said, closing the door and walking towards her desk.

She held up a hand. "Stop. I have too much work to do."

Galvin gave her a look. "I thought maybe you'd want to come back to my office. Soon to be your office. I'm sure you'll want to redecorate? Move things around?"

Danielle knew a pretext when she heard one. He certainly had missed her this weekend.

"I can't," she said. "I have to work. There's that stupid meeting Gabby's having."

"I know," Galvin said. "What is that about?"

"Galvin," Danielle said.

He held up his hand and ducked his head. "Don't say it."

"I have to," she said. "What did you think would happen when you moved to Alaska?"

Galvin put his hands in his pockets. He was quiet for a few beats. "I don't know. A long distance relationship?"

Danielle smiled. "Alaska is quite a long distance, Galvin."

"I know," he said. "But I thought for Christmas and, you know, vacations. We could at least try it."

Danielle shook her head. "I don't think it would be fair to either one of us."

He took a step back. "A clean break then?" Galvin's eyes looked a little shiny.

"Yes." To her surprise, her own eyes stung with tears. She held out her hand. Galvin took it.

"You'll probably meet some gorgeous Aleutian woman," she said. She dropped her hand.

Galvin didn't smile. "But I'll never forget you, Danielle."

"No," she said. "I'll never forget you either, Galvin."

There was a beep from her computer. "Time for Gabby's meeting," she said, rolling her eyes.

"Who authorized this meeting?" Galvin asked. "I certainly didn't."

"I didn't either," Danielle said.

Galvin opened the door for her, and they both stepped onto the purple carpet that led to the main meeting room, an open space beneath fluorescent lighting, surrounded by cubicles. Light without heat streamed through the insulated picture windows in streaks of banded gold. There was a large white screen at the front of the room. Gabby was already there, fiddling with her laptop computer and cursing under her breath.

Danielle and Galvin dragged chairs from two of the cubicles into the meeting room and sat down. They looked around at their colleagues. All of the trainers were there except Sara. Slowly, the call service reps, the technicians, the programmers, even the project managers took seats or dragged chairs in.

"Look," Danielle said, digging her elbow into Galvin's ribs. "Isn't that Nick Montana?"

Galvin looked. "I don't believe it."

Nick Montana, the reclusive founder and owner of InterTech, was 75 years old and preternaturally tall, towering over his employees at 6'9." Because of his height, his suits were all custom made with bohemian touches like lilac-colored linen and pastel cravats rather than ties. His hair was white and pulled back into a ponytail tied with what looked like braided rawhide. With him was a petite older woman, probably in her 70s. His companion wore a knee length black sheath which contrasted nicely with her silvery hair.

"Do you know who the woman is?" Danielle asked.

Galvin shook his head. "She looks familiar, though."

At that moment, Sara entered the room with a portly guy dressed in khakis, flip flops, and a green polo shirt. Danielle squinted at the couple. Sara walked directly to the older woman and embraced her. She sat down next to her, patting the adjacent seat for her male companion. Nick Montana leaned in and shook hands. He stayed in that position for a few minutes, talking to Sara and her companion.

"Oh," Galvin said. "That's Gran Rain. Sara's grandma."

"Who's the guy with Sara?" Danielle asked.

"I don't know," Galvin said. "He looks a little familiar."

"You keep saying that," Danielle said.

Galvin shrugged. "Maybe it will come to me."

Gabby finally adjusted the projector to her satisfaction. She walked up and down the center aisle of folding chairs that seated her colleagues, greeting people. She wore a black suit with white piping around the wrists and collar, giving her a vaguely nautical air.

She turned around with a flourish when she reached the front of the room. Even wearing high heels, she was only 5'1." Gabby's cherubic face and blonde ringlets, her high voice and apologetic manner did not inspire authority, and it was several minutes before the private conversations ended, and all eyes finally turned to the petite trainer. People in the audience several rows back strained to see her. She waited.

Skills like this drove Danielle crazy. She emphasized to each of her trainers they did not reward late comers and penalize the prompt by waiting to open the meeting. Talkers needed a direct stare and if that didn't work, Gabby should go and stand directly in front of them. There were many ways to tone down a crowd. Danielle reflected she may have to start sitting in on more of Gabby's training sessions just to see what was going on.

"I have things to do," she whispered to Galvin.

"Me too," he whispered back.

Danielle patted his hand. He grasped it and brought it to his lips. She snatched her hand away, but smiled at him. Looking around, she noticed the audience settling down. Silence, finally, descended except for the sound of a can of soda sliding down a chute in a vending machine in the lunchroom.

Gabby began speaking. She was small, but she had a pair of pipes on her, Danielle had to admit. "I think you all know me. I'm Gabrielle Finney." There was a murmur of acknowledgement. Gabby flicked a remote switch and the room darkened. The projector beamed an image on the white screen. It was sales figures. Danielle let out a bored yawn. 'Gabrielle' was making the case that training was carrying sales financially. Again, Danielle wondered why Gabby had not come to her before she scheduled this meeting. She had better facts and figures.

Abruptly, Gabby switched to another screen. There was a murmur from the seated employees. Danielle turned to Galvin and raised her eyebrows. Confronting the employees of Inter-Tech was an image of a swaddled baby.

"That's me," Gabby said. "I was adopted when I was three months old."

She was starting to sound a little nasal. "My girlfriend didn't understand why I was freaked out about the idea of having children? It made me start thinking. I work with you all," Gabby went on, "you should know me. You should know the main reason I work here. It isn't sales."

People were visibly squirming with embarrassment. Low-grade chatter broke out again.

"Being adopted always made me feel at sea," Gabby said. She clicked the projector and another slide displayed. It was Gabby in a cap and gown. "So I worked really hard in school? Got accepted on scholarship to Smith." She clicked the projector again and the room beheld a picture of a young Gabby in cutoffs and a bikini top working a hula hoop at what was, apparently, an outdoor concert.

Danielle almost stood at this point. "Who authorized this?" she whispered furiously to Galvin who lifted his shoulders and shook his head.

The image on the screen now was of an exultant Gabby, flinging open Venetian doors to a scene definitely taken on the Mediterranean during Gabby's winter vacation in Milan.

Gabby said, "I'm taking steps to claim my birthright." She stepped forward dramatically. "Thirty years ago, my biological father donated to a sperm bank. He's in this room right now."

"Oh my God," Danielle said under her breath.

Gabby walked up and down the aisles. "I've had a good year at InterTech. I want my real father to know it." Gabby was at the back of the room, and all eyes were upon her. For a moment, the nascent sunlight outlined her curls in gold. She walked along the perimeter of the rows and stopped suddenly in front of the older silver haired woman who said, "Hello, Gabby."

Gabby smiled reflexively and let her gaze move past Gran Rain, past Sara, past her companion, and finally to rest upon the tallest man in the room.

"Dad," she said and spread her arms for Nick Montana as she stumbled across the feet of the three people precluding him in the row. There was a collective intake of breath. The CEO rose, which was an impressive sight, and awkwardly accepted the embrace of his newly found daughter who crushed her face into the area just below his solar plexus. He stooped and addressed his employees. "The sperm bank was my first wife's idea."

Sara said, "Gabby, you're stepping on my toes."

The room broke out into an uproar of chatter as employees twisted around in their chairs to talk to seatmates, brows furrowed, speaking quickly, interrupting each other. They kept looking over at Nick Montana, who seemed to be making introductions to people who already knew each other. Eventually, he held up a hand.

"Folks," he said, "this is a surprise to me, but a good one, and I'm glad to share it. Of course, I want to see the documentation supporting this unknown offspring, but that is neither here nor there." He chuckled. "We're in the process of introducing my family, so why stop here?" He gestured to the silver-haired woman seated at the end of the row. "I'd like you to meet Felicia Rain. My fiancée."

Gran Rain, half stood, waved, and sat back down. "My new granddaughter," Nick Montana said, gesturing to Sara, whom, Danielle noted, looked somewhat shell shocked. Sara and Gabby scrambled out of the crowded row, tumbling over

Gran Rain. They stood with their backs to the wall, observing Nick Montana as he introduced the final member of their row. Danielle was not prepared for what came next.

"And this," Nick Montana said gesturing to the pudgy young man in WalMart clothing, "is our lost sheep. Stand up, son."

The young man stood. His hair hung lankly from a crooked part. His face was pretty badly scarred. Yet Danielle knew she had seen him somewhere before. Nick Montana hugged the young man around the shoulders. "It's the prodigal son, returned to us. It's…"

"Oh my God," Danielle gasped audibly around the same time several others in the audience did as their memories aligned with the present.

"Jay Hicks," Nick Montana said, enveloping the young man in an embrace. He patted Jay's back a few times. "It's okay. It's cool."

Danielle looked at Galvin. His eyes were fixed on Sara, and she was staring at Jay. She put a hand on his arm. "Hey."

He turned to her, but didn't even attempt to smile. "Pretty crazy, huh?"

"Galvin," Danielle said. "Did you even think of asking her to go with you?"

All around them people were leaving, talking loudly about the strangely entertaining and totally inappropriate meeting they'd just witnessed. Finally, he said, "I thought about it."

Danielle took his hand. "Sara is a really talented trainer. She may not have the career opportunities in Anchorage she has here. But…" She shrugged and squeezed his hand before she released it. "She always impressed me as someone who would do a lot for love."

Galvin shook his head. "Looks like she's back with Jay."

Danielle stood up briskly. "I can find out about that."

She headed in Sara's direction. She looked back at Galvin. He was looking at Sara. Danielle quickened her steps.

45
SARA

Sara wanted Jay to get a haircut before he came to the office, but he refused. After a night on her couch, he was groggy and sore, and she barely got him up in time to take a shower and down a cup of coffee. He sat down to breakfast in the same ratty t-shirt and the same filthy tattered shorts he'd worn the night before.

"Something has to be done about those clothes," she said, over the rim of her cup. She dragged him to WalMart and bought him an eight dollar cotton polo shirt and a sixteen dollar pair of khakis. And underwear. She made him change in the Men's restroom. Someone had to take charge.

Apparently, her ex-girlfriend had the same idea. By the time Sara and Jay arrived at the office, Gabby was about to begin a presentation.

"Sick," Sara said. She whispered to Jay, "Let's take seats in the back." She saw Gran Rain in the side row and had to look twice. "What the...?"

Sara ran over to her grandmother and embraced her. Her grandmother smelled of peach, as usual. "You look so nice." She held Gran out at arm's length, by the shoulders. She looked up, startled, as Nick Montana loomed over them.

Sara stood up straight, smoothed the cuffs of her white linen blouse, before offering her hand.

"Mr. Montana." She knew who he was, a legend at InterTech. He invented a necessary little gadget, a wireless router that worked with WIFI, and InterTech was the result.

Gran Rain was perfectly composed. "Nick, this is my granddaughter, Sara. "

Nick shook her hand. "A pleasure," he said. "Although I believe we've met once or twice." He looked over her shoulder at Jay who was trailing behind. "And your friend?"

"Oh," Sara said, "that's a long…"

Jay interrupted her, putting out his hand to the older man. "Jay Hicks. I used to work here." Nick Montana lifted his eyebrows, and Sara could see a kind of synthesis occur.

"You're not the fellow who was shipwrecked?"

"Guilty," Jay said and gestured for the CEO to proceed to his seat. Jay sat down next to him.

"What's going on?" Sara asked Gran Rain.

"I could ask you the same thing." Gran gestured for Sara to take her seat next to Jay. Sara sat down, and surveyed the room. She saw Galvin and Danielle sitting together in the back row, turned to each other in conversation. She saw Galvin take Danielle's hand and kiss it. Sara turned around quickly and stared straight ahead.

Gran was sitting to her left in the aisle seat. Sara bent her head and whispered in Gran's ear, "How do you know Nick Montana?"

Gran shook her head as though Sara were a fly. "Later," she hissed.

Gabby began her presentation, but no one seemed to be paying much attention. Sara's mind was on other things. But she snapped to attention when Gabby's baby picture displayed, a solemn swaddled image with a head as bald as an egg. For an instant Sara flashed on her baby, what it could look like. "A sight better than that," she thought.

Sara heard Gabby say, "My girlfriend didn't understand why I was freaked out about the idea of having children," and didn't hear anything else. People knew she and Gabby had been together. Although Gabby didn't explicitly say why they were discussing children, Sara went cold all over. She snuck a look at Gran who was staring straight ahead smiling a little, clearly not following the presentation closely. Sara didn't dare look back at Galvin and Danielle, but for once she hoped they were too engrossed in each other to listen.

Sara stretched out her legs. No one listened to these stupid meetings anyway. She hoped it would be over soon. She had to pee. She noticed Gabby was moving around the room as Danielle taught them to do in training sessions. Then Gabby stopped at her row.

Afterward, Sara couldn't believe what she witnessed. Gabby, the exhibitionist, thought it was a good idea to reveal her biological father in a business meeting. And there was no doubt she was related to Nick Montana because he picked up where she left off, announcing this mysterious engagement to Gran Rain. Her Gran. Then he exposed Jay's identity. Sara was starting to feel a little dizzy by the time the meeting broke up. She staggered out of her seat and leaned up against the wall. Gabby followed her.

"What the hell, Gabs?" Sara hissed from the side of her mouth.

"You can laugh. Laugh all you want. I've been doing a lot of self-introspection."

Sara was not even listening. Instead, her gaze was drawn once again to Galvin. He stood with Danielle, but he was looking intently at Sara. Sara felt her face color, hoping he had not put two and two together based on Gabby's stupid presentation.

"You almost ratted me out," she said to Gabby, her eyes still on Galvin. But it was not Galvin who moved towards her. It was Danielle.

For a minute, Sara's palms felt clammy. Danielle was smart. Sara respected her. She wouldn't want her boss to think she was trying to steal her boyfriend back just because she was pregnant and wasn't sure who the father was.

Danielle crossed the room and walked right past Sara to embrace Gabby. "Great presentation," she said. "What a surprise." Gabby looked up at her through her eyelashes and Sara hoped her ex was not planning a play for the boss. Wasn't it enough that the founder of the company was her biological father?

Sara stepped forward. "Danielle, Jay and I were hoping you could spare a little time for us."

Danielle turned to Sara. "Of course." There was no inflection in her voice.

Jay stepped forward. "I'll go, Sara. You talk to your grandmother." He leaned forward to shake Gran's hand. "Congratulations." Gran nodded, folded her hand over his and then released it.

Sara took a step forward and then stepped back. "Okay," she said. "I'll join you in a little bit." She watched Danielle lead the way to her office down the far end of the purple corridor. Gabby and Nick disappeared probably to catch up on their entire lives and compare DNA.

Sara sank into the seat next to Gran. "Nick was a blind date," Gran said before Sara could begin. "I didn't want to go, but my friend set it up."

"What friend?" Sara asked.

"Jackie Moates," Gran said, gesturing to the reception desk.

"Jackie Moates? I didn't even know you were friends."

Gran tucked a long strand of hair behind her ear. "Well, we are. We taught English together in Japan. When you've lived as long as I have, suddenly you're fond of someone because you've known them forever."

"That doesn't sound like a strong endorsement," Sara said. She found Jackie to be kind of nosy.

"I introduced Jackie to her late husband. They were happy. She wanted to return the favor."

Sara asked, "How did she get her boss to go on a blind date?"

"Well," Gran said. "Nick is her brother."

"Oh." All Sara could think of to say was, "But she's so short."

"They have different fathers. She set it up, so Nick and I met in a restaurant, which she neglected to tell me was unfathomably expensive. I'm talking 'take-your-wife-there-for-your-twenty-fifth-anniversary expensive. I had three glasses of wine."

Sara whistled.

Gran lifted her shoulders. "What can I say? Nick swept me off my feet."

"I find that hard to believe, Gran," Sara said.

"It's true. Jackie wanted Nick to retire for years so she can run InterTech openly. She has an MBA. But twenty years ago, when the business started, you rarely heard of women CEOs. She worked behind the scenes and let Nick be the figurehead."

"Why?" So innocuous Jackie sitting at the reception desk really ran the company. Sara thought of all the times she was late, and Roosevelt the doorman covered for her. How she walked right past the real boss. It was amazing she hadn't been fired.

"She runs the company behind the scenes to save Nick's reputation. He lived in the Keys. Developed a cocaine habit. If their investors knew, they would have been ruined. There were gaps in the accounting, and so on. So Jackie stepped in with her marketing experience. Discreetly. She was never really his secretary. Everyone just assumed that. She was good at staying under the radar and knowing everything that was going on. Saved his ass."

" How can you be with someone who screwed up that badly? " Sara asked.

"Everyone screws up," Gran said. "You will too."

Sara looked away. She wondered if Gran knew more than she was saying.

Gran said, "I thought we could use a man in the family. Nick is funny. He has a good heart."

"I'm sure," Sara said, thinking she would never feel comfortable around Gran's intimidating fiancee. She missed Gramp. She would never forget the brown-eyed man with the mop of red hair who volunteered at her school to coach 'Math Wizards,' who taught her how to swim, who took the training wheels off her bike. He died of a heart attack, a decade later, swimming laps in the pool. Which reminded her...

"About Jay," Sara said. "It's not what you think."

Gran said, "I should hope not. What happened with

Gabby?"

"Oh," Sara said vaguely. "We didn't get on. Besides... "

Gran looked at her totally not getting it. "We're kind of like sisters now," Sara said.

Gran laughed. "Really, Sara, you need to expand your social life."

She gestured to the beige walls, the blue cubicles, and the banks of computers in an adjacent training room.

Sara found it hard to smile back. "I know," she said. "I know." She rose and hugged Gran in a half crouch. "If I don't get to the bathroom quickly... "

Waving as she walked off, trying not to sprint, she reflected that she probably went to the bathroom every hour these days. Yet now was not the time to spill the news of her pregnancy to Gran. She would wait and see what happened.

Sara pushed open the door to the Woman's bathroom and dashed into a stall, banging the door shut behind her. She barely managed to hoist her shirt and lower her pants and underwear before her bladder gave out. "Sounds like a damn waterfall," she thought.

Sitting there, the walls close, Sara thought about all the things she had to do before she left today. She would be on leave for a month, but she wanted to take some work home. And Danielle needed her address.

Sara wondered if she should stop by Galvin's office on her way out. The way he stared at her from across the room was intense.

Perhaps it was the memory of Galvin's eyes upon her that made her leap up from the toilet seat. As she did, she heard a splash. In slow motion, she reached, too late, and saw her cell phone swirl in the water and automatically flush down the drain.

Sara cursed. Then she looked around the bathroom stall. Turning, she lifted one foot and kicked the stall door out. She stopped by the sink to wash her hands. Then she strode into the purple hallway and pressed the Down button for the elevator, ignoring Jackie Moates who sat, implacable as ever, behind the teak and cedar reception desk.

Stepping inside the elevator, Sara gave her a little wave as the doors closed, and she was transported to the InterTech lobby and subsequently out the door and onto the street. She reached for her phone once or twice on her way to the garage.

She was on the road before she remembered Jay stranded at the InterTech office.

46
JAY

Jay followed Danielle back to her windowless office. Entering, he detected the faint scent of patchouli. Darlyn used to burn incense. He felt at home and homesick at the same time.

Danielle motioned to a chair, closed the door, and sat down behind her desk. She leaned forward and said, "Condolences on your cousin."

Jay nodded, expecting her to lean back. "Thank you."

But Danielle stayed in the same position with her body tilted forward. "But Jay? What the hell? I mean, thank God you're all right. But what the hell?"

He saw her touch the locket she had at her neck. She was wearing some kind of dress with flowy fabric. Her face was tinged with red, a roseola Jay recognized from spending time with Ruby. His stomach muscles clenched a little, thinking of Ruby. He fingered the amulet in his pocket. He guessed whatever he said to Danielle he would have to repeat over and over to interested parties, to law enforcement, to lawyers. In all of these accounts, he would leave out his trafficking in drugs. Jay realized this omission could hamper the search for Truly. Had one of his former customers caught up with his cousin? He wanted to tell the truth to someone, especially if that someone was not the police, the Coast Guard, or even the FBI who likely suspected him of espionage. Even murder.

He wanted to tell the truth to Danielle. *Snap out of it*, he told himself. He sat up and leaned forward. He smiled, usually a deal breaker with attractive women like Danielle. She remained expressionless.

"Look, I'm just here to see about getting my old job back. I came to collect a few of my belongings. You're assuming I want to talk to you about what happened. I don't."

Danielle stood. "Then I guess we're through here."

Jay remained seated. "A lot of it is fuzzy. Truly, my cousin, inherited the boat from the old man, his father. He wanted to spread his father's ashes. You have to go three miles offshore to do it legally."

Danielle, sat down back down. Slowly.

"We hit a squall. I washed overboard. I had a life vest on, and I buoyed myself by creating a float out of my jeans. I washed up in the Keys near Hens and Chickens. That's a reef. A guy named Captain Tom saved my life. God, do I owe him."

Jay sat back and folded his hands over his stomach. He waited for Danielle to say something. There was a battery-operated clock somewhere in the office, and the ticking was loud.

"How horrible. What was Truly doing while you were steering through a squall?"

Jay shifted in his seat. The chair arm fell to the floor. "Oh sorry," he said. He picked it up and placed it on Danielle's desk. She continued to look at him, waiting for an answer.

"Truly was out of it," he said. "He fell asleep right after we took off from Fort Canaveral. I remember he lay down on the port side and rolled onto the floor during the height of the storm."

"Was he still alive?" Danielle asked.

Jay nodded. "He must have been. Why not?"

"He probably drowned, though."

Jay nodded again, his eyes filling with tears.

Danielle waited a moment and shoved a green box of tissues towards him. Jay shook his head and wiped his eyes on his hand.

"I'm sorry to be so blunt," she said. "But you were an InterTech employee. I have to consider the fallout."

Jay nodded; his eyes blinded by tears.

"And I have to tell you, you can spin to the police whatever you want, but parts of your story do not ring true to me."

Jay sniffed, tried to lean back, but the lack of a chair arm just made him roll a little.

"What's not true?" Jay meant it as a challenge, but his words were high pitched. Tears still leaked from his eyes.

Danielle smiled at him. "It just strikes me that you, and your cousin, maybe had different goals in mind. Did you know he received death threats prior to your trip?"

"No," Jay said.

"It was in all the papers. Also, police uncovered remnants of a lot of marijuana in a Porta Potty. Next to your house. Know anything about that?"

Jay said nothing.

Danielle finally leaned back and laced her fingers over her stomach. She hummed a little. "The really damning thing," she said, "is that you hung out in the Keys for six weeks. Without contacting anyone. How do you explain that?"

Jay cleared his throat. The clock ticked.

Danielle tried to help out. "You gave the pot to your cousin. Or she took it."

"No!" Jay said. "I mean…she was supposed to get rid of it. But I, I… damn." He hadn't stuttered since fifth grade. He took a deep breath.

"I let her take it. I didn't want Truly getting mixed up in anything."

"How did you plan on explaining that to him?"

"I was going to talk to him once we set out to sea. Scattered the old man's ashes. I thought that would be a good time. Truly, he would have forgiven me. Truly led this blame free life." He paused. "Except for the affair."

Danielle sighed. "Jay, I have to tell you, it sounds as though you and Truly had an altercation over the drugs. The Gold. Worth a few million bucks."

Jay squinted. "Eight million."

"People kill for a lot less."

"No! I didn't kill him! I didn't come home because- "

Danielle lifted an eyebrow waiting. The room was cool, dim, fragrant.

"I fell off the wagon," Jay said. "I'm in Alcoholics Anonymous. I'd been sober for almost a year. But when Captain Tom rescued me, he poured bourbon down my throat."

"What about your sponsor?" Danielle asked.

"I didn't have my cell," Jay said. Danielle knew about sponsors?

He took a chance.

"I'd like to go get my white chip. Know of any meetings around here?"

"Yes," Danielle said. "I do. But then you have to promise me we'll go to the police."

"The drugs are gone," Jay said. "Truly is gone, the boat is gone. I'll report for duty. But I'm not going to sully his name."

"Well," said Danielle, "I guess I'm going to have to accept what I cannot change."

Jay nodded, shifted, and almost fell off the chair again. He straightened up and took a deep breath. "You know, I feel better than I have in a long time. How did you get so smart?"

Danielle smiled. "Call it female intuition."

47
GALVIN

The ponies were back.

Galvin considered trying to locate Sara. It would make a smooth opening, a segue to previous conversations. Look! he'd say. There they are. Like in the old days. Or perhaps Galvin would just look pathetic.

He sat there tapping his chin, staring at the gamboling colts. Danielle had just broken up with him, but he couldn't get Sara off his mind. It wasn't that he didn't care about Danielle. Her decision was disappointing, but it was understandable for her to want her freedom when he was thousands of miles away. He was far from crushed. This set him apart from Sara who looked so unhappy lately. He found himself searching for words to make her smile. The ponies had come to mind. Engrossed in his own thoughts, he didn't hear the tap on his door. It wasn't until Gabby cleared her throat that Galvin turned around.

He felt himself recoil a little when he saw who it was. Galvin, who took a few psychology courses in college, pegged Gabby as a narcissist and the spectacle he'd witnessed today did nothing to change his opinion.

"What is it?" he asked, swiveling his office chair to face her.

"Galvin?" Gabby sat down and smoothed her skirt. "I've been wanting to talk to you."

"Really," Galvin said. "How can I help you?"

Gabby said, "It's kind of personal."

Galvin exhaled. "Then," he said, "I advise you to contact human resources."

Gabby's mouth tightened. "Meaning you are not human? Or a resource?"

Galvin's head started to pound. This blonde Kewpie doll, this shallow exhibitionist who made her workplace a soap opera playground... "Look," he said. "I'm not interested in drama."

Gabby crossed her legs. "What happened this morning? Was far from drama. It was research."

Galvin pulled his chair up to his desk. "Gabby..."

She cut him off. "How would you feel if the parents you grew up with lied to you about who your father was?"

"If they provided a good home for you, I'd say they desperately wanted a child."

Gabby's lower lip protruded the tiniest bit. "They shoulda told me."

"Yes," Galvin agreed. He drummed his fingers on his desk. "But this can't be what you want to discuss."

"I'm leading up to it." She paused. "It's about Sara."

Galvin finally met her gaze. "What about Sara." He was damned if he wanted a meeting of the minds between all of Sara's exes. Hell, why didn't they just get Jay in here, too?

For a minute Gabby looked as though she would burst. "I shouldn't tell you."

"Then don't," Galvin said. "Now if you'll excuse me... "

"She's pregnant," Gabby said.

Galvin stared at her. He opened his mouth, but no words came.

Gabby prattled on. "That's why we broke up. After what happened to me? I couldn't be with someone who was pregnant. And as irresponsible as Sara."

Galvin just looked at her.

Gabby fingered one of her curls, twisting it in an absent way. "She wouldn't say what she wanted to do. Have the baby? Not have the baby? You know Sara."

"Yes," Galvin said.

"I don't think she even knows who the father is," Gabby said.

Galvin had trouble getting his words out. In fact, he felt as though he were running a fever. "Did she say that?"

"No, but I figured it out. I could not stand by and see a child brought into this world not knowing who her real parents were."

"I see," Galvin said.

"Plus, do I look ready to help raise a child?"

Galvin coughed into his fist. "No."

Gabby stood up, brushing the back of her skirt.. "Well, there you are. Sara told me you're crazy about kids. Which I am not. I have five half brothers and sisters from five different sperm donors. Absolute bedlam growing up. And none of us look alike."

She walked to the door. "I have to say, though. Even if you're not the real dad, you would be a good one. Especially since Jay is not exactly Mr. Reliable right now?"

She got to the threshold. "Gabby," Galvin said. "Your dad? He raised you. How does he feel about Nick?"

Gabby turned, and her face softened a little. "My real dad is great. He encouraged me to find the sperm donor. I mean... Nick."

"Is that why you did it?"

Gabby smiled. "It drove my mom crazy."

She waited a moment, and when he did not speak, she said, "You see? It worked out. I guess I hit the jackpot." She waggled her fingers. "See you."

He nodded, and hoped not. When he was sure she was gone, he got up, and walked to Danielle's office. Her door was closed. He walked into the hall, to the window overlooking the parking lot that bordered the pasture. The Miata was gone. It was not like her to leave this early.

He didn't know what to do. Then he remembered a book he read many years ago. It wasn't a self-help book, it was more like philosophy, authored by a priest, a really intelligent guy. He said that when confronted with bewildering choices it was best to exist in the moment. Live with uncertainty and eventually a path opens.

Galvin wondered if that was true. The news that Sara was pregnant made him want to run to her doorstep, to run to her side. For the first time in his life, Galvin had a sense of destiny, of unconditional love. Screw paths.

He dug his cell out of his pocket. She was still on his Contact list. He listened to the ringing and eventually Sara's voicemail switched on. She never bothered to personalize it, so it was one of those robotic digital voices. Please leave a message.

"Sara," Galvin said. "Gabby..." He broke off, trying to get a grip on what he should say. "This is Galvin. Please call me back. Please. Thanks."

He sat there looking at the phone he held in his hand. He willed it to ring. Swallowing, he noticed his throat was a little sore.

48
LINK- A MONTH LATER

Link opened the door to the Sixth Street Restaurant, which was cool, dark, and noisy. On his left was a crowded bar, men and women in work clothes drinking, laughing, turning to meet friends with waves and shouts of camaraderie. On his right the restaurant looked empty, but it was still happy hour. "I'm meeting someone," he told the waitress who gave him the kind of evasive look someone gives when they are trying hard not to look at all. She was older with a towering hairdo, and she reminded him a little of Darlyn. She grabbed a couple of menus and guided him to a booth by a window.

"Thanks," he said and looked away. His voice was different, deeper as though he'd finally passed puberty. It was only a week since he was released, yet it seemed strange to be out of the hospital. There were more skin grafts in his future; eventually, the doctors promised, he would look fairly normal and lose some of the melted facial features of a severe burn victim. They couldn't guarantee he would ever get his eyelashes, eyebrows, or hair back. He was still moving to Hawaii, though. He'd used his time in the hospital to apply to a college in Honolulu. He received his letter of acceptance yesterday.

He looked out the window past the parking lot and wrought iron street lamps to the sculpted hedges and sodded expanse of green that made up the park. It butted the city hall of Lake Ann, which, according to gossip, was erected next to the grave of a beloved neighborhood horse who drank beer at the local bar.

It was 6:00, quitting time, a time of families and friends coming together. In the park, fathers pitched footballs to daughters. Teenagers strolled hand-in-hand. An older couple threw a few coins in a fountain. Link saw Matt park in front of the bike stand, get out of a police car, and walk across the street.

He was wearing street clothes, which Link had not seen him in very often. The past three weeks in the hospital, they both wore pajamas. And bandages. Matt was thinner, but he looked good in faded jeans and an open necked long sleeved polo shirt. His face was not as damaged as Link's, but Link knew Matt's arms were a lot worse where the flaming beam had fallen on him. As Matt drew closer, Link saw scar tissue across his friend's forehead and the bridge of his nose. He remembered the first time he met Matt three months ago. As always, some lines from a Shakespearian sonnet came to him:

> *Like as the waves make towards the pebbled shore,*
> *So do our minutes hasten to their end;*
> *Each changing place with that which goes before.*

Link stood when he heard the door hiss open and, keeping his face averted, waved. Matt waved back and strode to the booth. Still standing, Link put out his arms tentatively. They were both recovering from second and third degree burns, and it was difficult to determine how much a hug would hurt. They compromised by touching each other's elbows. Then they quickly slid into opposite sides of the booth.

"You look good," Link said.

"Yeah, well. "Matt hesitated. "Wish I could say the same, bro."

It hurt for Link to smile. "The doctor says I could get

my hair back. Or some of it. We'll just have to wait and see."

Tentatively, Matt reached over his side of the booth and covered Link's hand with his own bandaged one. "What were we thinking? Running into a burning building."

"We've discussed this. We were really high for one thing," Link said, trying not to laugh.

Matt leaned forward, "When you ran into that house? I never told you this. I couldn't not follow you. I don't know what that was about."

"Me neither." Link shrugged, but his heart began beating rapidly. Why was Matt telling him this? "Listen when the waitress shows up, order for me. Water and hamburger, medium rare."

Matt shook his head.

Link leaned in. "I don't like people looking at me, man."

Matt snorted. "Your face is messed up. But that fire didn't do nothing to your... build, if I may state so bold."

Link withdrew his hand. "Here she comes." His attention returned to the window. The father was walking off with his daughter, football in hand, both of them talking animatedly. He thought of his future students, how he would someday teach them to appreciate Shakespeare, Shelley, and Plath. For some reason, he missed the usual spark of excitement at that thought.

He heard Matt give their orders to the waitress. When he was sure she was gone, he turned back. "I'm leaving in a few weeks."

Matt avoided his eyes, the same way Link avoided the waitress. "I thought about what you said."

Link sighed. "You don't even have to tell me, man. I can see the writing on the wall."

He pretended to watch the Magic game on the overhead TV. He kept one eye on Matt.

Matt leaned forward, and his words came like bullets. "Look. The nights we were together in the hospital? Best of my life." He laughed shortly. "If you don't count the pain."

An image of Matt's face as Link slipped into his narrow hospital bed surfaced. The ward had been quiet with that weird odor of disinfectant. He almost laughed. Would his memories of Matt forever be triggered by the smell of Pine Sol? Link turned his gaze back to Matt. "But not good enough, right?" His tone was hard, and he looked away. He got through his recovery solely by seeing and thinking about Matt every minute of the day. His life would always be like that.

"I'm not like you," Matt said. "I want us to be together. Don't think there's anything I want more. But I can't do it. I can't. No one has any idea. I'm a police officer; I'm a son; I'm a brother; I'm…" he stopped suddenly and gave Link a stricken look.

"What," Link said, although he knew.

"I'm going to go ahead and marry Beverly Cleary. The wedding is this winter."

This was the worst outcome Link could imagine, but he maintained his composure.

"That's good. Congratulations."

The night he and Matt almost died the firemen said the building was too dangerous to enter. He thought of Officer Cleary, ignoring the confident men in hazmat, demanding their gear, entering that inferno, dragging Matt from the flames first and then going back for Link. How that woman found the strength to move him he would never understand. He supposed it had something to do with adrenalin. The police officer suffered some torn ligaments, but nothing serious. He was grateful to Officer Cleary. His own Viola.

He was sorry Darlyn was dead. Link thought her husband was a dog, sleeping with the maid. Here Darlyn was, organizing searches for that cheater, praying up a storm. He heard on the local news that the little girl, Ruby, survived the fire. While he was in the hospital, Darlyn's cousin, the one who was shipwrecked, came to ask him about her. He brought his bossy girlfriend with him, too. Link told him as far as he knew one of the neighbors was watching her. "Ruby called her Bef," he told the cousin who looked pretty rough. Well, they all did.

He came back to the present, to the dark cool booth and the raucous shouts from the bar. He looked Matt in the eye and said, "I'm happy for you, man. She's a good woman."

Matt grimaced. "She saved my life. I owe her."

Link could think of few successful relationships that began with the phrase, I owe her. He kept that insight to himself. The waitress came with their food, shoving the steaming platters across the booth. "You doing okay for drinks?" she asked and left without waiting for their answers.

Link shrugged. "I guess I make her nervous." He picked up his burger and took a bite. It was practically raw, cold in the middle. He dropped it back onto his plate.

"What about you, bro?" Matt asked, grabbing a chicken wing and dunking it in a plastic basin of blue cheese. "Excited about starting school?"

Link chewed for a minute. "I am. But I'm thinking of changing my major."

Matt put down his chicken wing. It was gnawed clear to the gristle. "Aw, bro? You a whiz at poetry. I never knew anyone who could say poetry like you do. Do some right now."

"I met a traveler from an antique land." Link grimaced, picked up his burger, looked at it, and put it down on his plate again.

"Bro, what're you thinking, changing your major? You told me all about teaching poems under a palm tree. Changing to what?"

"I don't know," Link said. "Maybe an Emergency Medical Technician? A paramedic?"

Matt shrugged. "Probably less school than an Education degree. You sure?"

"No," Link said and then wondered if that was true. He couldn't explain to Matt that the fire changed him.

He saw Matt watching him and guessed he'd have to say what he planned, get it out of the way. But Matt beat him to it.

"I love you, bro."

Tentatively their hands slid under the surface of the booth, as they laced fingers as well as they could. Link's throat was already aching with missing Matt, so he tried to memorize the shape and weight of his lover's grasp. It was all he had. It could be all he'd ever have.

He said, "I love you too, man." And then he let go, pushed back his plate, threw a bill on the table, stood, and walked out of the restaurant. He thought he heard Matt call his name. He pushed through the double doors and walked to his car, his head high, his damaged face out there for all to see. He got in his car, shut the door, locked it, and bowed his head on the wheel. As always, he took refuge in Shakespeare, whispering to himself:

And whether we shall meet again I know not.
Therefore our everlasting farewell take:

For ever, and for ever, farewell,
If we do meet again, why, we shall smile;
If not, why then, this parting was well made.

He sat up, took the key out of his pocket and put it in the ignition. He drove. He wasn't crying. He really had changed.

49

BEV- A MONTH LATER

Bev woke up, sat up in bed, and opened her eyes. Lately, she was experiencing flashes of light and wiggly lines in her vision.

It was still dark outside. A glance to her left told her Ruby was sleeping, on her side, her mouth open, knees tucked up. Bev checked her diaper for dampness, then swung her legs over the side of her bed and slipped her feet into her slippers. Noiselessly, she opened the night table drawer. She took out a pale blue blanket and wrapped Ruby in it. As she turned to her closet, she almost tripped over Ruby's pink backpack. She shoved it to the side and selected her signature white polo shirt and white shorts from the hangers. Colors were still too much trouble to bother with.

Creeping into the bathroom with the clothes she turned on the light and regarded her reflection. It was strange to see herself in the mirror after her sight was partially restored. She assumed she would still look like she did when she was seventeen. Instead, a grown woman on the other side of youth confronted her. She grew to like her looks, the sharp cheekbones and dark eyes, the slender body.

When she was a girl, Bev was interested in body building. She wanted to own weights and use them. But it was just unheard of for a girl to do that. So, she said she wanted to be a ballerina. She used to spend hours in the community room, bending and stretching to a scratchy 45 rpm of Tchaikovsky's

Nutcracker. How could she have known at six or seven that it was acceptable for her to develop agility not strength?

Quickly, she combed her hair, brushed her teeth, slipped her Braille watch on her wrist and dressed. She tiptoed down the stairs to the kitchen. Ruby's high chair sat in the corner. Bev ran her hand over the tray and turned away to make the coffee. At 4:40, Bev poured two cups of black coffee and set them on the small kitchen table. A minute later, she heard a key turn in her front door. She turned her head towards the sound.

A door opened and closed and then she heard footsteps. A man's voice said, "Bev?" and she stood.

"In here," she said. She switched on the stove light, and the man emerged from the foyer. His hair was clipped short, and there were red angry scars on his face.

"Hello Bev," he said. "The key was under the mat like you said. Here." He dropped it on the table. "I didn't wake her, did I?"

"Hello, Jay," Bev said. "I doubt it. Won't you have some coffee?"

Jay hesitated, but he sat down opposite Bev and folded his hands on the table.

"How're you holding up?" he asked.

"Okay, I guess," Bev said. She took a sip of her coffee, which was scalding hot. She put it down, the cup rattling on the bare table.

Jay blew on his cup, and the steam roiled a little. "I went down to the old house."

"Ashes, isn't it?" Bev said.

"Yep. I'm going to sell the lot, of course," Jay said.

Bev managed a smile. "Thank you." She would have

found it unendurable to live down the street from Jay's family.

Jay turned the cup around and around. "It's okay. Danielle wants to buy a bigger house."

Bev knew all about Danielle. Jenny Zinn found it easy to pry for information when she called under pretense as a census taker. The rest Bev uncovered through search engines. She knew about Danielle's alcoholism, and she had planned to use it against her. Meanwhile, Jay was all over the news for weeks, but Danielle quickly took charge of his media exposure and all his contacts. Because of her public relations ability, she managed to portray Jay as a bereaved relative, and a lost soul suffering from PTSD. He was never charged in connection with Truly's disappearance, and staring at him now across her kitchen table, Bev could believe he was as guileless as he appeared to be.

"Truly and I used to sit here," she said softly. "And drink coffee."

Jay drank some coffee. He fumbled in his back pocket for his phone, and turned off the ringer. Maybe he expected Danielle to check up on him.

"Don't worry," Bev said. "She won't be up for hours."

"I guess this is where we talk," Jay said.

Bev nodded. "What went wrong? What went so wrong that Truly and the boat just vanished into thin air?"

Jay was silent.

"I was supposed to be with Truly," Bev said. "Me and Ruby. We were going to be together. A fresh start."

Jay said, "You sure about that?"

Bev stared at him. His face was blurry in the half light.

"Because the way I figure it?" Jay gestured towards himself. "He was pretty miserable. Truly just wanted a fresh start.

Period."

Bev said, "What are you talking about?"

"Look," Jay said. "If it's any consolation I believe Truly would want you to have Ruby. Because Darlyn, let's face it, wasn't much of a mother." He hesitated. "But maybe…maybe he didn't mean to come back."

The floaters, little squiggly lines in her vision, were back. "You're wrong about that," she said.

"No, I'm not," Jay said. "He told me. In so many words. He wanted to get away."

Bev looked down and took long, slow, deep breaths. Her fists clenched and unclenched. Jay didn't know what he was talking about. She had to keep her cool. When she looked up, she said, "Will you change your mind about Ruby? About visitation?"

Jay grimaced. "We hashed this out with the mediator. Danielle agrees it's too confusing for Ruby to continue to see you. Especially since…" he trailed off.

Bev wanted to bite her nails, something she hadn't done since childhood. "I beg you to reconsider."

Jay shook his head.

"I'd still like to know what happened to Truly," Bev said. Her voice shook a little.

"Who knows?" Jay's mouth drew down. "He fell asleep on the boat. I fell off the boat."

"All right." Bev straightened up. If he didn't know about Truly's plan to abandon the boat, likely there was no foul play. She was deeply disconcerted to learn that Truly may have had another agenda. Especially since she could get in trouble if anyone ever found out she was the one leaving the death threats.

She began talking about Ruby's schedule, her likes and dislikes. Surely, Jay knew some of this information, but talking kept her from breaking down. As she talked, she felt as though she were underwater, all of her gestures exaggerated, slow, weighted down. She thought, "I can get through this step by step. If I try to jump ahead, I'm in trouble."

It was a month since Danielle and Jay hired a lawyer to mediate for permanent custody of Ruby. Jay was the child's only living relative, and if what Truly told her was correct, Jay was actually Ruby's half-brother. Still, Bev was inclined to fight it. She had advance warning of their intentions thanks to the uncanny resourcefulness of Jenny Zinn. Bev knew Truly wanted her to rear Ruby. Jay was young and not the most stable guy around. Who the hell was this Danielle anyway?

Then Bev teleconferenced with Dr. Dojo on what she thought was a routine checkup. Dr. Dojo's soulful face filled the screen, because he always stood too close to the camera. "Yes, yes, the operation was a success. Very successful. However, I have news. Other news."

It was the expression on his face that put Bev on the alert.

Dr. Dojo said, "I sent some extracted eye fluid and tissue to a lab. Just to be safe."

"What are you talking about?" Bev said.

Dr. Dojo took a deep breath. "As I suspected, something irregular."

"What?"

"Ocular cancer. Sorry, so sorry, Bev."

Remembering that moment, Bev realized she'd been talking, and now she wasn't. Jay was trying not to look at her. The silence in the kitchen pressed in on her.

"I appreciate you deciding not to fight for custody," he said.

She called him with the news she was withdrawing from the custody mediation. That he and Danielle could drop Ruby into whatever readymade family they'd hastily concocted. Bev thought she'd have a few days, maybe even a few weeks more with Ruby. But Jay and Danielle insisted on retrieving the child within twenty-four hours.

"Well," Bev said, her voice thickening a little. "Maybe I could have been a good mother with bad vision. But I do have cancer. So, if that's your version of gratitude, the pleasure was all mine." The words came out sharper than she'd intended.

Jay said, "Danielle and I would like to compensate you for taking care of Ruby." He pulled out his wallet and withdrew a folded check and pushed it across the table to her. Bev pushed it back. Hard.

"I'm not being noble," she said. "And I truly don't need this."

Jay nodded and picked up the folded slip of paper and returned it to his wallet. "I thought you might say that." He stood up. "We've got to get going."

The 'we' stung a little. Now that the moment was upon her, Bev realized she had not decided whether to watch Jay carry Ruby off or to look away.

"Follow me," she said to Jay and switched on the hall light. She thought of how many times she had mounted these stairs with Ruby in her arms. She felt actual pain in her chest as though her heart was finding it hard to continue to function.

The nightlight was on in her bedroom, and she pointed to the bundle curled up in the middle of her big bed, a bed where she'd lain with the girl's father. Well, this was her punishment now.

Jay scooped Ruby up, bent and retrieved the pink backpack without Bev even pointing it out. Then he hurried from the room.

"Wait," Bev said too loudly.

Ruby opened one eye. She stretched out one small hand. "Bef." Then the hand dropped and the eye closed. Bev sprang forward and kissed the child's forehead, stroked her curls. Then Jay walked quickly down the stairs. Bev stood at the top, her eyes watering so much she could barely see Jay carry off the small figure. The small dark head bobbed against his shoulder. Then he opened the door and shut it behind him.

"Ruby," she said and sank to the floor at the top of the stairs. She put her face in her hands and wished with every fiber of her being she had never gone to that neighborhood party, and she never met Truly Ravija.

50
DANIELLE - A MONTH LATER

Danielle worked at her desk in the deserted InterTech office. Some type of virus or flu had decimated the entire floor. Galvin was the first to succumb, then several of the trainers. The janitors were next. So in addition to the loss of personnel, garbage was piling up. One day Danielle opened the door of the refrigerator in the break room and almost threw up.

The next day she called the health department, and it fell to Danielle to shut everything down, arrange for a deep cleaning of the office, and wait two weeks for an inspection in order to reopen. Now it was just her and Jackie Moates walking the purple carpet. Nick Montana decamped to his fiancée's house, and the rumor was he was finally turning his title over to his half-sister.

It was a wonder Danielle found time to help Jay with his troubles, but with the training schedule suspended, she managed. Danielle would never presume to manage Galvin's affairs with the same authority, although to be fair, she was carrying his child without his knowledge or permission. But Jay was a blank slate; he was unformed clay. Danielle knew she could make a man out of him. Although AA frowned on relationships formed in haste, Danielle with her special gifts, knew the difference between enabling and fate.

It started when Sara embarked on her leave of absence without a word of notice, effectively deserting Jay. Danielle could have driven Jay to a hostel or called her own sponsor to find some kind of temporary shelter. But he was a former Inter-Tech employee who survived a horrendous tragedy only to find his cousins dead, and his house burned to the ground. Surely, Danielle could not pawn him off to strangers. So, after their first AA meeting together, she invited him into her home. And her bed.

They were a couple. It was as simple and as inevitable as that. And in order to make it work, Danielle had to do the hard work. She went with Jay to the police, and waited as he endured hours of questioning. The death threats Truly received on social media were troubling, but the police could not link them directly to Jay. Instead, thanks to Danielle's prodding, the men's military history was reviewed, and the police concluded it was unlikely Jay would dispatch the man who saved his life. Jay's story had some holes in it, but Lake Ann's PD budget was not exactly the stuff in-depth criminal investigations were made of.

There still remained the troubling question of Jay's toddler cousin Ruby who apparently was residing with her former babysitter down the block from the ashes of Jay's home. By this time the InterTech office shut down because of the flu epidemic. Danielle promptly hired Jay back as an IT consultant, even if he did have to work at home. She also hired a lawyer and filed a custody suit for mediation in order to return Ruby immediately to her only living relative.

The babysitter, Bev, actually hired a lawyer to fight for custody of the child. She claimed it was what Truly Ravija would have wanted. The woman clearly had her nerve in Danielle's opinion, especially when Bev's vision problems emerged as a result of a deposition she had to sit for. And then, Danielle's lawyer picked up on the report with child services about Bev's neglect to safely secure her swimming pool, leading to the incident where Ruby was removed from her home. The day Bev called Jay to tell him she was giving up her custody suit, Danielle had turned up the ten of cups on her Tarot deck. The card illustration displayed a happy family standing under a rainbow.

Now Danielle worked on the piled-up paperwork at her deck, worrying, because Jay had gone to pick Ruby up that morning. Would Ruby remember her cousin? Would she cry for Bev? How would she take to Danielle?

Her phone buzzed. She punched the red button and picked up. It was probably another employee wondering when he could come back to work. But it wasn't. Instead, Jackie Moates came on the line and said Galvin was in the foyer. He wanted to speak to her.

"Well, send him back," Danielle said. "Please." Jackie was strict about monitoring comings and goings until the health department gave InterTech the all clear. Still, everyone knew Galvin was leaving in a few days for Alaska. Clearly, he was tying up some loose ends.

She opened her desk drawer and removed a red face mask and fastened the straps behind her ears. In a few minutes, Galvin appeared at her door, dressed more casually than she had ever seen him in khakis, a pair of black Nikes, and a navy polo shirt, open at the collar. He was wearing a face mask, but Danielle thought she could detect a beard under the cloth barrier. He was thinner, of course, and pale as paper. She stood when she saw him.

"I would hug you," she said, "except physical contact is not a good idea right now."

Danielle couldn't tell if Galvin smiled or not, but she thought he did. "I'd like to hug you too," he said. "You look fantastic." He walked into her office and sat down in the chair facing her desk, avoiding putting any weight on the loose arm. "And healthy. Lucky you."

Seeing the deliberation with which he sat made Galvin very real to Danielle. For weeks, she thought of him as an abstraction, as a means to an end. Now, seeing him again in person, seeing the way he pursed his lips before speaking, a characteristic he may well pass down to a child, she suddenly realized how wrong she was. How could she think of having Galvin's baby without informing him of the fact? They didn't have to get married or anything. But he could be a part of the child's life.

"I have something to tell you," she and Galvin said at the same time. They both laughed and Galvin threw up his hands.

"You first," Galvin said.

Danielle shook her head. "No, no. You go." She clasped her hands and leaned in on her desk. This was a technique that worked to get interviewees talking.

"All right." Galvin took a deep breath. "I'm telling you this in strictest confidence. It's personal, not business."

Danielle had a sudden premonition. She touched the locket at her throat. "What is it?"

"Sara is pregnant." Galvin put his elbow on the loose arm chair, and it clattered to the floor. Danielle barely noticed.

"She's…"

"Yes," Galvin said, struggling with the chair arm. He dropped it abruptly, and it landed with a thud on the purple carpet. "Probably between two and three months." He hesitated. "Depending on who the father is."

"You don't know?"

"I don't know anything. I heard about this through the grapevine."

"Gabby," Danielle said and gave a short laugh.

"Do you think it's true?" Galvin asked. "I tried calling Sara, but her cell goes straight to voicemail. I went by her house, but it looks empty."

"That's right," Danielle said. "She was supposed to give me her new address."

"Did she?" Galvin asked.

Danielle shook her head.

"So, there you are," Galvin said. "She doesn't answer her phone, and she moved with no forwarding address."

It dawned on Danielle whose baby Sara would carry if it was not Galvin's.

"Aren't you supposed to be in Alaska?" she asked.

"I leave tomorrow." Galvin said. "Danielle, what should I do?"

"Let me ask you something," Danielle said. "Suppose you could get hold of Sara? Suppose she is pregnant? Suppose she tells you the baby's not yours?"

Galvin leaned back in his seat and laced his hands over his chest. "Yes?"

"Would it matter to you?"

Galvin waved a hand in the air. "I've asked myself that. When I was sick with the flu, I was constantly trying to find a cool spot on the bed. Sara is a cool spot in my life. Without her, I'm uncomfortable. Considering that, would it bother me if the child grew up resembling another man, a constant reminder of his origin? "Galvin rocked a little in his seat. "I thought of my own dad, how I favor him in appearance. Would it have bothered me if we didn't look alike?"

Danielle listened, barely breathing, her heart pounding.

"And I had to tell myself honestly. That no, I wouldn't mind. At all."

"You wouldn't mind?" Danielle asked.

Galvin leaned forward clasping his hands. "What made my dad so great wasn't how he looked. What made him great were the things we did together. The way he listened to me. How he took care of me. Good memories."

"He loved you," Danielle said.

Galvin nodded. "Love can overcome a lot."

"But," Danielle continued, "what if Sara's baby has a different biological father than you? It's great you are good with that. Would you want him to know?"

"I thought about that too," Galvin said. "Here's the thing. I really don't care how this baby got started. But I am willing, no, eager, to be a dad. If Sara will have me as her husband, then that, too. But a dad, regardless. And I see no need to find out who his biological father is. If there ever is a need to find out, I would rather deal with it then. There's a line from Macbeth I remember reading in high school. 'Fate will unwind as it must.' That's how I feel about it."

"What if," Danielle asked, "you found out in high school or in college your dad was not genetically related to you."

"I wouldn't care," Galvin said. "I think. I mean, who knows. But it wouldn't change much."

Danielle allowed herself a tiny smile. "That good a dad, eh?"

Galvin didn't smile back, but he looked her in the eye.

"That good."

Danielle straightened her chair and rearranged some paperwork on her desk. "I wish I could help. The only thing I can suggest is try Sara's Grandma Rain. I bet she knows where Sara is."

Galvin sat up. "That's a great idea. Got her address?"

Ordinarily, Danielle wouldn't give out personal information, but she was concerned for Sara's safety. True, she was on leave, but it was odd that Galvin couldn't reach her. Danielle rose and walked over to the file cabinet, opened it, and began rummaging around.

"Didn't you say you had something to tell me?" Galvin asked.

"Did I?" Danielle laughed, and then stopped abruptly. "I forgot what it was."

Her face reddened as she perused the manilla file folders. She remembered Denny teasing her about her tendency to blush when she was lying. Perhaps the red face mask camouflaged her complexion. She felt a pulse in her stomach, a flutter, as though something inside were asserting itself. But she plowed on, ignoring it. "Here it is," she said, plucking out a file. She handed it to Galvin who turned his attention to its contents. She took a deep breath. Her heart skidded to a slow and steady cadence.

51
GALVIN - A MONTH LATER

Galvin took a picture of Gran Rain's address with his phone and trotted across the parking lot to his car. He cast a look of regret at Danielle's Miata before climbing into his sensible sedan and starting the engine. "This is a better car for a family," he thought. Provided I can find Sara in time. His stomach cramped thinking about boarding the Air Alaska plane without seeing Sara again.

He set the GPS to Gran Rain's house. It started to rain, and steam rose from the asphalt parking lot. Follow the guided route. He signaled left and pulled into the stream of traffic. He turned on the radio and listened to the news. The flu bug was becoming more widespread as businesses and restaurants were closing down. He would have to wear a mask during the nine-hour flight tomorrow. However, Alaska seemed pretty remote from the flu circulating in the city of Lake Ann. It was safer there.

The roads were wet and largely deserted as Galvin drove to Gran Rain's house She lived in an old-fashioned Florida suburb six miles from the interstate. In less than twenty minutes, Galvin turned into Gran Rain's driveway and parked.

It stopped raining. As soon as he opened the car door, a suburban din manifested: painting, hammering, pressure washing. He walked up the driveway to the front door and noticed Gran Rain had the same ceramic frog perched in the corner of the brick ledge that Sara had at her house to hide her key. He resisted the urge to inspect the frog and instead rang the doorbell.

After a minute or two, and some distant shuffling, it opened.

The CEO of InterTech, Nick Montana, loomed over the doorway and cast his shadow over Galvin. Nick wore a crimson jogging suit with white stripes up the side of the pants and the long-sleeved jacket. He looked puzzled to see Galvin.

Quickly, Galvin held out his hand. "Sir?"

Nick Montana took it and drew Galvin into the house, clapping him on the back. "My boy." He raised his voice presumably to contact Gran Rain. "We have company." There was a faint odor of peach in the air and behind him bookshelves loomed.

Sara's grandmother appeared in the foyer, wearing an identical jogging suit, although, as always, less conspicuously than her fiancée.

"Galvin," she said smiling. She held out her arms to embrace him.

He held up a hand. "I just got over the flu. But it's great to see you." Galvin wondered if Sara would be as beautiful in forty-five years and thought the odds were good.

"Come in here," Gran Rain said, gesturing. Galvin walked through the kitchen and into a small sitting room overlooking a garden. He sat down on a leather couch, which whooshed and settled beneath him. He heard the thin wail of a saxophone, probably Kenny G.

"Alexa, lower the volume," Gran said loudly. "Can I get you anything, Galvin?"

Galvin shook his head and then nodded. "Well, maybe."

Gran Rain and Nick Montana sat perched in matching leather arm chairs facing Galvin.

"Should I leave?" Nick Montana asked.

"I don't know," Galvin said.

"Why don't you stay?" Gran Rain said, smiling at Nick. She turned to Galvin. "How are you dear? Can't I get you anything? Soda? A beer?"

Galvin sat on the edge of the plush seat, and held up a hand. "I'm fine. Now. I was sick, or I would have come sooner."

Gran waited for him to continue. "I'm better now," Galvin said. "And I just received some information that makes it important I contact Sara right away. But she's moved."

"Whoa," Nick Montana said. He squinted at Galvin. Then he glanced at Gran Rain. "You know what he's talking about?"

Gran smiled. "I reckon he found out our Sara is expecting a baby."

Nick Montana frowned. "I didn't know that."

"Well, pay attention," Gran said.

"I love it when she talks to me like a teacher," Nick Montana said to Galvin.

Galvin looked down. "She told you?"

"No," Gran Rain said. "I just knew. The constant peeing. She'd gone up a bra size. The glow."

"She looked exhausted when I saw her," Galvin said.

"I don't know," Gran said. "I just knew. Plus, I cornered Gabby before I left InterTech that day."

Nick Montana laughed at the same time Gran did. "She's a pistol, that one," he said. "Turns out she really is my daughter."

Gran Rain interjected, " I barely heard from Sara this month to tell the truth. I was trying to give her space."

"She moved," Galvin prodded.

Gran nodded. "And she flushed her phone down the

toilet. By mistake, she says." She picked up a large brown purse beside her leather armchair and rummaged through it. She took out a cell phone. "Give me your number, and I'll text you her address." She quickly recited her own number, although Galvin had already memorized it from Sara's personnel file.

Galvin took out his cell and typed in the digits. Gran's cell gave a brief ring. She typed for a minute, and Galvin saw 'Sara's new address' ding on his messages. He quickly transferred it to his contacts.

"Where did she move to?" he asked. "And why?"

Gran brushed imaginary lint off her crimson pants leg. "She bought a condominium downtown. On Lake Ann. Paid a fortune for it. Why? She got a raise. Sara is great at spending money. And maybe she wanted something permanent."

"You talked to her," Galvin said.

"Just once or twice," Gran said. "She hasn't confided in me. If I know Sara, she hasn't told me because she doesn't want to ruin my engagement. Or some nonsense."

"Well," Galvin said, "I guess there's something I should ask you."

Gran looked at Nick Montana who raised his bushy eyebrows. "Go ahead."

Galvin said, "She never talked about her mother or father."

Gran leaned back in her chair. "Mimi is in and out of rehab. Last I heard of the dad, he died of some alcohol related illness. They married, but never lived together. My late husband and I raised Sara."

"Well, congratulations," Galvin said. "You did a great…"

Gran cut him off again. "We did our best. Sara was

worth it."

"Well, that's my point," Galvin said. "I want to ask, that is, I want to know." He shook his head. "I'm going to ask her to marry me. Is that okay with you?"

Gran turned to Nick Montana. "He's asking for her hand." Her fiancé chuckled and shook his head. Galvin remembered cartoons from his childhood where a trap door would materialize with the stroke of a cartoonist's pen and drop the unfortunate toon from sight. "Lucky," he thought. He pressed on.

"I'd like her to come with me to Alaska."

"When are you leaving?"

"Tomorrow."

Gran Rain straightened up in her chair. "That sounds a little rushed."

"Let me worry about that," Galvin said. "Meanwhile, she doesn't have a phone, and I don't know where she lives." He stood.

"Well," said Gran Rain, "you're not going to find her at home."

Galvin sat down again. "I won't?"

"She went to a wedding," Gran said. "She called to ask me what dress she should wear. Not white, I told her. Or red."

"A wedding?"

"You should stop repeating everything I say," Gran said. "Or I won't give your marriage my blessing."

"Do you?" Galvin asked.

"Of course, she does," Nick Montana said. "And so do I. You're a steady young man. Just what Sara needs."

"Don't take words out of my mouth, Nick," Gran Rain

said. She turned to Galvin. "Of course, I approve. Jay was just an infatuation. And Gabby was a novelty. No offense Nick."

The older man lounged back in his chair. "None taken, my dear."

"But you two," Gran Rain said, "seem like you belong together. You're opposites, but in a good way. Strengths and weaknesses, you know. Do you love her?" Gran Rain's voice softened, and Galvin looked up. He didn't hesitate. "Are you always this nosy Ms. Montana?"

"Call me Gran," she said, straightening up. "You'd better hurry then."

"But where is she?" Galvin asked.

"I should think," Gran Rain said, "you'd have figured that out."

52
JAY - A MONTH LATER

Jay sat on Danielle's couch and wished he was anywhere else. He wished he was back at Captain Tom's or even adrift on the ocean, dying of thirst, terrified a shark was going to chomp off his legs. At least he didn't have to worry about anyone but himself.

He sat in a dim living room on a purple sectional sofa that must have cost Danielle ten grand. Silk screen shades covered the windows. Next to him was a glass of ice tea with crescent shaped ice cubes. At his feet, was his cousin Ruby.

She was lying on her back on a towel he fetched from the linen closet. Her thumb was in her mouth and her gray eyes were fixed on Jay. He didn't have the slightest idea what to do with her. Ruby knew few words. Her fingers were always in her mouth.

Getting custody was Danielle's idea. Jay argued, but not very hard. He knew by now it was best to give Danielle her way. And what could he really say? No, it was better to have a blind neighbor of no relation raise Darlyn and Truly's child?

Danielle made him go to visit that big guy in the hospital, the one who tried to save Darlyn's life. Link, his name was. He said he didn't think Ruby was at the house. Any time he'd seen her, she was with that blind chick, Bev.

Now Truly was gone, and now he had Ruby and Danielle. Jay already knew how he felt about Ruby. Danielle was another matter. She was beautiful. And smart. Single handedly, she'd kept him from being charged with Truly's disappearance. He absently rubbed the amulet he kept in his right hand pocket.

But it was this other airy-fairy stuff he found hard to take. The tarot cards. The incense. The huge astrological chart hung on the wall over her bed. The premonitions and the signs. No, he'd say this was not the high point of his life. Danielle was, after all, a woman he'd only just met, and he barely knew his young cousin. He had a stay-at-home job where he sat in front of a laptop all day instead of meeting people, meeting women. If Danielle was any indication, he hadn't yet lost his appeal. A lot of good it was doing him.

Still, he managed to stay sober since he returned, and he had Danielle to thank for that. They managed two meetings a day sometimes. It was one thing to be depressed and bored. It was another to be depressed, bored, and drunk. Still, there were days when he scarcely remembered the difference.

Ruby stirred at his feet. "Hey Rube," he said. "You hungry?"

She stared at him, like she always did. "Bef," she said.

"Bev's not here," he said. Jay sat on the floor next to Ruby. He covered her perspiring little hand with his own. They sat like that for a minute. Suddenly Ruby sat up. Jay realized she was grinning. "Jay Jay." She clapped her hands and squealed.

'Why they could be brother and sister', Jay realized. Same curly black hair, long lashes, and a dimple on the left cheek. He pointed, intuitively remembering an old game he used to play with her when she was very little. "Boo," he said.

Ruby screamed with laughter and got to her feet. She ran in the opposite direction, looked around, and got down on her hands and knees to hide behind the couch. Jay crawled on all fours over to the couch. He crouched down to Ruby's eye level. "Boo."

She collapsed laughing. Jay dragged her out from under the couch, laughing at himself. Ruby got to her feet and held her hands up to him. Well, she had never done that before.

Jay picked her up, marveling at how light she was, this tiny wisp of a girl. Someday, she would be a woman with her own likes and dislikes and a distinct personality. She put her head on his shoulder. He held onto her carefully as he sat down on the sofa and reached for the remote. One of his secret vices was watching reruns of *Downton Abbey*. Ruby fell asleep as Jay watched the imperious Mary make her sister's life a living hell. He thought Danielle looked a little like the actress who played Mary.

In the dim living room, his toddler cousin asleep in his lap, Jay pondered his options. He could stay with Danielle and raise Ruby. They would have more children. He would have a safe, suburban life, and a steady job. Or he could take off again. Go back to the Keys and Captain Tom. Take a freighter to Australia, or New Zealand, or around the world.

He thought about the ways he'd gotten out of entanglements in the past. Danielle had nursed him back to health so a fatal illness wouldn't work. She took care of herself and didn't care that he worked part time. She already bailed him out of legal trouble so she was not skittish or, based on her performance in bed, prim and proper. But she was maternal. Her insistence on rescuing Ruby could be interpreted in no other way.

He heard the key in the lock and knew he had to make a decision.

Danielle swept into the room. She was wearing a red jacket and a white dress with red sandals. Her hair was tousled and windswept, falling in thick brown waves inches below her shoulders. "I came home early." She stopped when she saw the child sprawled lengthwise next to Jay. "Oh, my God."

Danielle crouched down to eye level and looked intently at Ruby. She lifted a curl off Ruby's forehead and smoothed it back. She sat down next to Jay. "How'd it go?"

Earlier today, Jay imagined this moment with Danielle. He would say something like "I'm not happy." But that wasn't exactly true.

"It went fine," Jay said. Danielle took his hand and Jay laced his fingers through hers.

"You know?" he said. "I could maybe get into this kid thing." He almost clapped his hand over his mouth, but Danielle was holding it. She looked at him.

"Being a parent, I mean." He couldn't stop, it seemed.

Danielle said, "That is so great."

"Why's that?" Jay expected Danielle to compliment him on his maturity. But she withdrew her hand, and looked down. "I have something to tell you," she said.

53
SARA - A MONTH LATER

"Here, Tiger."

Sara watched as the cat inched closer and then abruptly swerved and walked the other way. She bent over and scooped her up, an action Tiger would have previously met with extreme repudiation and possibly bloodshed. Now she just squawked loudly and resigned herself to occupying Sara's lap.

"Who's a good girl?" she asked the petulant feline. Tiger mewed loudly. Sara scratched between her ears and rubbed under her furry chin. Tiger closed her eyes and lifted her head. She purred.

A month ago, this kind of interaction was impossible. Tiger, incensed at having to adjust to yet another new environment, inflicted new wounds on Sara and just about scratched her new sofa to ribbons. But things changed. The strangeness of the condo created a bond between them.

Their new home was a square white box with a window in each room, looking out on a city in a constant state of chaos and construction. Sirens whined, cars crashed, trucks backfired, and planes roared overhead. Tiger sat on the windowsill in the kitchen and watched the tumult, her tail twitching. Sara covered all the other windows with garbage bags duct taped to the wall. She knew the paint would come off when she peeled back the duct tape. She didn't care.

Her focus narrowed to the four walls of the unfamiliar

home she'd moved to; a space she shared with a feral, possibly homicidal, cat. She did not replace her phone. She did not set up internet service, and she used her laptop to write instead of surfing social media. She didn't set up cable either, and her forty-two-inch-wide screen TV sat dark and dusty in a corner of the room.

She was reading a book, titled *Even Cowgirls Get the Blues* by nineties writer, Tom Robbins. His character, Bonanza Jellybean, was so outrageous, she made Sara feel brave. Courage inspired her to approach Tiger in benevolent gestures of peace, like sharing a whole chicken with her and feeding her potato chips.

Food was accepted, but her affectionate efforts were spurned until one night she was awakened by a heavy thud of something landing on the foot of her mattress. Her eyes flew open, and she sat up. Tiger inched her way up the bed, purring loudly. Sara put out her hand. The cat didn't bite it. Instead, she ran her jaw, teeth sheathed by gums, along her knuckles. The cat's eyes glinted. Apparently, they'd bonded.

Sara did not unpack. She removed a single plate, a fork, a knife, and a cup from a box marked Kitchen. She located a public telephone across the street from the Lake Ann police station, not far from the condo. From there, she called Gran Rain.

Sara wondered if she could go on this way forever. Live in the city, never go out, and keep a cat. But following that course did not seem practical. There was the baby, after all. Maybe she could move out west as Mimi did when she was young. Sara remembered a trip she'd taken with her mother when she was really little. "Hop in the van, ma'am," Mimi used to say. This memory gave Sara a little catch in her throat.

If she wanted to move, she could sublet the condo. She had money in a 401k with InterTech. She could teach school anywhere. She thought about Galvin and how she caught him staring at her during Gabby's stupid presentation.

She found the invitation to Meryl's wedding in her purse, as she was looking for hand disinfectant to ward off infection from Tiger's scratches. She held the embossed card in her hand. She wasn't sure she wanted to go. She knew that a wedding invitation to one person meant that another person was not invited. Galvin had probably already left for Alaska. That was two wasted invitations.

Sara decided if she was going to come out of her shell, Meryl's wedding was as good a place as any. She could dress up a little. How long since her last shower anyway?

After consulting Gran Rain, she decided on a ecru lace dress, an empire waisted frock she bought years ago at a consignment store. She located it with some difficulty, as she ripped into boxes marked Closet. She pulled it over her head, and ran to the adjoining bathroom where Tiger sat on the vanity, dipping her paw under the leaky faucet, and then licking her paw. The cat watched as Sara smoothed the dress over her hips and turned to see how it looked in the back.

The dress concealed a barely noticeable rounding of her belly. The fabric strained a bit across her chest. The color picked up glints of gold in her red hair, which had grown and now touched the tops of her shoulders. She would wear Gran's platinum ring and opal earrings. She had a pair of Melanio black pumps. Somewhere.

She stood over the bathroom sink applying makeup, humming along with Etta James on Pandora: "My love has come along, my lonely days are over…" Tiger looked at her, adjacent to her vanity, and looked away. Sara giggled. She was glad she was doing this. It showed initiative, a readiness to get on with her life whatever that may be. She put a bowl of water and kibble down for Tiger in the kitchen. The cat ducked as Sara stooped and tried to pet her. She stole one last look in the mirror, gathered her keys and purse, and stepped outside her condo, locking the door behind her.

She turned around and faced the long unfamiliar corridor. The carpet was gray and still so new she could smell the scotch guard. She walked to the elevator and pressed the button with the arrow pointing down. She checked her purse to make sure she had the invitation. No one would know her at this wedding. She never actually met Meryl.

The elevator rumbled down to the garage where she would retrieve the car she hadn't driven in a month except to get cat food. She set the GPS for the obscure chapel in Lake Ann. She shook off her misgivings. If it was a bore, she would leave after the first toast.

She was a little late. The valets were on the point of leaving, and there were no other cars lined up for the parking lot. Sara braked, put the car in park, grabbed her purse, and gave the keys to the valet, a guy about her age and clearly grumpy over having to park one last car.

Sara turned around to face the church. She remembered this place, sitting in the pews, the prayers, the processions. Most churches in Lake Ann, regardless of denomination, were built in the sixties so they all had the same boxy modern look. Sara hurried up the steps and one of ushers held the glass door open for her.

She remembered the smell, too, as soon as she walked through the door. A trace of incense, old books, and a comingling of perfumes and aftershave from the congregation. Hot wax emanated from the candles flickering under a plain wooden cross.

Gran and Gramps Rain had taken her to Paris when she was fourteen, to a church service at Notre Dame. She prayed her mother would stop doing drugs. Broached from the antique church, Sara believed for a little while that God heard her prayers. She wondered if belief was still possible. Mimi still used drugs as far as she knew.

She was so late, the wedding party was poised in the front of the sanctuary. Sara saw the bride draped in a lace veil and managed a tentative smile before she bolted down the aisle, squeezing herself beside a matron with a toddler on her lap.

A few minutes later the wedding party started down the aisle. The organist pounded out "Here Comes the Bride." The groom stood at the foot of the procession, a wiry guy with slicked down blonde hair, wearing an aloha shirt and a dark blue suit. The bridesmaids and groomsmen advanced, two couples, the men wearing blue suits and flowered shirts, with yellow rose boutonnieres. The women wore tight velvet sheaths of autumn brown and carried white and yellow roses.

"I have to go potty." The toddler fidgeted just as the bride began to process. Everyone stood and the mother took the opportunity to scramble past Sara. The kid, no lightweight, stepped squarely on one of her Melanio pumps, and Sara suppressed a scream.

Meryl walked alone to the strains of "Here Comes the Bride," a veil covering her face. For such a traditional wedding, the lack of a relative to walk her down aisle seemed poignant. Perhaps her father and mother were dead or estranged. Sara wondered who would escort Gran Rain when she married Nick Montana.

Meryl made it to the end of the aisle and handed her bouquet of roses to a bridesmaid. She and her groom knelt at the altar while the minister asked the congregation to bow their heads. Sara felt movement on her right and, without looking up, stood and stepped to the left to make room for the young mother and her child. Best to give them the aisle.

Instead, she felt an arm around her waist. She looked up. Galvin stood beside her wearing a polo shirt, khakis, and sneakers. He had a beard. They were around the same height and without meaning to Sara looked directly into his amber eyes.

"Dearly beloved we are gathered here..." Galvin's right hand covered the gauzy fabric that hid the swell of her belly. He continued staring at Sara instead of the wedding taking place at the foot of the altar. There were only a few seconds to react, but Sara knew immediately what she wanted to say to Galvin.

ONE YEAR LATER...
LINK

Interstate H-1 is the longest and busiest highway in the state of Hawaii. Located on the island of O'ahu, it should take 15 minutes, sans traffic, for Link to drive to the Honolulu International airport from the South Street Workforce Housing Project where he lives. The trouble is there is always traffic. The airport is right near the Navy Marine course where he golfs with some vets from work. The traffic is murder.

He's lived on the island for almost a year. Aside from the gridlock, Link loves everything about Honolulu. It is still quiet enough to hear the birds, when he strolls to Yama's Fish Market mornings for boiled peanuts or some haupia, a coconut pudding.

"Aloha, Macai," he says to the teenager doling out brown bags wet with salt and squishy peanuts.

"Aloha, Link." He smiles at her, she looks away, and puts a cookie in his bag.

"Mahalo, Macai." And then she smiles back at him.

From the volcanic mountains to the underwater depths of the Pacific Ocean, Link finds Hawaii more exotic than Florida. Instead of swamp, springs, and scrub, Hawaii has rain forests, waterfalls, and deserts . Much of Florida is just above sea level, a white sand peninsula. Hawaii has islands of black volcanic ash. Link prefers the kama'aina, Hawaii's gap-toothed, and cheery native to the unsmiling Florida cracker with dots of melanoma on his neck.

What he doesn't love about Hawaii is the loneliness. It's like he has a hole somewhere in his heart and soul, and it hurts. Still, not all the guys he works with are straight. He dated one handsome Irish lad for six months. They used to surf and snorkel together at 'Pops' on the South Shore. But the relationship was like treading water. He was not willing to attribute the sense of buoyancy to more than physical science.

Link Zooms his parents once a week. He misses them, but he is glad to be in charge of his own life. He never looks back on his decision to get his EMT and paramedics license instead of his English degree. He still loves words and during rigorous training sessions he amuses his fellow firefighters by quoting Frost: "Some say the world will end in fire."

Well qualified with his certificates and degrees, he is already Assistant Deputy Fire Chief of the Honolulu Fire department. He gets along well with the guys just as he did when he was a construction foreman. His face will never be the same, and he is permanently bald. But his burn scars are a plus in the fire department as a mark of bravery.

Link can't deny he is dazed by the abrupt turn life has taken. He experienced a kind of spiritual awakening when he ran into Darlyn's burning house. Not everyone knows what he would do in a moment of extreme risk. He failed to save Darlyn, and probably endangered the lives of Matt and Officer Cleary, but that does not deter Link from marveling; he ran towards danger rather than away from it. Reading poetry under a palm tree is a cop out for a man with the special gift he possesses.

He drums his fingers on the steering wheel. The island of O'ahu holds ninety five million people and most of them own two cars. The gridlock on highways is even more terrible than usual. Is he actually going to be late? He drives aggressively, cutting into lanes, laying on his horn, making gestures out of the driver's window. The digital clock on his dash flicks off minutes anyway. He thinks, "Oh my fur and whiskers! I'm late, I'm late, I'm late!"

There is no opening ahead. He keeps pressing Seek on his stereo, but all he gets are ads. Finally, traffic starts moving inch by inch. Sweat runs down Link's neck in spite of the blasting air conditioner.

He thinks of Matt, and his breathing eases. The best mornings are the ones where he wakes up from a dream about Matt. The best nights are when he goes to sleep with his memories; the hospital where they made room for each other in their narrow beds. The ward was quiet as a church, and the two men were afraid to even whisper. Being together was good. It was enough.

Link noses the car into the left lane. Ahead lies the airport ramp exit. For one crazy second, Link contemplates just driving on. Then he pushes down the left blinker, and inches off the highway, behind one luxury sedan after another.

There is nowhere to park as usual, and by the time Link finds a spot it is already past the ETA. He leaps out of the car without even noting his location and sprints towards the elevators, then up escalators, then dashes between travelers, all the while frantically scanning the counters for on time arrivals and gate numbers.

The flight is delayed. "Thank you, Jesus," Link whispers. He takes his place amid the crowd. They are standing at the end of a long corridor where the passengers will appear within minutes. Never, in all the times that Link picked people up at airports, has the person he came to meet come out first. Except this time.

As though it is a reward for his hot, traffic-snarled journey, he sees a passenger, first one off the plane, carrying a military style duffle bag on his shoulder. Link can barely keep from rushing forward, but he does, contenting himself with waving his arm and calling out the passenger's name. The tall man drops the duffle bag and leaps forward. Link moves forward too, although it seems as though it's in slow motion or as if he were in a dream. The men reach each other, embrace. Link closes his eyes and the busy airport vanishes. Everything else vanishes. It is quiet in this space like being in a church, or the burn ward of a hospital late on a quiet night.

Link holds the man by the shoulders, and they look at each other and smile. "Matt," he says.

Matt says, "We meet again."

Link looks away, blinks hard. "Let's get that duffle bag."

"Where we going, bro?"

"Home, man. Let's go home."

For the first time in a year, Link feels light, the small aching sore in his heart and soul suddenly and miraculously healed.

THE WEDDING

"I think the babies need to be changed," Danielle says.

Jay springs into action even though they're just entering the church. Danielle thinks it's a mistake to bring the children to the wedding, but Jay persuades her.

"I'll take care of the child care," he says.

Now Jay lifts the babies from their double stroller, one under each arm. Danielle hands him the diaper bag from the stroller basket. "Be right back," he says, bending to kiss Danielle and Ruby. Humming he makes his way to the Men's room and Danielle leans against the poured concrete wall of the church, fanning her face with her wide brimmed hat.

People pour into the building. She nods at several employees she knows from InterTech. Everyone who works there is invited. It looks like they are all showing up. Ruby plucks at her skirt. "Where Jay go?"

Danielle crouches down to her heels. "He's changing those pesky boys, sweetie. He'll be right back." She smooths the curls away from the child's flushed face. She wanted to put a blue ribbon in her hair to go with her dotted swiss dress, but Ruby balked, and Jay backed her up as usual.

Ruby still asks for 'Bef,' and brightens whenever she sees a tall African American woman. But Danielle hopes Ruby harbors no lasting damage from the past year. She touches the locket at her throat.

Jay has taken to fathering in a way that seems like talent. They formally adopted Ruby last spring. At two and a half, she seems like any other toddler. A bit precocious, perhaps. She likes to play with Danielle's tarot cards.

The twins are only four months old, two bouncing baby boys, blessed with the family hair, jet black and curly. The boys, Denny and Danny, are a lot of work, but Jay seems to be thriving. He still works at home, part time.

Jay deposits the babies in their twin stroller and turns to Danielle. "You look nice," he says. Danielle is wearing a green silk sheath with an emerald green fedora. She lost a lot of weight since she had twins. When her maternity leave ended, she handed them over to Jay. Between work and moving into their big new home in Algonquin Acres, she seldom has time to eat anymore. She is tired all the time. Jay feeds and bathes the kids before she gets home. It's all she can do to read Ruby a story at night.

They are a handsome family, even Jay, although he still has visible scars on his face, and he's gained a lot of weight. His belly hangs over the belt holding up the pants of his blue suit. Danielle pats his canary yellow tie and starts to herd her family towards the door. She stops. Jay turns and follows her gaze. Three people approach, and Danielle and Jay recognize two of them.

A woman with long red hair and a floor length yellow gown rushes over.

"Danielle, Jay!" She hugs them both, then turns to her entourage. "This is my mother, Mimi." Mimi looks like an older used version of Sara. Her red hair is dull and stringy. She is wearing the same gown as Sara, but it is not as flattering with her thick waist and broad posterior.

"Pleased to meet you," Mimi says in a monotone. To

Sara, she says, "I'm hungry. I need to eat." Sara pulls a granola bar out of her clutch bag and hands it to her. Mimi tears it open and drops the wrapper on the ground. Ruby steps forward cautiously and picks it up, handing it to Jay who puts it in his pocket

"And you know Galvin," Sara says, gesturing.

Galvin steps forward, hand extended. He is wearing a shiny gray suit, but it's hard to see. Strapped to his torso is a blue cloth baby carrier and, in the carrier, nestles an infant with a pink bow tied to a carefully gathered strand of red hair.

Jay steps forward, and shakes Galvin's hand, kisses Sara on the cheek. Galvin kisses Danielle.

Danielle colors a little. "Congratulations. And who is this?" She gestures towards the infant.

Sara says, "This is Rain. It's a family name."

Galvin motions towards Ruby and the twins. "You guys have been busy."

"Oh sorry," Danielle says. "This is Ruby. And Denny and Danny. Denny is named after my brother."

"I remember," Galvin says.

Mimi says, "I need a drink."

"There's a water fountain inside, Mom," Sara says. She glances at Galvin. He has taken her place peering at the twins. Galvin pokes a finger at the boys, and Danny grabs it and tries to bring it to his mouth.

"Your baby is pretty," Jay says. "She looks like you." They both admire Rain who is goggle eyed by the rambunctious twins, who writhe and whine in their carriage seats.

"Thanks," Sara says. "Your family is beautiful."

"Yeah." Jay gives her the version of his old smile. As always, his amulet is in his pocket, and he touches it briefly. "Still have that killer cat?"

Sara says, "Tiger? Yeah. She's adapted pretty well to the Great Frontier." She doesn't mention Tiger falls asleep between her and Galvin every night, which causes them to sleep gingerly and with nascent dread.

Mimi jostles her elbow. "I need to go in."

"How's Alaska?" Danielle asks. "I hear nothing but good things from Jackie."

"Oh, we love it," Galvin says. "Sara has a new job teaching school in Anchorage."

Sara says, "It's so weird to think of Jackie Moates officially in charge at InterTech."

"Why?" Danielle asks.

"Because it makes so much sense." Sara and Danielle smile at each other.

"You guys still live around here?" Galvin asks Jay.

He nods. "We go to the Keys a lot. Deep sea fishing with an old friend of mine."

Danielle laughs. "Captain Tom is counting on helping the twins find their sea legs."

"He helped me find mine," Jay says. "I owe him big time."

"Sara," Mimi whimpers.

"I have to go in," Sara says. "Gabby just texted me she's already here. I'll see you guys later?"

"Oh," Danielle says. "We may leave after the ceremony." She gestures towards the babies.

"Totally understandable," Galvin says. He hugs Danielle. Then he holds out his hand to Jay, who takes it and shakes.

"Take care," Jay says. "Of both your pretty ladies."

"I will," Galvin says. He steps forward addressing the boys and Ruby. "You guys be good." Ruby nods and looks down, but the babies stare brazenly at him, then turn away fretting.

Danielle and Jay sit in a pew with Ruby between them and a squirming baby on each lap. They watch Sara, then Mimi, then Gabby proceed down the aisle carrying white baskets of sunflowers. Galvin is already at the altar standing up, with a rose in his lapel. He is best man for Nick Montana, who towers over him.

"Steady old man," he says in a low voice.

Nick Montana peers over Galvin's head. The organ player's fingers descend on the keyboard. The church fills with the notes to "Here Comes the Bride."

"It's corny," Nick Montana says. "But I like the tune."

The double doors open and Gran Rain begins to mince down the aisle, accompanied by Jackie Moates. The bride wears a floor length silk suit of goldenrod yellow, and Gabby has twined daisies into the chignon of her silver hair. Her yellow Jimmy Choos are perhaps a bit much for a woman in her 70s to carry off, but she says she needs the height, and she's damned if she's going to look like a child standing up beside Nick.

She carries two white roses, one of which she hands to Nick Montana when she gets to the altar. He stoops and kisses her. Danielle and Sara each recall that moment at their own weddings, almost a year ago, and how their husbands looked at them.

Jay and Galvin recall that moment too, and their eyes squint as though they are smiling although their faces remain impassive. Jay proposed when Danielle told him she was pregnant. Galvin never proposed. There was no need after Sara turned to him at Meryl's wedding and simply said, "At last."

Jackie Moats takes a seat in the first pew and Gran Rain hands Sara her bouquet. The wedding party turns and faces the altar. The Episcopal priest, a woman in her forties, spreads her arms wide and smiles broadly. She begins:"Dearly beloved…"

BEV

Cherie stands in her driveway with arms crossed and watches a figure approaching on the half mile loop around the neighborhood. Her husband Toby stands beside her, smoking. Bears were spotted in the neighborhood recently, and they are in the habit of standing guard as the sun comes up. It is still early morning, garbage day in Harrison Parke. They watch the distant figure swerve to the curb and pick something up. Cherie makes a clicking sound with her tongue. "The hoarding is getting out of control."

"It's the same every Thursday," Toby agrees. Their neighbor makes the rounds before the garbage trucks, sometimes hauling a child's red Radio Flyer. She isn't particular. Anything that isn't broken is salvaged: lamps, hot wheels, books, and knick knacks.

"I saw her walking off with a kids' bike frame last week," Cherie says.

"Not any worse than your collectible Barbie dolls," Toby says.

"Oh stop." Cherie pretends to slap him. Toby laughs. He crushes the cigarette butt beneath his heel. Cherie looks at it. She quit smoking six months ago, and she misses it. "Seriously," Cherie says as the figure comes closer. "She's been our neighbor for years. Aren't we kind of responsible?"

"For what?" Toby asks. "We're not kin."

"Even so. She's obviously sick." Cherie squints, trying

to detect further deterioration in her approaching neighbor. "I have nightmares worrying about her dying alone in that house."

Toby says, "She told Will it's some kind of cancer."

Cherie nods. "That's what it looks like. It's a shame."

Toby says. "You were never friends. She came to our house, what, once?"

"She's a neighbor," Cherie repeats shortly.

"Well, I can see why she doesn't have us over." Turning their heads, they can just see the eyesore Bev's house has become. The porch, visible from the road, crammed to the ceiling with furniture. The lawn chairs and rattan tables spilled out into the backyard. Neighbors note the air conditioner has not been on in months, even at the height of summer. Her pool turned black. There is a big No Trespassing sign planted amid the scrub grass, weeds, and milkweed that passes for a front lawn.

The woman is within hailing distance and Cherie sees she carries a cloth bag and a cane. She is dressed all in dingy white and wears sunglasses and a face mask. She is thin, scary, emaciated thin. Cherie waves and calls out, "Morning, Bev."

Bev looks up and at that moment a thin black cat darts out of the common area and runs right between her legs. Bev drops her bag and gasps. Toby calls out, "Everything all right?"

Bev fans her bony chest and crosses the street, her cane tapping back and forth. She stops at the foot of the driveway.

"What was that?"

"Why that's Shadow," Cherie says. "Don't let him scare you."

"Shadow is the one who should be scared," Bev says with a laugh.

Cherie and Toby laugh along companionably. "Everything all right?" Toby asks.

"About as well as it can be." Bev hesitates. "You ever hear from Truly?"

"No," Cherie says as gently as she can. She and Toby exchange a look. "You let us know if you need anything."

"Okay," Bev says.

"You need to come over when the tomatoes are ripe," Toby says. "There's more than we can eat."

"Sure," Bev says. "Thanks." She turns and heads around the corner past the cleared lot that belonged to the Ravijas, past the corner lot that never resold. Swishing her cane back and forth, she finally turns into her own driveway. The neighbors say when she opens the garage door, things fall out. But she goes in through the front door after depositing her bag next to the bedraggled hedge that hasn't seen the side of the pruning blade in a year.

"That's sad," Cherie says.

"Shadow," Toby calls. The black cat saunters up drive, his tail straight in the air.

"Both of you get inside now," Cherie says. They all head up the driveway. Cherie turns around once to look at Bev's house. Then she enters her own. It is still partially dark, and the house doesn't get much sun anyway on the east side of the neighborhood. She turns on the electric light in her kitchen, but that doesn't seem to be enough. She goes around to the living room and dining room, snapping on lamps.

"What're ya doin', Cherie?" Toby yells.

"Nothing," Cherie yells back. Then she goes into the room with her dolls after turning on the big overhead light. She needs to sew a doll weave and those synthetic monofilaments require really delicate exacting work. It can take up an entire day. She threads her needle and gets to work.

MERE' BYRD

One of New Orleans' simple pleasures is a muffuletta with a Pimm's Cup in the courtyard of the Bone House near Conti Street. The old woman is a regular, and the young waiter knows her well enough to bring her standing order fifteen minutes after she is seated. He puts the plate before her and sets down her drink. He is sweating. "Bon Appetit, ma mere," he says.

She gives him a fleeting smile. It is only in New Orleans she gets the respect she deserves. Elsewhere, no one believes in her, but that's okay. She knows the truth. She knows the power. She has spent the last forty five years claiming her power, refining it, learning how to use it.

At first, even amidst her grief, there was rage, there was incredulity. Who would dare do this to a premier family, a family with roots in an ancient religion, a religion whose members routinely disavowed with a laugh that was not entirely authentic?

She was not a fool. No one who lived in New Orleans would dare steal the child of the Mere'. The only explanation was the child was taken – not by her enemies- but by strangers. Everything pointed to a random kidnapping. And the child was just-gone. Her boy, her baby, with the big gray eyes and tawny curls. Early Byrd. She left him napping in his stroller next to the counter while she attended her store. When she finished, she actually raised the hem of her blouse, preparing to feed him before she realized the stroller was empty.

She appealed to the sky, she made sacrifices, she grew adept in her knowledge and strong in her powers. But she could not see the face of the kidnapper. It was ironic, she acknowledged, that it was the contemporary fad of genetic testing and analysis that finally located her Early Byrd.

He contacted her. He thought she was dead. He was married with a child. His father was still alive. Could she explain her connection to his old man?

She gave no hint of her intentions. They chatted freely, they met. She asked for pictures, and he sent them to a messenger account she kept on the internet. There was that picture of him, cheek to cheek with his child, his wife pressed in close, holding the brim of her hat in a jaunty salute.

She asked her son to send her something personal of the old man, something that could remind her of him. He texted a picture of a Mardi Gras T-shirt, and that was enough.

People who don't believe in her power will say that Arthur Ravija was struck by lightning that cloudy day when he fished off the side of the dock. Or people may say he had a heart attack. The day Arthur Ravija died, she sprinkled corn meal and gin into water boiling in a barrel and then dropped a wax ball studded with pins, which contained the chopped picture of the old man in his scrappy t-shirt. Later, she pinpointed the old man's collapse into water the moment she dropped the wax ball.

After he died, she told her boy the truth, that it couldn't be helped, and that his place was with her. It was preordained, and he needed to let go of his silly attachments. The wife, for one thing. The child, Ruby, she would forgo for the moment, but at some point, she would be reeled back in. She explained the power passed from generation to generation.

A different waiter comes back, with a complementary Shrimp Remoulade Stuffed Avocado. He places it to the side, bows from the waist and backs off. She notices he is wearing a face mask. She gestures toward his face and cocks her head.

"It's the flu," the waiter says, hoarsely. "There've been a few cases. We're careful around customers."

She nods dismissively. A nice boy, doing his job. Her own son didn't understand his duty or hers. He stopped taking her calls. He blocked her from his social media. But she already had a picture of his wife and her name. So, she contacted the wife, Darlyn, and got all kinds of information, including the name of her son's mistress. She told her about sprinkling salt on Bev's threshold as a curse.

Darlyn was lonely, talked too much. She spilled the date and time her husband planned the voyage to scatter the old man's ashes. Smelling a rat, Mere' Byrd recommended putting some kind of sleeping potion in his food. She painted a crude facsimile of the Florida seal on the side of her truck. She drove all night to get to Florida in time, pulling up just as he and his friend were getting in the boat.

She recognized Early, the taller of the two, and she spoke to them coarsely from a distance to avoid recognition. She never meant to harm her boy. Not now, and not in the past. Sometimes the spirit was so strong in her that she lashed out. That was all.

People who don't believe in her power will say that the storm would have occurred anyway, that bad weather was predicted in the forecast. It was summer, and there were always squalls in the summer. All she knew was after she pulled away, she parked, got out of the truck, and made a hole in the ground close to the shore. It filled with sea water, and she twirled her finger in the brine. Looking up, she chanted, "Master, we ask Your protection. The water, which is able to hear mortals, deliver our children to us."

Storm clouds showed up a few minutes later. Then she pulled a map of the Southeast out of the glove compartment, took a marker from the center console, and drew an outline around the perimeter, ensuring that the pressure systems stayed out of that area. If it all went as she planned, the boat would be drawn to clear passage and temperate weather. If the friend was still on board, she'd deal with him when she had to.

She went to JaxPort in Jacksonville the night Truly and Jay disappeared at sea. Nothing. She studied maps. She studied the Gulf Stream. She listened to the news. She helped organize the search party at Cocoa Beach, bringing some of her acolytes along in the truck. They stopped at the Brevard mall to buy beach clothes. Lily Pulitzer was having a sale.

She thought he would come north of Jacksonville. Then following the map, she thought otherwise. In 1562, Jean Ribault was sent from France to Florida to begin a new colony. He built a monument on St. Johns Bluff to honor France. Looking at the tidal flow, and following her own intuition, Mere Byrd was convinced Early's boat would show up near that historic spot eighteen miles downstream from Jacksonville.

If she were right, how long would it take for the capricious tides to deliver the *Early Byrd*? After marching up and down on the beach all day, she drove to Fernandina Beach at night. Out of her truck she loaded a pickaxe, a dolly, a rubber raft, rope, and oars. Then she waited, staring out past the monument to the dark waters, looking for movement. Occasionally she heard a splash, and she would leap to her feet an odd skinny caricature against the star-studded sky.

On the second night, it was not a leaping fish disturbing the waters. Instead, she saw a signal, a wispy wave of vapor. There was the sound of a bridge clanging open in the distance. Then of moonlit water lapping against a wooden surface. A boat appeared.

The boat, neared, listing, wooden planks bulging. It came closer to shore. Jenny, her hands fumbling, threw herself into the raft and rowed 100 feet to meet it. It would have been too bad for her if it was some poacher. But it was Early. Her son showed up alone, on schedule, half-dead from exposure. Spread eagle on the deck, his head lolled. Jenny couldn't be sure if he was alive or dead. But she attached the rope to her waist and to the boat's transom eye. It took close to an hour to row to shore.

The boat was almost submerged. She undid the rope and splashed into the water and clambered onto the boat. She checked Early's pulse and felt the faint scattered tremors of his heart. Putting both hands under his arms, she dragged her son, inch by inch across the deck, over the side, through the water and finally to the small sandy inlet where she placed him on his back.

She felt the power, the strength emanating as she waded back in with the pickaxe, she brought in a backpack, puncturing the hull and sending it back out to the Atlantic. It didn't get far before it sank. Someone conducting a powerful drone search might see the boat underwater. But she didn't think it was likely they would search there. She piled Early onto her dolly and then hoisted him into her truck bed. She drove straight back to New Orleans in about seven hours.

She hoped Early would recover. There was no question of taking him to the hospital and risking him being recognized as one of missing men from Fort Canaveral. She prepared some poultices and special teas. She left him in the care of the servants and immediately drove back to Florida. Her son needed time to convalesce.

She joined in the search efforts at Fort Canaveral, thinking they would taper off soon. But the wife liked the attention and would not relinquish the search. Jenny grew impatient. She had recruited everyone in Truly's life into her web, but it was Bev's idea to ply Darlyn with Seconal. Mere Byrd saw a lethal advantage.

People who don't believe in her power will say the wife died of a drug overdose, and the fire was an accident. All Mere Byrd knows is the weeks spent with the wife, masquerading as Jenny Zinn, she collected all kinds of things from Darlyn -strands of hair, a lighter, used Kleenex. These were wrapped in red flannel and set on fire. And just like that, the Darlyn problem went away. Poof.

When she returned home, her son seemed much more pliable, and she set about teaching him, making up for forty-five years of ignorance and the abandonment of his heritage. This time he spoke no more of his daughter, his wife, and his mistress. The wife was dead, the daughter would come to her later. She set a call back curse on the mistress, who should lose everything she had ever been given by any man. In fact, she should have died by now. But the mistress is strong and is hanging on. But not for long.

Finished with her lunch, she wipes her lips with the paper napkin, crumples it, and drops it on her plate. There is no need to wait for a check because there never is a check. For this, and other tributes of respect, she will extend her protection.

Mere Byrd rises and slowly, she pushes open the door and starts home. She is limping slightly and finds it hard to catch her breath. It is later than she thought and there is much to do before the evening ceremony. She hurries.

EARLY BYRD

The Men's Room in The Bone House is small as a closet and smells of urine and disinfectant. The old man always said you can tell how good business is by the rest rooms. Truly looks at himself in the mottled mirror and removes a brown wig and a face mask. He throws the items in the metal bin for garbage and throws about a million paper towels on top. Then he removes the clip-on bow tie the waiters wear and stuffs it in his pocket, opening the top three buttons of his shirt. Whistling slightly, he opens the door and slips into the breezeway. Sidling along the wall he makes it to the street. He takes a few hurried steps, and then he starts running.

He stays in the street, avoiding the cracked uneven sidewalks of New Orleans. The massive tree roots play havoc with the walkways, even the asphalt; he has to watch his feet every minute. At any moment he can encounter inches of separation between adjoining segments of poured concrete. A man can trip, fall, and crack his head open.

A year ago, he was Truly Ravija, looking for a new life. Now he had one quite against his will. He was Early Byrd, long-lost heir to Mere' Byrd. Now he knew to be more careful about what he wished for.

A year ago the old man was still alive; Darlyn was alive; Bev was healthy; Ruby was under his care. He took the genetics test to please Darlyn because she bought it for his birthday. No one was more surprised when the list of relatives showed up in his email. He hadn't expected any. They were all from New Orleans. The one at the top shared fifty percent DNA. It was Jenny.

He contacted her by email. He actually flew to New Orleans to meet her. Why not? But he got the jitters walking through the city. Before he got to her shop of souvenirs and religious artifacts, the famous *Authentica*, he stopped in front of the St. Louis Cathedral, wanting to go in. Instead, he walked on, turned on Dumaine Street and entered the dark stuffy shop.

It was full of old books, primitive statues made of wood, cards of the saints, even a real human skull. Near the wooden statues and the cloth dolls there were dollar bills, notes requesting love, money, revenge. Truly almost turned and walked out.

"Can I help you?" The woman had a sharp narrow face, was dressed in black, and wound her hair in a purple turban.

"I was told to come here," he said.

The woman embraced him with her spidery arms. She took him to the Bone House, and he noticed at once the deference she was shown. The waiter scooted people out of a terrace table to make room. He supposed it had to do with her status as a longtime customer.

"You went missing," she said when they settled. "Practically an infant, you didn't just walk off." There was rebuke implied in her remark. She reached in her bag and took out a cigarette holder of black onyx into which she fitted a slim clove cigarette. She blew smoke in his face.

She wanted him to move in with her. Her family had roots in New Orleans, yet she would say nothing about his biological father. Truly fiddled with silverware, wanting to flee.

"I have a home," he said. "And a flight to catch."

She nodded and had one request. "Send me a picture of

the man, the old man," she said. "Maybe I will remember him. Maybe he is your real father."

Truly nodded. "What harm could it do?" he thought.

Shortly after he texted her the picture, the old man was struck down on the dock. Truly fished him out of the water, performed CPR, and sat with him in the hospital while he died. In the last hours of his life, the old man finally came clean about Truly's past.

His voice was whispery, punctuated by the ebb and flow of the ventilator working on another patient behind the curtain. He coughed often in a terrible lung rattling way. He told Truly how his wife left him when she was pregnant. How Darlyn turned up 35 years later.

He said, " DNA? That don't lie, I reckon. Turns out, Darlyn is my daughter. Jay is my grandson. But I guess…" Here he struggled, sitting up, coughing, gripping the iron railings of the bed. Finally, he stopped. "I guess you knew about summat."

Truly nodded. He had guessed about Jay, but he did not know Darlyn had a biological connection to the old man. "Go on," he said. "Go on, if you can."

The old man took a long shuddering breath. With difficulty he lifted his hand and Truly took it. The stanchioned TV was on, and he heard a late-night host welcome a guest.

"Tell me," Truly said. "Don't die yet, old man," Truly thought.

The old man said,. "I went off on a tear. I was young. Ended up in New Orleans for Mardi Gras. Drink, whore, gamble all night, sleep all day. Took a walk one day on the way to Tropical Isle. I saw this little…it was a witchcraft shop. I go in. There was a lady, the owner, I guess." He paused.

Truly said. "What happened?"

The old man took some time, his mouth forming the words, without any sound.

"Please," Truly said.

"I just come in and was kind of standing in the shadows. I saw this woman, dressed in black with some kind of wrap on her head. She was holding you, jiggling you. You were crying.

"Can't feed you now," she said. 'Can't pop a boob with work to do." But you went on crying. 'You're a devil child, Early Byrd,' she said. Then she slapped you. She slapped a baby. Hard. Your head hit the counter. You went quiet. She kind of threw you in your stroller and went on about her business. A crazy woman.

The old man took a deep shuddering breath, his chest rising and falling. "I seen child abuse before. It's different from a spanking. I saw a man in a train station slap his daughter across the face so hard, thought he broke her neck. I dint say nuthin.' I dreamt about that poor child for years. I swore, if I ever saw a child abused agin, I would do something.' But I dint know what."

The old man's breathing was hoarser and his words came with difficulty. "An she hadn't seen me… standing there. She was in another room. I kind of …went over to where you was. I stood over you. There was a red mark on your face. An a lump… the size of an egg on your forehead. I thought. 'I kin point to that when I call up tha police… I wasn't even sure you was…still breathing. So, I bent over and picked you up."

The old man made a feeble attempt to grip Early's hand, but all he could manage was slight pressure. "You was a hand-ful… a big boy. An you opened your eyes and stared straight at me. I have never seen a baby with gray eyes before. You put your little arms aroun' my neck. Head on my shoulder. It... done something to me. I don't know what. But then your face screwed up like you was... fixing to cry again. She would hear. Come out. Afraid... you would get hurt." Here the old man's words trailed off, and he closed his eyes.

Truly's nightmare rose up before him. "You don't have to finish, old man."

The old man opened his eyes and stared at Truly. "Before I knew it. I was on the sidewalk. Then I was running with you bawling... running... bawling... running." By now, the old man was gasping and wheezing.

"Stop," Truly said. "Just stop." The old man was describing Truly's dream.

"I threw you in the back of my car. Probly scared... the shit out of you. I remember you rolled onto the floor. I took off. Couldn't help it. Went straight to Harrah's. Packed my bags. Took the next flight home with you wrapped in a hotel towel. Tole everyone that m'wife died in childbirth. No one knowed any better. She kept to herself. Had no friends."

The old man's face was slightly blue. Above them, on the TV, the audience laughed at a joke told by the late-night host. "Named you Truly," he said. "Couldn't call you Early. But named the boat after you. There's money in a boat. You take it after I go. Jay is selling weed off of it. He takes it out to the Gulf and loads and unloads. He's my grandson. You gotta stop him."

The old man gripped Truly's hand. Then, just like that, he leaned back in the hospital bed. Truly knew the life was gone from him, knew it by the grotesque way his mouth hung open. The sudden stiffness. Truly marveled how little a human body mattered. What he faced now was a shell of a man.

How odd that their journey together began where it

did and ended in this hospital room where the secrets the old man revealed changed everything forever.

He got a call from Jenny that night. All she said was, "See what happens?"

"Leave me alone," he said and hung up.

She sent him stuff in the mail, horrible stuff: bones, chicken feathers, a real tail of a cat. And notes, which got worse and worse. He talked it over with Bev.

"You're a psychologist," he said. "Do you think she's dangerous?"

Bev hesitated, then nodded. "I don't like to diagnose based on speculation. But this one is pretty clear. She's delusional. Grandiose delusional. Possibly schizophrenic. I had a patient like that once. I'd say, 'Have a nice day,' and he'd say, 'I will make it so.' He thought he had control over the weather. Your mother thinks she has some kind of mystical power from an ancient bloodline."

Truly swallowed. "Should I...worry?"

Bev stared him straight in the eye, although he knew she couldn't see a thing. Her eyes were large, dark, opaque. "I would say she's dangerous. Yes."

They discussed getting the police involved, but Truly doubted there was much they could do. A restraining order meant nothing to a crazy person. Besides, Bev and Truly wanted to be together to make a fresh start with Ruby. They talked for a long time, brainstorming. The idea they finally came up with was crazy by anyone's standards. Truly would fake his own death and disappear.

Bev sent the death threats to his Facebook account to provide a red herring for his disappearance. She was a good enough coder that it wouldn't be traced back to her. Truly would take Jay out in the boat to scatter the old man's ashes three miles out to sea. He needed a witness.

When Jay wasn't looking, Truly would dive over the side of the boat. If he could hold his breath and stay under for two minutes, he could hook up the ExtraLung, an underwater breathing device. And put on his mask. Following a GPS map on his waterproof Apple Watch, he could monitor his blood oxygen level and make it, with luck, back to shore in less than three hours. If Jay fell under suspicion because of Truly's disappearance, it would serve him right for selling dope off the old man's boat.

For months, Truly practiced holding his breath underwater in Bev's pool. Then he would swim laps, twenty, thirty, forty. He lost the layer of fat around his waist, the slightly stooped posture that made him look apologetic. He was hard and muscled. He was going to seize what he wanted, what he deserved. His plan would succeed.

Instead, everything went wrong. The last thing he remembered was boarding the boat with Jay. When he awoke, shivering, all he could see was water. He couldn't even remember what he was doing out to sea. All he knew for sure was that he was in terrible trouble. He was right.

He had no memory of Mere Byrd rescuing him. For a year, he was a prisoner in her smelly unventilated house with the squawks of chickens who roamed around as if they owned the place. And the huge black snake who lived in a cage and was released once a day to slither around at will. The servants forced him to drink tea, which made him lethargic and drowsy.

Truly refused to call Jenny 'mother' or Mere' Byrd. She had a loyal servant, Lega, whose family had been with her for generations. She was his guard, essentially, stoic and unmovable. Truly wasn't going anywhere.

It was the maid that gave him a reason to go on living. She was young, and when his head cleared a little, he slipped her a note asking for specific newspapers. She got them to him late at night when Jenny was leading some godforsaken ritual over in Congo Square, the same kind of ritual that made it impossible for her to identify one man as Truly's father. From the newspapers he learned what happened to Darlyn, to his home, to Jay, to Ruby.

Jenny claimed responsibility for Darlyn's death and warned him of the things she would do to Bev, even to Ruby, if Truly abandoned her. So, he feigned interest in the family religion. In fact, after doing some reading, he was certain that Jenny's black powers had more to do with a prosaic and deadly element. Poison. There was poison everywhere in New Orleans, old stuff, hard to trace, used for generations.

That was why he pretended to be a waiter at the Bone House. Away from Lega's watchful eye, he mixed some of that poison into an order for Shrimp Rinaldo and delivered it to Mere' Byrd. He remembered she was particularly taken with that dish. All he needed was for her to take a bite. He timed how long it had taken them to eat lunch when they dined at the outdoor restaurant. The poison would take effect within forty five minutes. Her throat would become dry, and she would cough. Soon, it would be hard to breathe. She would lose consciousness. Truly figured out to the mathematical second where she will collapse.

He quickens his pace. He will find her near Brennan's Restaurant a block and a half away on Royal Street. And sure enough, there she is, a dark huddled figure, sprawled on the sidewalk. He is lucky he is fresh on the scene and the first to find her.

There is no one around. She must have tripped on the sidewalk. Her face is scraped and a piece of her tooth lies on the pavement next to an outstretched arm. Truly checks her pulse, but her arm is already still and cool as marble, as though death were always inside her.

Truly feels his heart speed up. He can go back to Bev. He can reclaim Ruby. But he can't just leave her here, lying in the dirt. He stoops, and with great effort, manages to get one arm under her knees and the other under her head. He hitches her up and begins walking towards her shop. He plans to leave her there. In the confusion, he will slip away. *Ding Dong the witch is dead.* He quickens his pace. Her head lolls under his arms.

People begin to recognize him on the street. They gasp, cover their mouths, cross themselves. And they speak. They say, "Papa Byrd."

Truly hurries on. More people line the streets. Some of them are kneeling now. Their voices broaden in multitude and volume. "Papa Byrd, Papa Byrd, Papa Byrd, PAPA BRYD."

Out of breath, Truly sees the *Authentica* up ahead. Now there are dozens of people on Dumaine Street. "PAPA BYRD, PAPA BYRD, PAPA BYRD." Someone spits gin in his face, and he almost drops the corpse. He hurries on much as the old man did forty five years ago, but in a different direction. Staggering, he makes it past the threshold. He stands there and looks out at the throng of people in the street chanting his name. Behind him stands the primitive lore of his ancestors, a world he wants no part of.

He lays Jenny down roughly, on the floor. The chanting from the streets grows louder. Truly thinks of Bev, Ruby, and escape. Can he survive by using the old man's standbys of diligence, subservience, and fear? He catches a glimpse of himself in the mottled glass of an ancient mirror. He sinks to the floor, his legs straight out in front of him with his back to the wall. The words of the people are making the walls shake.

Perhaps he will wait here until things die down a little.

About the Author

Elizabeth Randall is a widely published freelance writer and a retired high school English teacher. She is the author of seven books. Her most recent publication was a book about the Florida environment, titled *An Ocklawaha River Odyssey*. She and her husband, Bob, live in Lake Mary with their cat Princess Calypso.

elizabethrandallauthor.com

CPSIA information can be obtained
at www.ICGtesting.com
Printed in the USA
BVHW080533250922
647691BV00003B/130

9 781737 841197